THE FIRE GOSPELS

THE FIRE GOSPELS

a novel

mike magnuson

HarperFlamingo
An Imprint of HarperCollins*Publishers*

HarperCollins books may be purchased for educational, business, or sales promotional use. For information, please write: Special Markets Department, HarperCollins Publishers, Inc., 10 East 53rd Street, New York, NY 10022.

FIRST EDITION

Designed by Kyoko Watanabe

Library of Congress Cataloging-in-Publication Data

Magnuson, Mike, 1963–
    The fire gospels : a novel / Mike Magnuson. — 1st ed.
      p. cm.
    ISBN 0-06-017595-8
    I. Title
  PS3563.A35214F57 1998
  813'.54—dc21   97-50352

---

98 99 00 01 02 ❖/RRD 10 9 8 7 6 5 4 3 2 1

THE AUTHOR EXTENDS MUCH THANKS TO THESE: R. S. Jones, for his colored pencils and Post-it notes, for his friendship and faith; Lisa Bankoff, for the wisecracks, for knowing when to give a guy a break; Beth Magnuson, for the long walks, for the patience; Jack T. and Mary Louise Magnuson, for haiku and canoeing, for everything that's good; Deborah and Sandra Magnuson, for being the only sisters, the best sisters; Colonel Padgett Powell, for his Tactical Arson Brigade at the University of Florida; Godfather Paul Reyes, for duct tape and bourbon.

To the original Mankato Seven: Clark, Davis, Higbie, Lohre, Mauch, Micus, Pratt. AND Dr. Petersen. Goddammit.

To these fellows—Tony Earley, David Gessner, Brady Udall—who know how to make a couple weeks on a mountain action-packed.

To Jeff Anderson, artisan, historian.

To the Sutherlands, Jim and Libby.

To the Hardwigs, Bill and Peggy.

To the Franks, Jim and Patty.

To Troy and Deanna Pflanz.

To Venus and Taylor.

To Garth Kutzke.

To Ibbetson.

And to the Liquid Forest. Everyone. Let us drink there together, and laugh, and call it a lifetime.

In memory of
Marguaret Ann Vaughn
March 27, 1905–June 11, 1997
Storyteller

We stayed till . . . we saw the fire as only one entire arch of fire from this to the other side of the bridge, and in a bow up the hill, for an arch above a mile long. It made me weep to see it. The churches, houses, and all on fire and flaming at once, and a horrid noise the flames made, and the crack of houses at their ruine.

— SAMUEL PEPYS, LONDON, 1666

You could hear the shrieks of women, the wailing of infants, and the shouting of men; some were calling their parents, others their children or their wives, trying to recognize them by their voices. People bewailed their own fate or that of their relatives, and there were some who prayed for death in the terror of their dying.

— PLINY THE YOUNGER, POMPEII, 79 A.D.

It began in the circus . . . then it climbed the hills — but returned to ravage the lower ground again.

— TACITUS, ROME, 64 A.D.

PRELUDE

AND THIS IS HOW FOLKS IN THE NORTHERN WISCONSIN valley town of McCutcheon believe the drought began:

Three months ago God made the clouds disappear. People prayed for a change in the weather, and God gave it to them.

And this is how they came to praying:

All spring the daytime McCutcheon County sky was the color of a tombstone, always cloudy, drizzling, or threatening to drizzle. Once every day, usually in the early afternoon, a sullen, spitty shower fell, not a heavy rain but rain enough to keep people indoors. And for five months of winter the people had been confined indoors, shivering under their comforters and drinking and eating and growing fat from doing not one blessed thing. Winter was over with, and still the people were stuck indoors.

And they were tired of looking at the world through a window, or through their TV screens, which showed pictures, nearly all day, of the great wide worried-about world that wasn't McCutcheon, and would never be McCutcheon.

And in the front yards, in the open spaces between the hardwoods and the pines, the ground was gray and covered with flattened leaves, and along the McCutcheon streets the snowplow drifts melted into long uneven mounds of dirty ice. The streets were covered with road salt, sand, tailpipe drippings, the grit of five months' winter traffic. And everything in McCutcheon was gray: trees, buildings, cars, heavens, ground. Even the people were gray and pasty-faced from living so long indoors, so long without fresh air and the comforting sun.

And God saw the truth in this. His people were irked with living the life He provided them. They were tired of getting wet feet every time they went outside. They wanted to rake their lawns again, and hang their clothes on the line, and sweep their driveways clean, and push their baby strollers through the park on a sunny afternoon. They were tired of these endless dreary days, of living with never a feeling of warmth in their bones.

And God said, "If My people despise the clouds, they can do without."

And He cleared the skies on Memorial Day morning.

And the skies have been cloudless since.

At first, because nobody thought this would last, folks were well pleased with the dry weather. The clear skies, the gentle breezes, the temperatures each day in the high seventies: Who couldn't this weather make happy? This finally was summer. And folks thanked God for hearing their prayers.

One evening that first dry week, on the six o'clock broadcast of McCutcheon Action 9 Cable News, Lucky Littlefield, the weatherman, forecasted a big high-pressure system to stay over the region indefinitely. Lucky Littlefield was originally from the South, from somewhere, he was fond of mentioning during his reports, in the pecan-grove region of south Georgia, and on this evening he concluded his forecast with a few words from his heart: "Friends and brethren," he said, "during these unfortunate months of weather, I imagine the last thing you've needed, after a hard day at your job or a hard day at home tending to your young, is to hear Lucky Littlefield telling you that tomorrow will not be a nice day. It hasn't caused me any joy, either, forecasting weather such as that we've had. But tonight I can promise not only will tomorrow be beautiful but we're fixing to have nice days for at least a week, days as clear and temperate as any there've been on this earth. I say, Git yourselves outside this next week and enjoy this weather. I say, You deserve it."

This was the first of June, and the lakes in the countryside surrounding the valley were pure and free of weeds, a month after ice-out, and folks could go swimming again, and could fish again for northern pike and walleye and smallmouth bass. In the hay fields that week the sun matured the alfalfa, and farmers cut, baled, and barned their first crop, and their feed corn stood as high as a fellow's ankles. Everywhere in the county people fished or worked in their gardens or took to the woods to cut down trees for next winter's woodstove fires. And in the evenings they drank beer in their backyards, played softball in the parks, pitched horseshoes behind the taverns. They laughed and enjoyed themselves and made toasts to Lucky Littlefield and to God and to all the good He had done for them.

Lucky said, "There's nothing like a dry June week in northern Wisconsin."

And everyone in McCutcheon County agreed.

Lucky had red hair, closely cropped and newsman neat, and a large red beard, which wasn't so neat, and no matter the weather he wore a Hawaiian shirt for every broadcast: sometimes a peach-colored one with dancing girls on it, sometimes a blue one with pineapples on it, sometimes a shirt that was plain old lemon yellow. Folks in McCutcheon had never seen him do the weather looking any other way. He had come to them a couple years back, and over time they had grown used to him and had come to feel he was somehow part of their lives. And his forecasts were never inaccurate, which generated considerable respect for what he had to say. When Lucky spoke, he had a way of making the movements of the jet stream and the passing-through of frontal systems seem personal to him, like he was responsible for the weather and wanted it to make everyone's lives more worth the living.

"It's magnificent," he would say, when the weather was fine.

Or "Our crops will flourish in all this sun, sure enough."

His voice had that lilting, Southern quality that for folks in rural regions of the Far North has always suggested religion, a fantastical, frenzied religion, the kind where believers holler and writhe in church, and handle snakes, and speak in tongues, and get cured of their blindnesses and of their palsies and other diseases of the Soul. When Lucky would say "Friends and brethren," folks could not help but feel, just for an instant, as if they were participating in a Christian faith far more exciting and miraculous than the stoic Catholicism in which nearly everybody in McCutcheon County was raised. Lucky would speak, and those who heard him automatically turned their thoughts, in ways large or small, to prayer. They couldn't help it. Almost no one in McCutcheon County objected to prayer.

But by the third week the dry life became a worry. The daily McCutcheon sky was blue as a bluebird, and the nighttimes were all firmament twinkling, shooting stars and passing satellites visible even under the townlight. Late every evening, at tavern close, folks saw the ruffling green drapery of the northern lights, giant arcing displays where a fellow could witness the earth hurtling through the particles of outer space. Sun to stars to northern lights to sun again, that was the sky. Something was out of kilter in McCutcheon, and in the taverns and farmhouses and grocery stores and nursing homes folks began trying to remember what clouds looked like.

On Friday night that third week Lucky Littlefield began his weather report with an ominous shake of his beard. "Friends and brethren," he said, "all this forecasting equipment I have here at the station, and I still see no end to the dry. I believe it's time we might could consider asking the Higher Power for all this blue weather to go away. Yessir. It's time to consider praying together."

And folks did pray that evening, right then, right in front of their televisions. They nodded their heads and put in a humble request for rain. Not everybody prayed that evening, but gradually, as people couldn't avoid noticing that something profound had gone wrong with the weather, they began gathering in small groups to pray, clusters of five and then ten or twenty gathering in the store parking lots and on the town sidewalks or in midday vigils at Saint Joseph the Worker Roman Catholic Church.

By the fifth week spontaneous evening rosaries took place at the William Olson City Park band shell, some nights with several hundred people at a time, chanting and thumbing their beads. Then even in the taverns, the last Godless refuges in town, some people started crossing themselves and saying a Glory Be before taking their shot of bourbon and mouthful of beer to wash it back. McCutcheon became a festival of hope and prayer, but still it did not rain.

On the Fourth of July, when McCutcheon was so parched and brittle the city fathers had to cancel the fireworks for fear of setting the town ablaze, two thousand people gathered after sunset at William Olson City Park, and they howled their prayers to God for rain. Lucky Littlefield himself led the praying from a rostrum in front of the band shell. "We need low pressure, dearest God," he said, "or the jet stream shifting near. Anything, merciful God. Just make it rain." Lucky wore a blue Hawaiian shirt sprinkled with bright yellow bananas. The holiday skies were freckly with stars. From time to time an airplane crossed the sky, a small blinking light way overhead.

And God wasn't ready to listen.

Fierce heat came then, and all that which is a precursor to fire: gusty days and odd windy nights, the tall grass turning brown and tinderish, oaks and maples becoming so dry they commenced dropping their leaves. Piles of leaves formed in the street gutters. Lawns turned white. And the hot winds blew. The city fathers banned public burning: no more weenie roasts, no more smoking cigarettes on the back porch and chewing the bull. A stray spark could reduce McCutcheon to ash. Most evenings Lucky Littlefield called for temperatures near one hundred the next day, and he delivered his forecast as though it were a death sentence for the town.

And on August 3, when Henry Nordstrom walked into the IGA on Mitchell Street and shotgunned his brains out in the produce aisle, Lucky appeared on TV, in lime green, looking haggard, and he said, "Friends, we cannot grow weak in our hour of crisis. We must remain strong. We must keep believing that prayer, and prayer alone, will get us through these difficult times."

Henry Nordstrom was a geography professor at McCutcheon University and by all accounts a solid citizen. When he died he had a handwritten note pinned to his chest, and it said this: "One cloud. Let me see one cloud." Word spread of the note, and folks visited the IGA like they might a martyr's shrine, praying and fingering their beads, resolving in their hearts to remain strong.

And by this last week in August, when the still ankle-high corn shoots have shriveled to toothpicky points lining the dusty fields above the valley, when the second crop of alfalfa hasn't come in, and won't, and the milk in the dairy case has begun tasting withered and chalky, it's obvious what used to make McCutcheon County a pleasant, picture-postcard gem in the Far North—the friendly town in the valley, the good farming, the fine forests, the clear lakes and streams—is near to complete ruin. All the vegetation is dead or will be. The McCutcheon River is threatening to dry up within two weeks.

And fights break out in the taverns and in the streets.

And those in prayer pray themselves into a frenzy.

FRIDAY

1

LATE THIS AUGUST FRIDAY AFTERNOON, THE SUN SHINES
hot and steady over McCutcheon County, and Grady McCann
drives his Pinto wagon along Highway 50 toward the
McCutcheon River Valley. He's burning his third after-work
cigarette, you bet, and he's drumming a happy rhythm on his
steering wheel, because today he just got paid, and all the rainless months in the world couldn't bother him. Up ahead the
road is dusty white, lined with dead cornfields and tag-elder
thickets turned to crisp sticks. And the countryside is deathy
brown. Even the jack-pine stands sectioning off the farms are
brown and brittle-looking in the wind. This is Wisconsin, for
chrissakes, and it looks like Egypt.

But Grady McCann is not bummed out about what he sees.
No way. He's got an indoor gig, climate-controlled, that the
drought can't touch. For ten years now, he's worked maintenance at the Shady Glen Convalescent Center, twenty miles
north of McCutcheon, in Window Falls, and the drought, no
matter how bad it is, doesn't change one bit what Grady does
best: fix wheelchairs, mechanical beds, air-conditioning systems, boilers, phone lines, and fire alarms; and unplug toilets;

and mop up various forms of body fluids powersprayed onto the nursing-home tile. Shady Glen without water would be a filth-fest beyond belief, but with Grady on maintenance, Shady Glen's pumps run tip-top. The old wizzlers get their baths on time. Their mash gets mixed for lunch. Their ostomy bags get properly dumped and irrigated. And Shady Glen's water supply is gigantic, sure enough, the McCutcheon Aquifer, which extends from McCutcheon and Window Falls a hundred miles in every direction—north to Duluth, west to the Mississippi River, east to the piney wastes of the Chequamegon Forest, south into the Driftless Area, where Grady knows for a fact that the glaciers of the last Ice Age never crossed. It could take three drought years for the aquifer to run dry, and Grady figures the rain will come long before then. Folks thought the winter would never end, right? But it ended. Grady figures this means the drought will end, too. To Grady's way of thinking, the weather tweaks with his life about the same way his Pinto does: The Pinto is junk, orange and rust-eaten and rickety, but it's running, which is good enough for Grady, gets him the twenty miles home from work each day. Having a lousy car, having a drought going on, either way, Grady's wallet gauge is reading Maximum Full.

Where Highway 50 intersects with Midland Mall Drive, Grady gets stopped for a moment at the red light. This is the crest of the valley, and from here Grady can see the entire spread of McCutcheon bleached in the sun. Here's the new McCutcheon Mall: two hundred shiny cars surrounding a Sears, a Farm & Fleet, a Northwest Fabrics, and some littler stores that won't get Grady's paycheck tonight. And here's the valley itself: so dry it's gone beyond brown into hot wintry gray, bare lilac hedges, the spruce and balsam crisp as Christmas trees on their sixth week in the living room. Billboards and dead pines line Highway 50's descent to the McCutcheon River, once a hundred yards wide, now barely twenty, and Grady thinks the river, from the view on the valley crest, looks like a small glint of urine dribbling across the valley. Sure, the valley looks destroyed, but no way will it look like this forever. Rain will come. It always has.

And Grady is bored nutless thinking about the drought, or hearing about it. For weeks nobody at work or at the tavern has talked about anything else, no more bullshitting about musky fishing or deer hunting or the Green Bay Packers. Everything's drought this, drought that, or, the worst of the worst, all these Sheepheads in town getting together and praying for rain.

When he's halfway to the valley floor he passes a billboard featuring a solemn Lucky Littlefield, bushy beard and foo-foo shirt, and these words: PRAY FOR RAIN, MY DEAR FRIENDS. This billboard wasn't up yesterday evening when Grady drove here, and the sight of Lucky Littlefield now, plastered up there and looking sanctimonious, sends a quake of vinegar through Grady's shoulders, causing him to veer slightly in the road. That goddam Lucky Littlefield is everywhere these days—on T-shirts and key chains, on posters in grocery stores and in taverns— which would be bad enough (that buttplugger shirt he wears, that goddam Southern preacher twang of his, the way he's turned everybody in McCutcheon into Dipsticks for Jesus), but Grady hears about Lucky all the time, not just the public Lucky, but the inner nauseating wonderful Lucky, because Grady's wife Erica works at Channel 9. Erica is Lucky's personal assistant, in fact, and works close with Lucky all the time.

Maybe even right now, while Grady innocently drives his Pinto to the tavern, Erica is nudging near Lucky in her sundress, that black cedar-smelling hair of hers two inches from his beard, and she's telling him ways to better fit Jesus into his Six O'clock Sheepcall, or she's reminding Lucky how terrific it is that he's leading McCutcheon to Christ. Surely later, when Erica comes home from work at eleven o'clock, Grady will hear some Lucky stories. *Oh, he's got such strength during these hard times. He's started a nationwide fund to save McCutcheon's farmers. He's leading a care rally tomorrow.*

At the valley floor Grady drives over the McCutcheon River Bridge, sees the rocks and stumps covering the riverbed, and he takes the standard turn off Highway 50 onto Mitchell Street, the road to his house and the road to the Liquid Forest Bar, where, until eleven o'clock, he *will* have fun, goddammit. He just got paid.

2

THE LIQUID FOREST BAR IS A NARROW, GLASS-FRONTED, thirty-stool moosepiss-and-peanuts place: one pool table, one pinball machine, one jukebox, a beer-can collection over the bar, a bar-length mirror, and one rotund fellow named Lennart Anderson pouring the Leinenkugel's taps. Lennart Anderson has been tending bar at the Liquid Forest for as long as Grady can remember, more than ten years, and all this time Lennart's been reading the same book, which is the size of a dictionary and which he's got with him behind the bar right now, leaning against the cash register: *The Decline and Fall of the Roman Empire, Part One.* Grady doesn't know what's so fascinating about the book, and he doesn't really care. Lennart and Rome are just part of the Liquid Forest, just like the fifteen other folks who drink here during happy hour each day and who know about Lennart and his big book but don't care what's in it. Folks in this tavern are here to drink, not to think. And Grady has always been comfortable here. He even likes how the tavern smells, that smoke-and-Lysol odor the wood floors give off, the smell of happiness.

"Well, if it isn't Citizen McCann," Lennart says, "ready to

exercise his tavern privileges for yet another evening."

Grady is ready with the Insult of the Day: "If you'd drop some tonnage, Lennart, you'd be getting your fudge packed more often."

Lennart is six feet tall, greasy blond, handlebar mustachioed, and three hundred pounds of Velveeta packaged in bib overalls and a black T-shirt. He says, "I get some when I need some."

"We all get some sooner or later," Grady says, pulls out a stool from along the bar and kicks peanut shells and pink Floor-Dry away from the spot where he wants the stool to rest. Grady doesn't want to drink with his stool legs teetering on other people's crud.

"You good today?" Lennart says.

"Now that I'm here, I'd say I'm better than good."

"You didn't have an unfortunate outing at Shady Glen?"

"Nope. Worst was, fixed a mechanical bed so sticky its hydraulics jammed. Grim. I'm telling you: the residents are tough on the equipment."

"Sticky, you say?"

"A little sticky never stops Grady McCann. I had that bed fixed by one P.M. For the rest of the afternoon I went ahead and loafed in my boiler room, watched my pumps running."

Lennart winks, twitches his mustache. "Then how about tonight, Grady, you go ahead and be a respectable citizen in here?"

"Fear not, my man. It's payday."

"Then no tantrums about Lucky Littlefield?"

"Fuck that Southern-fried Chickenhead," Grady says.

Lennart sighs dreamily, and says, "I'd love to."

"You, Bud, are one sick puppy," Grady says, and gives a

yearning glance at the booze bottles lined up next to the cash register. "Anyhow, folks in town aren't, like, dying of thirst."

"Certainly not you, Grady." With a tubby elegance Lennart sets a tap beer in front of Grady. Grady takes the beer, drains it, and thuds a twenty on the bar.

"You bet I'm not dying," Grady says. "There's plenty liquid left in this town."

"You do have a limited imagination, but I'm fond of you all the same."

"Goodness H God. I'm a married man."

"A shame, truly," Lennart says, and winks again, and when he ambles off to make change, Grady sits up straight in his stool, wingflexes his shoulders, presses his palms flat together, and checks himself out in the bar mirror. He's impressed how pale he's stayed through all this sun and heat, how his arms and face look thick and droughtless and watered and cool. Here is a man, thirty years old and pigtailed, whose job the drought can't touch.

Up and down the bar the regulars play horses or shake-a-day or 7-14-21, rapping their dice cups on the bar with the regular violence, hooting at the victory or loss, and the only reminder of drought in the Liquid Forest comes when a dice winner tosses back a shot: the unsmiling sign of the cross before the booze goes down the hatch. Since late June folks have been crossing themselves in here, and Grady longs for the days when a tavern was a tavern, not a fucking cathedral.

"Gimme a big bourbon while you're at it, Lennart," Grady says. "And I ain't crossing myself for Lucky Littlefield."

"Enough about Lucky already," Lennart says.

Grady doesn't look into Lennart's eyes, instead into his thick hairless forearms and hands pouring Grady's double Jim Beam. "Goddammit, Lennart. The whole town's turned meek. Either a guy's gonna see rain or he's not."

Grady's glance shifts over Lennart's shoulder to a plastic Number 10 candy jar half full of small bills and coins, and affixed to it a note card that says, "Cash for Lucky's Farmers." Everywhere, no shit, absolutely everywhere there's Lucky. Grady hoists his drink, gulps it all down, the full double making him gag a little, and he raps the glass hard on the bar, like a dice cup. "The fuck I'm bowing to that Lucky Littlefield."

Lennart leans over the bar, places a heavy hand on Grady's shoulder, and says, "Look outside, sister." And Grady does, looks through the glass barfront. The view is sunbathed and gray, the way it would look on a clear day in January, everything desolate. "We have a disaster going on here, and Lucky's the only guy in town who's stepping up to do something about it."

Grady sees a small speck in the sky, what he thinks is a hawk circling out there.

"Lucky can't make it rain, whatever it is."

The big Lennart hand moves to Grady's face, pats him softly twice: a smell of cigarettes, peanuts, and dish soap. "Somebody's got to try, Grady." They meet eyes momentarily, Lennart's yellowed around the greens, and Grady decides he's too bent on relaxing to bicker.

"We do got booze in the meantime," Grady says, and he gestures for a beer refill with a pistolpoint of his index finger.

"True," says Lennart.

Led Zeppelin comes on the juke—"When the Levee Breaks"—a gutpounder tune for Grady if there ever was one, bass drum booming enough to sledge out a guy's teeth, harmon-

ica, too, like a chainsaw wailing, and Grady shucks and shimmies some in his stool. Lennart shucks and shimmies some, too.

Grady says, "This is bullshit: listening to a flood song during
a drought."

"It's historical, Grady. The Roman Legions, for instance,
were required to listen to battle music, even when they weren't
in battle. And here *we* are, listening to music about rain."

A flash in the glass bar door then, a noise of feet shuffling,
and it's soft personnel entering the barroom, three girls, back-
packs and pastel T-shirts and shorts and sandals, from
McCutcheon University. Grady eyeballs them through the mirror. Plookworthy, all three. Two of them are munchkinlike,
short and brown-haired, with pointy noses so much the same
Grady figures them to be sisters. The third, a half foot taller,
freckly and blonde, sidles up in the stool next to Grady, giving
him a no-lipstick smile in the mirror when she clunks her backpack on the floor and sits. She flounces her hair back over her
shoulders with a jerk of her head. The other two assume their
drinking position the same way: backpack on the floor, smile at
Grady, flounce hair. As one, they place their hands on the bar
and look expectantly toward Lennart.

"Ladies," Lennart says, with a girly voice, way too cheery, and
he reaches to a rack of pitchers behind the bar. "A pitcher?"
When the three nod yes, a happy look comes over Lennart, and
Grady thinks this is for a couple of reasons: Lennart's pegged
them as students and correctly guessed they want a pitcher; and
Lennart's always pleased to serve women, who think about the
world in a roughly Lennartish way.

The tall girl pays for the pitcher, flourishing a twenty-dollar
bill at Lennart, and Grady smells in the wind of her movements

a cooking spice he can't identify. Coriander, maybe. Marjoram. His wife would know. The tall girl fills three glasses, hers last. Then the girls cross themselves and drink.

Here's Grady's opportunity to speak: "Wait one second there, ladies. You're only supposed to cross yourself before the hard stuff."

The blonde turns a half glance toward him: gray eyes, wide set, a somewhat bulbous nose. She says, "I beg your pardon." She has an arching forehead covered in freckles, and cheekbones square and mannish enough to make Grady guess she looks like her father.

"That Lucky Littlefield crossing-yourself bullshit," Grady says, "should only be done before bourbon. Fuck that beeswax before beer."

The blonde says, "We'll cross ourselves when we like. But you may buy me a bourbon, if you want me to do things properly."

Ho! She's got moxie, this one. And listen to that way she says *You may*. This is a cultured schoolgirl, sure enough.

"Lennart," Grady says, and the big boy's been standing right there watching, twizzling his handlebar mustache and grinning. "Give this lady a belt of brown."

Lennart pats the blonde's hand and says, "Grady here's exceptionally abrasive sometimes, but he means well."

"I'm certain he does," says the girl. "But I'll have my bourbon just the same."

Lennart performs a dipping movement, a graceful reach for a glass and the bottle of Beam that makes him look like a ballet-gifted musk ox. He makes both bourbons doubles. "This round's on the Liquid Forest," he says.

The blonde swivels on her stool so she faces Grady straight up, pressuring her knees against his thigh. Her neck is so freckled it looks tanned, sturdy collarbones on this one, thick, and she wears a thin leather necklace that suspends a polished agate over her throat. "Well," she says—with the word, widening her eyes—"shall we cross ourselves now?"

Something in this girl, her indefinable smell or the sharp curve of her chin or the flexing and widening her eyes do, makes Grady consider for an instant actually crossing. His index and birdflip fingers press together, preparing for the motion. He notices he has involuntarily stuffed his marriage-ring hand in his pocket, and the thought that his wife's probably right this minute cooing and slobbering next to Lucky Littlefield snaps him to.

"Fuck the crossing," Grady says. "Bourbon's for bourbon's sake."

She nods in the affirmative, but crosses herself anyway, clinks glasses with Grady, and they belt their shots at equal rates.

From deep down Grady feels a body gag, a shuddering from too much booze too quickly. His eyes water, and he raps his glass hard on the bar, picks up his beer, and takes three swallows to kill the Beam taste. He has a cloudy thought of work, geezers in wheelchairs lining Shady Glen's halls, the pasty faces, the residents he sees and greets every day but who never remember meeting him before, the ones who die without knowing who they used to be, the clumps of mashed potatoes he mops off the dining room floor, the canned peas, the chicken-skin clumps he scrapes off wheelchair tires. He calipers his forehead with his hand, closes his eyes, and begins massaging his temples with his pinky and thumb.

The blonde's voice, cheerful and upturning: "Hey, that shot too much for you?" She's leaning over, elbows to knees and hands cupping her chin.

"Things on my mind," Grady says.

"I understand." She flexes her eyes, extends a hand to him, and says, "I'm Kate."

Her hand when she shakes is firm and salesman-strong, but at the release she slides her fingertips across Grady's palm, like she's making a pass.

"Grady," he says. "That's me."

Kate says, "I'm perfectly capable of reading, you know." She pokes his chest where his name is embroidered into his work shirt. "I'm so pleased you're a real person, Grady. I do enjoy meeting real people."

"*Real* people? You talk to mannequins all day, or what?"

"I mean, someone who actually works in the world. Someone who's actually out there on the planet."

When Kate speaks Grady hears mostly what her breasts say. *Twen-ty*, that's what her breasts say. *Twen-ty*. He decides if Kate wants to talk to a *real* person, well, he for damn sure can check out her number all he likes. Grady lights a cigarette, tilting his head upward on the first exhale, keeping his eyes fixed on the prize. "Nobody you know works. Is that it?"

"Not really. I mean, they don't *actually* work at a *real* job."

"All jobs are real," Grady says, "and they all suck."

"Is that what you think?"

"That's what I'm telling you."

One of the sisterlies calls Kate's name, and Kate shrugs her shoulders and twists herself toward these girls she came with, still keeping her knees pressed against Grady's thigh. He squares himself to the rail and pretends to concentrate on his cigarette, though he watches Kate's hair bounce in the mirror. Funny, she's a pie slice, no question, and maybe innocent enough to con into some unspeakables out in the forest behind the tavern, but Grady doesn't care, not that much. But this isn't completely because he's married. It's the nature of his marriage that's made him disinterested. Erica has been his wife for a little more than two years now, and they're childless, and they're childless as a result of constant effort to *remain* childless. One of the stipulations of their marriage is that Erica can continue her strict Catholic ways. And to plook, in Catholic terms, is not to sheathe or to take the pill or to insert a diaphragm, any of that. And to impregnate, forget that. Erica's not ready for *that*. Goodness! Her job is strain enough, and what with Grady working days and her working evenings, a child would be a train wreck, no question of it. Or at least that's the way Erica's line of malarkey runs concerning her feelings about children—not that Grady disagrees or anything. So Grady and Erica have been practicing what the church calls Natural Family Planning, a process—at least till a couple of months ago, when Grady gave up matters of plook with Erica altogether—that requires Grady to check Erica's body temperature and to monitor the consistency of her cervical mucus. Tacky and stringy between the fingertips means she's ovulating; slippery means she's safe to mount. Think about it: Cervical Mucus. For the entire twelve years of Grady's adult life, and maybe the five years before that, he has devoted incredible time and effort, not to the pursuit of making First-Class Love with a First-Class Lady, but to sticking his dick into an envelope of snot. Snot! Lordy, that's unsettled him, enough so that some days he considers retiring from women altogether. But something anyway about this Kate, slippery between the fingertips or not, sets Grady's heart to stirring.

He hears Kate say to her friend, "Grady's not bothering me. He's nice." Then she faces him again, wobbles her head to and fro in a smile. "So," she says, "what is it you do in the *real* world?"

"Not enough," he says.

"I'm serious," she says, and she fingertips his forearm. "You look like you work in a service station or something."

Grady checks himself over in the mirror again, the hair in a pigtail, the blue work shirt, the thick forearms, and he feels a tinge of sadness. Somehow, when he thinks of himself, he never pictures the maintenance sort he is. Not that he wishes he were somebody else; Grady simply has an inner version of himself that looks maybe like a TV insurance-commercial person, not suave and hip necessarily, but somebody going his way through life, owning a car and having a wife and making payments on a house, and hard as he might try to say, *I'm Grady McCann, I do maintenance, I look like maintenance*, he can't make it add up to something he can precisely see. He's Grady McCann all right, but a different Grady than Kate imagines.

"I fix toilets in a nursing home," Grady says.

"I'm sure that's very valuable work," Kate says, and she jerks her knees forward to the bar and waves for Lennart. "It's my turn to buy *you* a drink."

Lennart arrives and pours two more doubles, saying as he does, "Are you enjoying this gentleman's company?"

When Kate nods, Lennart says, "I enjoy him, too." He winks at Grady, sticks out his tongue and wiggles the purple tip.

Grady says, "Goodness H God!"

Lennart pretends hurt, pouts and puts his hands to his cheeks. "It's so hard for a girl in this world." He laughs then, makes change for Kate, and skips down to the other end of the bar, near the television, and he ogles the screen. It's almost time for Action 9 News.

Get this straight: Action 9 News is the Lucky Littlefield Show, nothing else but.

"Is Lennart," Kate says, raising her glass to toast Grady, "one of *those?*"

"That big boy," Grady says, "is the mayor of Fudge City."

"In a working-class tavern like this? I never would have guessed."

"He's the best bartender in town. What can I say?"

They clink glasses and slam their shots, Kate not crossing herself this time.

She winces, swallows so hard that the agate on her necklace vibrates, and she says, "I can belt better than you thought, eh?"

This young girl has all the hard-core bar qualities of a pulp-wood hauler, yet the way she looks at him, or the bone-brained questions she asks, or her breasts that say *twen-ty*, the shine her freckly skin has in the barlight—Grady wonders if he's hallucinating her. He slumps in his stool, smoke clouds sinking and rising in his view of the barroom, drunks adjusting their feed caps up and down and from side to side, everything double and then not double. Grady squints to hold the world in focus.

"I half expected something like this," he hears Kate say, and she's using a chitchattier tone, probably talking to her friends. "A tavern like this is a memorable experience for sure."

Along the bar, each head is facing the television, which is mounted over the pay phone and is now flashing the logo of

Channel 9 Action News: a whitetail buck frozen in time, leaping over a fence line of joined-together nines. And, presto, there's Lucky Littlefield on the screen, a pink Hawaiian shirt dotted with coconuts today.

"Friends and brethren," Lucky says. "We're at a dry ninety degrees here in the McCutcheon Valley this afternoon, winds steady from the west at fifteen. And, friends, something inside me—in the part of me that knows about the goodness overwatching our mortal souls—*that* part of me believes the Lord might could relieve our suffering soon."

Lucky's voice through the barroom is tinny and echoing off the smoke-stained beer-can collection and the drunks and their glasses suspended before their mouths. The ice machine ticks. The ceiling fans scratch and thump overhead.

"That's right. I can now see an end to this drought. It's not all my forecasting equipment that's telling me this, either. It's what's happening in my heart when I pray. I *know* He's listening. He'll bring us relief, but only if we purify, purify, if we believe our prayers with more than just our bodies and minds. We must pray directly and honestly now. We must pray with our spirits. We must have no doubts but that He will finally bring in the clouds and the rain and make McCutcheon the wonderful place it once was."

A solemn bow from Lucky, and from all in the Liquid Forest except Grady, and in this extended quiet moment Grady sees ten years of wrench-pulling and toilet-fixing at Shady Glen, old toothless faces spitting up their orange mash, legions of geezers, who are mere packages of bone, who were people with jobs once, who slouch afternoons in the activity room now, who convulse or scream or strike at him with their canes, who have gone through their drying-up long ago. He thinks about his wife with her small hands folded, standing on the wings of the Action 9 News set in her sundress, her eyes closed, just like on Sundays, back when Grady was first married to her and would go with her to Saint Joseph the Worker's. What pisses off Grady about his wife is that she really believes, in her tilted-head way, that whatever happens in the world is a result of something miraculous, something dictated by God, not something that human beings do, or that happens simply because of freak fate in the natural world.

And there it is: Lucky and the drought and his wife and his job and the Jim Beam wheedling the backs of his eyeballs. Grady can't take it anymore.

He dismounts his bar stool and shouts, "You ignorant motherfuckers." He expects heads to turn toward him, but none do. "You think that weatherman's gonna save us?"

On the TV screen Lucky's head remains bowed, his hair combed and clean. Along the bar everybody—even Lennart and Kate and her two friends—continues their headnod.

Grady shouts, "Rain's gonna come or it won't. Lucky or no Lucky." And he kicks over his stool for emphasis.

A humming sound emits from the neon Leinenkugel's sign over the cash register. The drunks up and down the bar keep their beer glasses suspended before their mouths. Their feed caps do not move. Through the bar walls Grady hears water rushing through the pipes; the urinal in the men's bathroom has just gone on automatic flush.

For a moment Grady considers whether he'd be better off participating. Join the crowd. Go along. It won't hurt anything to bow. But Lucky up there on the screen, his beard probably perfumed, that goof commands so much and knows so little. Grady ain't playing any part in Lucky's bullshit.

"All you fuckers are sheep," he shouts, and stomps down the length of the bar, cussing under his breath and bleating, goes past the pool table and the bathroom doors, bleats his way down the narrow hallway to the back door, and he opens the door and steps out into the alley, into the heat, into the dulling light of evening coming on.

3

WHEN LUCKY LITTLEFIELD CONCLUDES HIS MOMENT OF on-air silence, Erica McCann inscribes the Holy Trinity over her chest so slowly and with so much concentration she can feel the Holy Spirit entering her hands and spreading into her arms and body and eyes, and when she looks up from her prayer, the Holy Spirit gives her a perfect view of the Action 9 News set. The flood lamps bathe Lucky in white light, making his Hawaiian shirt somehow pinker, his beard redder than it truly is. He sits in his broadcasting chair behind his desk, spreads his arms, and says, "Now, you could feel it today. Couldn't you, my friends? You could feel that He's listening. Yes, the clouds *will* come back. You *know* they will. And rain will be part of our lives again. This is Lucky Littlefield, and I am praying for you." The red lights on the two cameras blink off, then the set lights blink off, and Lucky becomes a dimmer figure, a chunky rectangular man who points to Erica, and curls his finger in, summoning her to duty.

She steps up onto the red-carpeted news-set riser, clasps her hands at her waist, and awaits instructions, because it is Erica's professional obligation to do what Lucky asks.

Lucky's eyes are a bit bloodshot around the corners. When he smiles, lines form on his upper cheeks, and he glances at Erica from her feet to her neck. She wishes he would look into her eyes.

"Nice dress," he says.

It is pale blue, a sundress, and not a new one. She doesn't know why she wears this dress today, doesn't know why it's any concern of Lucky's what she wears. "You did well this evening," she says, which is the kind of thing she's expected to say.

Lucky reacts the way he always does. "I owe everything to *you*."

He doesn't: Lucky owes everything to the drought and to the Cable 9 ownership—a corporation in Minneapolis that owns dozens of cable companies in dozens of small towns—deciding that the McCutcheon market doesn't require its own full-production news program, because the weather, according to the ownership, is the only thing that interests people in the area in the first place.

Lucky rubs his hands together and says, "Write up something good and Godly for the ten o'clock." His voice, whenever he's off the air, is considerably less Southern-sounding. "I've been getting stale lately—too much gloom and doom."

Erica suppresses what she wants to say—*If you would ever read the copy I write for you*—nods and forces a smile instead. "I'll have something by eight-thirty."

Lucky claps his hands together, shakes his beard. "I've said it once, and I'll say it again: You're the perfect assistant for me."

"Eight-thirty, then?"

"Perfect."

And when she turns to leave the news set and head back to

her desk, she feels a breeze at her rump, hears laughter from Jimbo and Pete, the cameramen. Probably Lucky has taken a swipe at her rump for Jimbo and Pete's amusement, but she doesn't look back. These things happen too often for her to look back. Her posture is straight, her strides even, and she makes her way to her cubicle, which is made of four portable work-area dividers and is situated near the front exit of the Action 9 building, about thirty feet from Lucky's office.

The Action 9 building itself is a large warehouse originally built for the manufacture of bayonets during World War II, and the floors are shiny concrete, the kind of concrete floors on which Erica used to stand at Peterson Products, plastics factory, Window Falls, Wisconsin, USA, where, during her four years studying public relations at the University of McCutcheon, she spent her summers placing plastic bottles into cardboard boxes. When she packed plastic bottles, she carried herself with dignity, did her best to smile and keep her poise through all the vulgar talk and obscene gestures of the factory men she worked with, and she carries herself with dignity now. She concentrates on keeping her face placid-seeming, no grimace, no smile, no face muscles tensing whatsoever. She knows her faith can help her through anything; her faith gives her the power to be serene. But the way Lucky leers at her, the way he's always making innuendoes—this is wrong, and she knows it. She could bring sexual-harassment charges against Lucky anytime, and the great Lucky Littlefield would be out of a job. But *anytime* can't be now, because just now the people of McCutcheon really need Lucky. Every evening he musters thousands to prayer, and, without prayer, will this drought ever end? Erica doesn't think so. True, Lucky is not a priest. He's not even

Catholic, which irks Erica somewhat, but the people are genuinely moved by Lucky all the same. Whether Erica likes it or not, all she can hope is that it's God's Will she's Lucky's assistant.

God's Will. That's odd she'd think a thing like God's Will now: makes her seem more like a Charismatic than a Catholic. But these days, in Erica's belief, Catholics have every right to express their relationship with Christ in the same enthusiastic way people from other Christian faiths do. So when she steps into her cubicle, she asks God, because she feels free to ask Him whatever she wishes, to give her strength.

Her cubicle contains a medium-sized gray desk, on top of which is her computer terminal, a telephone, and two wire in-out boxes, both crammed with copy she's written for Lucky to ignore, and above the desk hangs a cork bulletin board, which, when she sits in her roller chair, draws her eye the way it always does. For in the center of the bulletin board is a photograph of Grady sitting on the hood of his Pinto and swigging from a bottle of Leinenkugel's. She took the photograph not long after she married Grady, and he looks in the photograph about the same as he does nowadays—hair in a ponytail, blue work shirt, a bit of stubble on his chin—and he's smiling a half smile, lips open to show the teeth but the nose crinkled and the brow furrowed. That's an unusual aspect of Grady: He's always smiling that half smile, whether he's happy or upset, which makes it difficult to know what's going on in his brain. At the time she took this photograph, she thought his half smile meant he was coming to appreciate a marriage in which the church is central. Grady would go with her to Saint Joseph's back then—wouldn't take Communion, of course, because he wouldn't go to the reaffirmation classes on Tuesday nights. He would be at least friendly about her commitment to living her life in the faith. Erica even thought, back then, that Grady would make an excellent father. But what she thought and what God told her to think were two different things entirely. After she married Grady, he still went to his tavern every day after work; he still hung out with his friend Lennart the homosexual, who, to this day, Erica has never seen. And after six months of marriage, Grady quit going to Saint Joseph's and started picking on her for being a Catholic: for going to confession twice a month, for saying her rosary every day, for hanging her picture of the Virgin Mary in the bathroom hallway. And by the time, a year ago, she was promoted to be Lucky's assistant, she couldn't tell what hackled Grady more, Lucky Littlefield or her faith.

She turns on her computer, opens a fresh file to begin writing more copy that Lucky will never use, and instead she begins typing a list of the things that bother her, and what she thinks the Lord would like her to do about them.

1. The drought is horrendous. Lucky Littlefield is a pig. Solution: Don't take action on Lucky till the drought breaks. But do take action when it seems appropriate.

2. Grady hates Lucky, but he can't be told anything bad about Lucky, because A) that would prove Grady's point, which wouldn't do Grady any good, because Grady won't be a better man by being right; being wrong, and about a lot of things, is the only way Grady will learn to be better; and B) if Grady finds out what the real Lucky is like, he might tell everybody he knows, which might somehow expose the real Lucky to

the community. People might not trust Lucky anymore, and keeping the community's trust is more
important than anything right now.

3. If Lucky can't be punished just now, Grady can.
   Solution: ?

She lifts her hands from the keyboard, examines her nails
briefly, and stares at Grady's picture, the half smile, the bottle of
Leinenkugel's, and she asks God to tell her what she can do to
teach Grady a lesson. It needs to be something exceptional,
something that will really make Grady stand up and take
notice. But nothing comes to her. She concentrates on this
problem and begins absently rolling her chair forward and
backward and from side to side in the sign of the cross.

4

BEHIND THE LIQUID FOREST IS A BLUE DUMPSTER, WHICH stinks bad, the way a Dumpster in hot weather will, and it's covered with strips of dried gunk and surrounded by flies, clouds and clouds of them. Over the years Grady McCann has stood by this Dumpster and smoked dope more times than he can remember, but he's dopeless now, and that's a shame. A couple hits off a doobie, a few laughs standing out here with Lennart, that will calm Grady down every time. Ain't no Lennart out here now, though. Probably Lennart's got the McCann Ban on the Liquid Forest for the rest of the night, just on the principle that a tavern can't operate smoothly with a maintenance man hollering at everybody and knocking around the bar stools.

Grady goddam sure shouldn't have gone belligerent like that. Most days he'll bitch a little bit when Lucky's on the TV, a couple of zingers delivered mostly under his breath. A guy does have the right to recognize the fact that Lucky Littlefield is full of crap. But to call all them people assholes and sheep? Really an amateur move. Really third-rate behavior. A man holds his rage inside, takes the bullshit for what it is, and says nothing about it. Grady kicks at the ground so much that his boot forms a rut. Once in a while he pauses from kicking and spits.

Beyond the Dumpster the alley is dusty and pebble-covered, and the hundred-acre stretch of forest across the alley quakes with dryness, needles falling from the pines in the late-afternoon breeze, a sound almost like light drizzle. Twenty yards into the woods, Grady sees a red squirrel foraging near a cinder block. The squirrel digs and sits still, digs and sits still. And Grady kicks at the ground. He hears engines running in the distance, a car horn here and there, an occasional barking dog, but each distant sound is dim compared with the dinging sound pebbles make when he kicks them against the Dumpster's side. Embarrassments creep through Grady like termites in his bones, and however much he kicks his feet or spits toward the alley or thumps his thighs with his fists, Grady can't make himself calm down, because the proof is in, folks: Grady McCann can't behave himself like a grown man. Left his cigarettes and his lighter on the bar, too. Even left money on the bar. But going back in: That's out of the question. Them folks have seen enough of Grady McCann the Pussy today.

But he's not ready to go on home. He focuses his ears on the bar door, hoping to hear Lennart cludding down the hall, and then the door opening, because Lennart is the kind of guy who might just step outside the bar to see if Grady's okay. Lennart does things like that; he's bighearted to folks, even if they're being shitheads. It's possible, maybe, that Lennart could take Grady right back into the bar, like nothing happened at all. But Grady doesn't face the doorway. He concentrates on looking like he's concentrating, one hand in his pocket, the other cupped to his chin. Through the balding pines he sees the sky fading into the bland, pale color of early evening.

This happens just the way Grady figured it would: footsteps in the bar hallway, and the sound of the opening door. He fixes his gaze out into the forest, tries to appear deep in thought, and says, "Lennart, I'm just going a little crazy. You understand."

"I don't understand *anything* about you. We've just met." This is not Lennart's girlycue voice but Kate's, and Grady does a heelspin toward her, which causes him to lose his balance. He wobbles but doesn't fall.

"Lennart told me you'd be standing out here," Kate says. In the outside light she looks smaller and paler than she did on her bar stool. Grady's guess: She's five six, maybe 120 pounds. Her backpack straps give her shoulders a smallness, a more delicate construction than Grady had imagined. She clutches Grady's cigarettes and lighter in her hands.

Grady says, "That goddam Lennart knows everything about me, don't he?"

She takes a step toward him and extends Grady's smokes to him. "He didn't think you could get by without these."

Kate's soft hand brushes Grady's in the exchange.

He says, "What about my money?"

"Lennart put it in Lucky's fund. That's what I'm supposed to tell you."

"That fat fucker," Grady says. "I had a lot of money there."

"Nine bucks," she says, smiles at Grady through her hair. "He said nine bucks is the price you have to pay for being a bad citizen."

"I should go in there and fuck him with a crowbar, is what I should do."

"I know you don't want any advice from me, but I would leave the money go."

"That's *my* goddam money."

"Look," Kate says, and now she smoothes her hair back behind her neck. "I do understand what you said in there. The thing with Lucky gets ridiculous sometimes."

Off somewhere in the valley a police siren sounds. The woods rustle behind Grady, a drum-roll noise in the hot breeze. Grady jacks a cigarette from the pack and lights up, which is an expensive crime these days, a two-hundred-dollar fine for burning a grit outside. With the inhale Grady's mood elevates to the small joy that comes with doing what he shouldn't.

Kate's eyes widen and scrutinize his cigarette. She says, "I think Lucky's taking advantage of the disaster for his own good."

"Well, what are you praying and crossing yourself for, then?"

"I'm praying," she says, "for the same reason you're complaining. I don't know what else to do with myself."

"These days, who the hell does?" Grady says, and he breaks into a bewildered chuckling, because Kate's probably right. Grady doesn't know what else to do with himself. Though he would never admit it to anybody, he wishes way inside that he was getting all the attention and adoration Lucky gets. Grady is as smart and has by God as much to say as Lucky; that *must* be the truth. But Grady's obscure by profession, a pigtailed guy in a blue uniform, whose lot in this disaster is to line up with the concerned townsfolk and pitch in. Sheep stuff is what he's supposed to do; he's supposed to have what he thinks dictated to him by a weatherman who isn't even from McCutcheon. It's all a manure crock, and if Grady could change his station in life, or even bring on the rain, as easily as he can rewire a sump pump, he would.

He says, "Maybe a guy should move somewhere rainy. That's the answer."

"Oh, it'll rain again. You said so yourself." Kate moves close and nods two knowing nods that seem like alliance-making to Grady. She hums then, a formless and sad tune, and sashays into the center of the alley with a kind of side-to-side dance, a jerk this way and kick a pebble, a jerk that way and bend her knees. She turns to face him and curtsies.

Booze, Grady thinks. She's drunk after all.

She says, "Let's walk down to the river."

A brief gust of wind blows her hair both backward and sky-ward, revealing the squareness of her face, a face that strikes Grady as an old soul's face placed on a young body. No wrinkles, she merely possesses something wise about her, a way of listen-ing to him, and understanding him, without using her ears.

"My wife," Grady says, and he can't believe he's mentioning her, "doesn't get too excited about me going for walks with beautiful young girls."

Kate droops her shoulders and tips her head forward, making a double chin. "Pretend I'm an old hag then." She rolls her eyes so that only the whites show, a freakish display, flapping her lids like she's near to a seizure. "Come on. Let's walk the booze off." She makes her face normal again and laughs.

"What about your friends?" Grady says.

"They'll live without me for a while."

Her hair in the breeze, her wise gray eyes, her neck freck-les—Grady can't decide why he can't refuse her, but he takes the first step her way, a tentative kick in the dirt. When she waves him forward, he walks to her, and they fall into a slow loping stroll toward the shrunken McCutcheon River. Grady looks into the woods and sees, maybe thirty yards in, a dead woodchuck covered with flies.

It's not far to the river, a half mile at most, and Grady is grateful they can walk the whole way on the dirt alley, out of sight from anybody who might know him, because this looks too obvious. She's taken his arm in the old-fashioned promenading way, gone giggly on him and superserious all at once, the way young girls do when they fall in love. Leafless lilac bushes line the alley, and here and there a wilted cypress stands, browning near its base. Beyond the lilacs, tall grasses waver in the breeze, like geezer hair, white and thin. Sparse vegetation, for sure, but it's enough to keep anybody from seeing Grady and the girl walking back here. The air is hot, and Grady's breaking into an uncomfortable sweat, getting sticky skin that makes him somewhat anxious about being touched, but he does nothing to remove Kate's hands from his arm.

"I feel so bad," she says. "I really admire the way you spoke up in the tavern."

"If you admired it, *you* should have said something, too," Grady says.

"Wasn't strong enough, I guess." When she tugs at his arm, he tries making a comparison between the size and feel of Kate's hand with Erica's hand, and to his surprise he decides Erica's hand is softer and smaller, an odd thought, since Erica must have ten years on Kate. In her own way Erica is a fine woman, good-looking enough to stir Lucky Littlefield's loins; Grady's certain of *that*. Maybe that's why he's walking young Kate now to a spot where he can test *her* cervical-mucus consistency, maybe just to get back at Erica for all that slavering she does over Lucky. Erica loves Lucky; Grady hates Lucky; therefore, Grady should plook Kate. This is making marvelous sense.

Grady says, "Don't worry about the tavern. I been drinking in there for years. They're used to me."

Her hand moves up and down his forearm, though Grady doesn't think it's in a suggestive way. She's comforting him. She's his ally. "Looked to me those people were pissed at you," she says. "A couple of fellows in the tavern said you need a sound beating."

"Drunk talk is all it was," Grady says. "Them guys always talk tough but never do a thing about it."

"I suppose you're right," Kate says, and she hums her form- less tune again. "You seem to know a lot about bars."

Grady catches an insulting edge to her voice, and this hack- les him some—he knows a truckload more about the Planet Earth than what happens in its taverns—but he keeps walking with her anyway. Underneath their strides pebbles pop, and small sticks and leaves. They sound like they're walking on a crisp fall day.

And Grady can smell the river now, a sourish odor, and up ahead are the only truly green trees in town, poplars whose tap- roots are buried deep in the wet sediment of the riverbed. As long as the McCutcheon flows, those trees will live, and the sight of greenery in the midst of the gray valley, the way the leaves here seem so healthy in the fading daylight, fluttering, gives the riverbank an artificial look, like Grady is watching a cartoon of McCutcheon. He feels short-circuitings through his system: wrist twitches, eyeballs failing focus, memories fading. He tries remembering a time when he had decency and judg- ment, a way of prefiguring what he might do next, and all he can see is how his life's becoming nothing more than moment- to-moment life. Okay: He wants to walk arm-in-arm with a college chick and maybe plook her. No problem. He wants to throw a snit in the bar. No problem. He can't remember thinking like this. Could be the drought's finally getting to him. Could be the rest of McCutcheon's got their shit together, and Grady alone is doing a lidflip.

Grady says, "You seeing something funny about the trees?"

"You know," Kate says, and she yanks him to a halt. "Everything's looking weird." She points to the crest of the valley, over which the sky has dimmed to an unsettling beige. "You look weird, too." When she says this she reaches to his face and pincers his nose, one solid wiggle, and this sends a lightning pain through Grady's face. He yelps, rears away from her, slaps his hands to his face and bends over.

"I didn't mean to hurt you," Kate says, a vague sound to her voice, a partial laugh.

From Grady's upper cheekbones to the tip of his nose he throbs, and he stares through his fingers at Kate's toes, which are gray with dust. He feels her hand on his shoulder, feels the pain in his face tapering, and when he stands he looks into Kate's eyes, bloodshot but wide open with alarm.

"Geez, I *did* hurt you," she says, and stares at his nose.

In his hands he sees blood, and with the sight he notices the runny-nose sensation of a nosebleed. He cups his hands to his nose and pinches.

Kate begins saying, "I'm sorry," and she says it over and over.

And his hands become loose, then his body does, and he knows he's about to faint, has everything going on in him that leads to fainting—the eyefade, the blinking—but he doesn't pass out. Kate squeezes her arms around him and holds him up. He begins sniffing, one sniff, then two, a sandpaper sound. He wonders why he can't smell Kate when she's so near.

"Look," she says. "I can't hold you much longer. Can you walk?"

"I can't do *anything*," he says, but he has power in his legs, and he straightens his knees, throws his head back, and Kate releases him.

The sky is paler, weaker, and barn swallows circle up there, swooping higgledy-piggledy at insects Grady cannot see. He thinks he sees a star but is not certain it's a star. Pinpoint lights come to him, and tinkling sounds from the rushing-back of blood into his head. He has an urge to spit a red fountain into the air.

"That's just it," he says. "I can't do *anything*."

Kate leads him forward like he's a blind man, clutching his arm and cooing at him. "Come to the riverbed," she says. "You can sit down there."

Behind him he hears the click of the streetlights snapping on, and he searches the ground with his feet. He feels an indecipherable calm throughout his body. When they descend the levee of limestone slag above the river, he peers down and carefully places his feet from rock to rock, putting his foot in the places where Kate put hers.

"I can't believe I did this to you," Kate says.

On the riverbed rocks large and small are scattered about: Some are boulders, some the size of bowling balls. Stumps and logs jut up from the dried mud. From the far bank comes a chanting noise, and the cluster of lights from William Olson City Park shine two silver girders across the riverflow, which is barely a flow at all. Folks are gathered at the park band shell to chant the rosary. They want Mary Herself to pass over

McCutcheon on her shaft of light and make it rain.

Kate directs Grady to an enormous barkless log fifty feet from the water. She sits Grady down, rummages a bandanna from her backpack, then wipes his face.

"Looks like you're drying up," Kate says, and sits next to him, her thigh pressing against his. "Hold the rag to yourself a while longer, and you'll be fine."

He nods and takes the rag, gently wipes his nose with it.

Across the river the rosary chant is gaining force:

> O my Jesus, forgive us our sins,
> save us from the fire of Hell.

Maybe four hundred voices make up the chant, and Grady imagines he can see their words vibrating the river water. A big fish jumps through the surface, a sturgeon maybe, and it twists miserably in the parklight, then splashes back into the murk.

Kate says, "That's the Fatima prayer they're doing now."

Grady grunts, begins drawing the bandanna back and forth over his nostrils. He sniffs to test his nose.

"You Catholic?" Kate says.

Grady snorts once, so forcefully he feels chunks of something collect in his throat, and he hacks, curls his tongue, and launches his loogey toward the park. "My wife is Catholic," he says. He contorts his face in a left-to-right motion, putting muscular pressure on his nose.

"Doesn't marrying a Catholic mean you're a Catholic?"

"Nope."

"Oh," Kate says, and hums momentarily. "But are you a believer?" With a textbook drive-in–theater date movement, she leans her shoulder into his side and sets her hand on his leg.

"I am a believer in the fact it quit raining."

"Tell me the truth, Grady." She grips his leg good and tight, and Grady remembers a mechanical bed he repaired just this afternoon so geezer-sticky he nearly gacked working on it. His pants rubbed against that bed. "What do you *really* think about God?"

"At this moment," he says, and absently pockets Kate's bandanna, "I don't believe there's a God any more than I believe those righteous women on the other side of the river can summon the Virgin Mary. Pure-D Manure, all of this."

"Sometimes I think that way, too."

Somewhere in Grady's damaged nose the death stench of the riverbed comes to him, rancid and loamy like bad compost. He tips his head to Kate's, and what was spicy before smells astringent now. She smells like Shady Glen. Her hand moves along his thigh, to the kneecap and squeeze, back to his hip and squeeze, and when the inevitable crotch-stir starts in him, he twists his body to her, reaches one hand around her waist, and he places the other on her thigh, such a muscular thigh, so young yet.

"You know what?" Kate says, and turns her hand palm up and opens her fingers, like she's holding an invisible globe. "You remind me a lot of my brother."

Grady ignores what she says, feels her body tense under his grasp, and in a mudless, clear space, with the rosary chant in the distance, with the lights of McCutcheon aglow all over the valleysides, the blackest drought sky overhead, the truest stars, he applies the French Clamp to young Kate, thumb in the hard bone over her snatch, middle finger pressing through her shorts to the gold itself. With his other hand he reaches around and gives her left breast a stronger-than-dirt one-hander. She bucks then, throws her torso forward, and Grady keeps her gripped, won't let her go. He feels her muscles straining to stand up, the lower abdomen jerking, her thighs clapping in on his hand and her legs kicking forward. Everything is movement and soft struggling grunts and muscles flexing, and she lets out one pure piccolo scream. But the French Clamp is infallible, his maintenance hands so powerful from years of the wrenching life. No way he's letting her get away. Then an elbow blow to his chin, and another to his eye, and another to his cheek—purple pains, blotchy lights all through his head—she's doing an eggbeater with her arms, and she flips her weight into him so hard that he falls backward off the log, and in the flipping back, he releases the French Clamp and he lands hard, his shoulder slamming into a river stone. Whatever strength Grady has fails him. He can't sit up.

The sky is the sky. The sky is what nighttime is, black and temporary. He hears two quick zipperings near, and the scratchy nylon sound of Kate hoisting her backpack to her shoulders. Footsteps then, drumthuds on the riverbed. Then this: "You had no right." Her voice is calm as a snowdrift. "Just because I was nice to you doesn't give you the rights to *me*."

Footsteps again, steady and fading, and Grady closes his eyes.

He breathes. That's good. Each breath has an even, calculated quality to it. That's good. He's under control now. He's planning his air. He can operate an arc welder, a TIG welder, an acetylene torch, a band saw, a power sander. He can spackle drywall, can lay tile, run conduit, repipe bathrooms, fix water chillers, telephones, lawnmowers, food processors, electric wheelchairs, mechanical beds. He can smile at nurses and geezers and do any maintenance task anybody asks of him, and he can collect his paycheck each Friday. But right now he can't do anything. He can't make it rain, can't shut down the rosary festival on the far side of the river. He can't take it back that he did what he did to Kate. What the hell was he thinking? Jesus, thirty years old, and he behaves like a brutal boy with boning on the brain. When a man comes to this, what the hell good is he?

A man, still, can make fact out of fact. Fact: The McCutcheon's not going to rise anytime soon. Look at the sky: stars. Rain is not what tonight is. A man can sit up and stand, and Grady does, and with little pain. He is not wounded, just cuffed around, maybe just beaten into making sense. A man can unfuckup his fuckups. A man can walk to his car and drive home.

Across the river, the chanters say,

> *Hail Mary, full of grace,*
> *the Lord is with thee;*
> *blessed art thou among women,*
> *and blessed is the fruit of thy womb, Jesus.*
> *Holy Mary, Mother Of God,*
> *pray for us sinners,*
> *now and at the hour of our death. Amen.*

5

BY THE TIME KATE MURPHY CLIMBS BACK UP THE LEVEE rocks, her anger has already three-quarters faded, and when she reaches level ground and starts walking back to the Liquid Forest to find her friends Judith and Tammy, it really bothers her that her anger can fade the way it has. How come she's not still furious?

Overhead the moon is a dull dusty blue. She stops underneath a streetlight and looks back at the trees bordering the river, half expecting Grady to come lumbering up the levee, and to be yelling for her to wait, wait: *I apologize for getting rough with you, Kate.* The trees have a strange purple hue in the streetlight, but Grady does not appear.

The streetlight she's standing under borders Second Avenue and its sidewalk, the safe, well-lit path to Mitchell Street and back to the Liquid Forest Bar, but instead of taking the sidewalk, she strolls down the alley, a gray sliver of pebbles narrowing off into dark distance lined with dead hedge. She can defend herself through the darkness up ahead. She's just proved it. The safest route to wherever she's going is whatever route she takes.

While she walks her sandals make crunching noises, and she tries to listen to herself breathing. Steady breaths, calm, she's under control. She should be mad enough to want to cut Grady's balls off. How could he grab her like that? But she's not mad. With each stride she feels a little throb coming from her underside, a little tickly feeling, which, try as she might to ascribe it to other causes, she can only ascribe to her thinking about Grady, about the hardness of Grady's hands—the rough palms, the small cuts on the thick knuckles and thumbs—and about the heavy muscles in his forearms and shoulders, how she could feel the power in Grady's body when she walked next to him, and how, while she listened to Grady and held his arm, she couldn't get over it that a man who fixes toilets in a nursing home could smell so pleasantly of soap. No, she shouldn't have a tickly feeling about Grady, but she does, which is a terrible feeling for her to have.

Kate is no foreigner to males and their sudden urges. She's had boyfriends by the classroomful her first two years at the university, most recently a boy named Brian, nineteen, who's thinking about majoring in political science so he can become a lawyer. She dumped Brian three weeks ago after he dropped his pants in front of her. And Eddie, who was Kate's boyfriend before Brian, was the same kind of unimaginative dolt, a biology major who wanted to become a rich doctor someday, and who—the reason Kate dumped him—always wanted Kate to stroke him off, in the middle of the afternoon, in the dimly lit cartography stacks of the university library's third floor. What a dismal experience Kate's had with boyfriends: all of them under twenty years old, with soft hands, with nothing interesting to talk about, in college so they can be rich someday, and always wanting to get off. Boys from the college, this is it, are living in a self-centered, artificial world, which Kate understands; they *are* boys after all. Henceforward, she will spit out all college boys like cherry pits.

But Grady, nothing about *him* is phony. Feel *him*! Listen to *him*! Here is a man, probably in his thirties already, with a full-time real job working with geriatrics, a very commendable occupation, very noble (he can't be in it for the money), and obviously, without having an education or anything, Grady can see right into this whole fraud that Lucky Littlefield is perpetrating on McCutcheon. And Grady is an unhappy man, too, a man stuck with a wife he must not love. Kate imagines what Grady's wife must be like: probably fat, or at least chunky, probably collects Hummels or Elvis plates, probably spends her weekends going to garage sales and looking for old plastic pinwheel flowers to display in her double-wide's backyard.

When Kate reaches the back entrance of the Liquid Forest, she stops walking for a moment by the Dumpster. The faint, thudding sound of the tavern's jukebox, and the rustling wind passing through the woods across the alley—that's all that's here now. She tries remembering the way Grady's face looked when she brought him his cigarettes and lighter. He had a smile that Kate isn't quite sure now was a smile, and when he talked to her, just at first, he talked to her like she was his best friend. Sure, Grady thought she was Lennart the bartender. Lennart must be Grady's best friend, and who would ever think a friendship like that could be possible: a workingman and a homosexual being best buddies? Just thinking about this brings on that tickly feeling again. Grady is a richly complicated man.

She opens the tavern's back door, letting out the sounds of

men shouting and a Judas Priest tune she's heard before but can't recall its name, and she walks through the narrow back hallway. There's Lennart behind the bar, in his bib overalls and pouring drinks, and it looks like he's joking around with his customers. He laughs and makes quick strutting movements and theatrical gestures toward the ceiling.

Everything is neon light and men in feed caps, and, despite the drinkers being mostly men, nobody really looks at Kate, which somehow she finds agreeable. She hasn't spent much time in taverns (she's not even of age, not for eleven more months), but what she has assumed of a bar like this is that all the men would be whistling and catcalling at a young woman in shorts. Yet these tavern men are far less overt than, say, a frathouse full of college boys. Here there is clinking and dice-playing and men crossing themselves before doing a shot, and, below the lamps that hang from the ceiling by cables, smoke hovers and seethes. The smoke in the Liquid Forest seems much more menacing than the men. She can hear the men talking about Lucky Littlefield and about the rain disappearing, but she doesn't hear the words she expects to hear: *nice ass, great legs, super tits.*

She finds a stool near the beer taps, takes off her backpack, and sits. She takes a cursory glance around the bar for Judith and Tammy, but they're not here, which suits Kate just fine. She's got some investigations to do.

In a moment Lennart looms across the bar from her. His eyes are shiny and sharp-looking. His handlebar mustache is so greased that, when he speaks, the mustache seems to be suspended in midair.

"What did you do with Grady? You didn't have to kill him,

did you?" His voice has a dignified quality to it, chesty and low.

"Nope. I didn't kill him. I sure thought about it though." The smile Lennart has, all thick lips and surprisingly white teeth, makes Kate feel like she's known him for a hundred years. She feels like she can say *anything* to Lennart. "I really enjoyed meeting Grady."

"Of course you did," Lennart says. "They *all* do." He flips up a beer glass from a rack underneath the bar, fills it with Leinenkugel's—a perfect pour, there's barely any foam on the full glass—and he sets the glass down in front of Kate. "This one's on me personally, because, as the Emperor Commodus used to say to the Roman Senate, I must tell you the truth for your own good."

When he leans his face close to Kate's, she can smell something sausagy about him, something salty and ripe. She rears away from the smell and attempts a preemptive stab at the truth. "Grady's married. That's what you want to tell me, right?"

"Very bright deduction," Lennart says. "You're not a student of history, are you?"

"Only recent history," Kate says. "Grady *told* me he was married."

"That's a new one. He might be turning into a decent citizen of the empire after all."

A customer yells for Lennart from near the pool table, and Lennart's smile gets even bigger. He squares his shoulders back, almost like a showgirl. He shouts, in a stagey voice, "I'm coming!"

But before tending to his customer, he winks at Kate, pats her forearm with his huge hand, and says, "Stick around awhile. You won't have to pay for a thing." He produces a glass the size of a jelly jar, along with a bottle of Jim Beam. He fills the glass halfway, winks at her again, and saunters off to his customer.

She takes a tentative sip. Unlike this afternoon, when she downed three whiskeys this size with Grady, the stuff tastes like gasoline now, makes her gag a bit. But the whiskey is free, and the tap beer tastes bready and somehow older-worldly, the taste of a new element to living she's getting to know this evening, the tavern life, the life wherein folks get to drink and to do whatever they want whenever they feel like it. She takes healthy swigs from her beer and takes the clinical observer's view of the bar: Lennart mixing screwdrivers for two men with beards; Lennart such a large man but a man whose arms move with speed and, Kate thinks, grace. On the TV above the bar some commercials play; probably it's not too long before Lucky Littlefield comes back on the air for the ten o'clock show. And in the mirror merely an ordinary woman is what Kate sees, long blond hair she doesn't comb often enough, regular-looking face, regular-looking freckled arms. She doesn't see herself as ugly, just not stunning, not like the way Judith and Tammy are stunning. They're both so petite and have those narrow faces and that unblemished skin men always seem to stare at and want to hold on to. When Judith and Tammy have boyfriends they don't get bluntly asked to wander off to the cartography stacks. No, boys want to *touch* Judith and Tammy, to do whatever Judith and Tammy want. With Kate and boys it's the opposite; boys want to *get touched* by Kate, not necessarily to touch *her*, because Kate is the type of girl who is so plain old essentially ordinary that boys believe it's, like, a major privilege for her to hang around them in the first place. Grady, on the other hand, showed patience, at least for a while, and without doubt showed a genuine interest in Kate and in what she had to say. Maybe that's how it is with older men; they don't care if you're not Judith-and-Tammy stunning, only that you make for good company.

Music plays, and men talk and smoke cigarettes, and Kate's beer tastes like a life with some mileage on it. She feels like she's suddenly become thirty years old and attractive in gratifying ways she never thought possible before. She straightens her spine and holds her tummy muscles in, clenches her jaw in what she believes is the beautiful, seasoned person's way to make a face taut.

Here's Lennart standing across from her again, holding a remote control, which he points at the jukebox to turn down the volume. "For once," he says, "we'll be able to watch Lucky Littlefield without your pal Grady throwing a snit."

Kate folds her hands and smiles a no-teeth smile, tries to appear calculating and educated in how she speaks. "You know, I rather admired what Grady had to say about Lucky."

"*Rather?*" Lennart says. "That's lovely."

Kate doesn't change her posture one titch. "I mean it. I can appreciate Grady's point of view."

"What you're missing is that your pal Grady has a difficult time—how shall I say it?—a difficult time comprehending the momentous."

"Are you saying Lucky Littlefield is *momentous?*"

"Well, I would say Lucky Littlefield is as momentous as a person can get, at least hereabouts. It takes an extraordinary human being to convince all these folks in McCutcheon County to pray the way Lucky Littlefield has."

"That doesn't mean Grady can't speak against him."

"Pah! Your imagination is as limited as Grady's. Listen, what I'm trying to tell you is this: Grady's wife works for Lucky Littlefield at Action 9. Assistant to Lucky Littlefield, that's her title. And *that title*, I would say, muddles considerably Grady's perception of our great weatherman. Grady McCann is not a genius, my dear. He's a jealous husband." Lennart stares for a moment at the ceiling, jutting his chin regally, as if he's accepting a crowd's applause. "Quid, I say, quid pro quo."

With the jukebox turned down, the sound of men in the tavern is echoey, their glass-clink much more distinct than before, and Kate is speechless.

"Amazing, isn't it?" Lennart says, and chuckles a rush of air through his nose.

Kate nods and stares awkwardly at her fingers. She's been chewing her nails too much.

Lennart says, "But listen: I'm half toying with you. Grady never brings her around *here*. Nobody brings their wives *here*. I've only heard mention of the woman, is all."

From along the bar come hollers and hoots, for Lucky's ten o'clock program has begun, and Lennart has forgotten to turn up the volume.

"Forgive me, citizens," Lennart shouts, and he points the remote control to the TV and cranks up the sound.

Lucky says, "Friends, can you still feel what I'm feeling? Can you feel that rain is finally coming around the corner? And that all these months we've been devoting ourselves to prayer are finally going to give us an answer? Yes! I know you can feel it. Relief at last! Let us bow our heads and feel the relief together."

Brief, Southern-twangy, direct to the praying—Kate recognizes the classic Lucky Littlefield style, a style that has become as much a part of life in McCutcheon as the lack of rain. But for this moment of prayer Kate keeps her head upright, watches the side view of Lennart bowing, his head tipped forward, making a triple chin, and all the drinkers in the tavern, on either side of Kate, bow. On the TV Lucky Littlefield bows, too. His beard is as red as fresh hamburger.

At first Kate wonders if she should stand up, like Grady did this afternoon, and yell at all the sheep in the bar. But making a scene would attract attention, and she doesn't want to leave this place, especially doesn't want to get thrown out. She likes it here. She's feeling at home among the life-worn folks.

The barroom is as silent as Kate figures a barroom can get. The ice machine makes clickity noises. The ceiling fans scratch and grind. And Lucky continues his bow, and the bar patrons do, and Lennart does, and what Kate decides is this: No doubt, Grady is a major improvement over any boyfriend she's had. Trouble is, she has to find a way to forgive him for that grab he gave her. And of course the only way to forgive is to get even first. She's going to call Action 9, get Grady's wife on the line, and tell her she's been having an affair with her husband. Not only will a call to his wife get Grady in trouble, but, this is the best part, trouble with his wife might facilitate the breakup that, deep down, Grady probably wishes would happen. In this manner Kate might cause temporary pain for Grady—much like the grab he gave—but in the long run she will be doing him a favor.

She reaches across the bar and nudges Lennart. "Hey," she whispers, "you really gonna let me drink free all night?"

"Certainly," he whispers back. "Anything for a friend of Grady's."

"I gotta make a phone call then, okay?"

"Anything."

She eases herself gingerly off her stool, digs in her backpack for a quarter, and walks the length of the bar to the pay phone, which is situated next to the pool table and directly below the TV. From here she can see the praying faces better than from the vantage point of her stool. Each man's eyes are tightly shut, and though most wear raggedy shirts and have faces in need of a shave, these men appear to be a hundred times more serious about praying than Kate has ever seen anybody praying inside a Catholic church. Lennart's right: Lucky Littlefield really has had a momentous effect on these folks, if they'll pray this earnestly in a tavern.

Through the bar window Kate has a clear view of the IGA parking lot, where it seems a crowd of women is gathering. Probably the rosary chanters from the park have come to the IGA to say a rosary for Professor Henry Nordstrom. Kate has heard around that his soul needs intercession from the community.

Now Lucky says, "From the heavens our relief will come. Soon. Soon. Raise your heads now so we may devote our hours now to rejoicing. Relief is on its way at last."

And the heads along the bar raise and appear uniformly content. One of the men, a small man with a sketchy blond beard, even says, "On its way at last! I'll drink to that."

The men begin talking again and ordering drinks from Lennart and shooting dice. Nobody, not even Lennart, seems to be watching Kate standing by the phone.

Okay: Kate is going to make this call without delay. She fumbles not long with the phone book that is attached to the phone with a wire, and it doesn't take her but a second to find the general number for Channel 9, and it doesn't take but a second for somebody, a young-sounding guy, to answer the phone. Kate is unsettled some that she's gotten through on the first try, but she asks politely if she may speak with Mrs. McCann.

And here Kate is now: on hold. Nothing new about that.

She shifts her weight from foot to foot and watches the women in the IGA parking lot forming into orderly lines, preparing themselves for the vigil. Cars and an occasional pickup truck pass along Mitchell Street, and sometimes a group of men walk the sidewalk past the Liquid Forest's window. Friday night in McCutcheon during the drought, and Mitchell Street is where the action is, if anything could actually qualify as *action* in a town this small.

And here's Grady's wife on the line: "This is Erica McCann." A curt voice, flat and unwelcoming.

For too long Kate watches two men in flannel shirts shouting at each other on the sidewalk.

"Are you there?" Grady's wife says.

Kate says, "Yes."

One of the flannel-shirted men shoves the other, and several patrons from the Liquid Forest slide off their stools and head for the door, saying, "Fight! Fight!"

Mrs. McCann says, "Please, if you have business with the station, don't call from a tavern."

"How do you know I'm in a tavern?"

"I can hear it."

A circle of men has formed now in front of the Liquid Forest. They smoke cigarettes and lean in against each other, but Kate can't see the fistfight they're jostling to watch.

"Please call back tomorrow if you have a concern," Mrs. McCann says.

"I have something to tell you, Mrs. McCann."

Now Kate hears nothing through the phone line. Kate says, "Are you still there?"

"I am."

"I just wanted you to know that Grady and me, we're in love, and I don't think Grady has the heart to tell you. So here I am, telling you myself."

"Who are you?"

"Kate. Ask Grady about all the fun we've been having by the riverbank."

And that's it. Kate hangs up. Done.

She wanders back to her stool, sees Lennart frowning in the direction of the sidewalk brawl. AC/DC sings "The Girl's Got Rhythm." That's cool. Kate's got rhythm. She's got nerves, too. Steel nerves. And she's got a big whiskey in front of her. And men on the sidewalk are beating each other. And women across the street are chanting together. Crazy, all these folks.

6

HOME, THE HEART'S HERE: AND THE CRISP BROWN LAWN
out front, and the lawnmower and gas can in the garage unused
for two months, and the new kitchen cabinets Grady installed
in January, and the green living-room carpet Grady installed in
May, and the walls he painted beige in June, and the burgundy
Ethan Allen sofa where Grady's stretched out and waking up,
and the streetlight shining through the picture window, and
Erica pulling his pants down and placing her mouth to his
wang. Home is where Grady's rising is. He angles his head on
the sofa arm to watch his wife. She seems luminous, her skin
absorbing the streetlight glow. Her head bobs but Grady can't
see her hair, only brief glimpses of her cheeks, her elbows
chickening outward. In his liquid mind he sees broad purple
tapestries of worklife, arc lights from the welding rod to the
angle iron, the slagbead over steel, how the bead flows and
binds. He sees acetylene flames go from yellow to blue at the
cutting nozzle, the curling away stainless steel does under the
torch. Heat and liquid he sees, and everything in him is dry and
wet simultaneously—a dried-up old biddy flooding her diapers
at Shady Glen; a dried-up riverbed and a moist young girl and

the French Clamp; the dry blue streetlight shining in his living room and the heat and wetness of his wife.

And he forms his thoughts into a raining flame.

And he lets it all go.

After a time, Erica rises from him, pats him twice on the belly, and she moves to the doorway and switches on the lights. Her black hair is tied back, her eyes green and bugged at him.

"So?" she says. "What happened to you?"

Grady tugs his underwear up, fiddles with his pants, and when he sits up he shrugs, his right shoulder feeling tight and sore.

"Did you get in a fistfight?" She folds her arms and throws out her chin, looking away from Grady, maybe at a point of some significance in the kitchen, like the full garbage can. Her nose is small and shiny at the tip, and the nostrils are flared. Just above her upper lip she has an inchlong pinkish crease.

"I don't get in fights," Grady says. "You know that."

"Don't lie to me. You've got blood all over you. Go look at yourself."

He leans forward and squints, his mind doing a quick recon-struction of his evening. *Kate, Kate, Kate,* that's what he thinks, and he does his best to formulate a quality husbandly lie. He tugs his work shirt out and sees the blood spatters. He feels the lump of Kate's bandanna in his pocket.

"Goddam nosebleed," he says. "I should have changed my shirt when I got home. Too tired, I guess."

Erica steps to him and smiles in a way that wrinkles her smooth brow. "Come with me, Grady," she says, and this is a voice she might use talking to a dog or a six-year-old, singsongy and instructive. She takes him by the hand and hoists him up, leads him to the bathroom. Grady walks behind her with a hip-sore limp and with that boyguilt she wants him to feel, and he holds his pants up with his free hand.

Theatrics are key to such a moment. She leads him into the dark bathroom, positions him in front of the mirror, holding him by the back of his shirt, then she flicks on the lights. Here are the man and wife, the owners of this peach scallop-shaped sink and this tile countertop, these peach towels racked neatly behind them. The wife is beautiful, dressed with simple elegance, her narrow fingers resting on the sink. The green eyes meet the husband's briefly in the mirror. His face is a filthy gray, beard stubble and dust, and around the left eye is a hefty red bruise. On his chest, near his embroidered name, are several splotches of blood, a deep purple color on a field of light blue.

"Now tell me the truth," Erica says.

Grady stares into himself, into his black eye coming on. Guilty. She's got him. He releases his grip on his pants, and they slide down his legs to his ankles.

"I suppose it hurts your manhood too much to admit you got your ass kicked," she says.

Grady winces when she says this, because he anticipates she'll fill in the true blank: *by a schoolgirl*. He gets an eyelock with Erica in the mirror, and he winks, which is how he usually wins her over: look at her; get her to laugh; she still loves him. But she can't hold his stare. Her mouth twitches in a peculiar way, a spasm from the lower lip, and she reaches to the cold-water tap over the sink and turns it on, a short splash, then turns it off, then turns it on again. She continues this—on, short splash, off; on, short splash, off—and her head tips forward so Grady cannot connect with her eyes. He can't decide whether

Erica has found out about Kate, a possibility that seems at best remote, or whether Erica herself has done something bad, which seems a stronger possibility, for she *is* acting odd. It's been at least a year since she blew him, and then, like tonight, she blew him as a surprise—came in the door from work, found him on the couch, left the lights off and got straight to it, didn't even look at him till she was done—and afterward informed him she was transferring from day copyediting to evenings, which, at the time, she worried could ruin their marriage. But if he launches an attack now, tries to find out what she's done wrong, she could suspect *he's* done something wrong; or worse, if he attacks, and she knows about Kate, he'll flat-out prove his guilt, and he'll be toast. The best thing he can do, he decides, is to use misdirection.

"You keep turning that tap like that, and you'll fuck up the gasket."

Nothing. She twists the tap back and forth with the evenness of a self-timed impeller pump.

"You're wasting water," Grady says.

Presto! She turns the water off, and keeps it off.

"I know," she says. "I know." She gives Grady a smile he thinks is phony and forced, too much teeth, something too vague in the eyes. "Of *all* people, I should know better."

She begins rubbing her hands now, and looking studiously into them. "But maybe we could waste some water on *you*," she says, "and *then* we can talk."

Okay: Time can get him off the hook, give him the chance to fabricate.

He says, "I'll shower. No problem."

But when Erica bursts into action, slides behind him and

gets the water running, fetches him a clean towel from the hall closet, takes his clothes from him while he undresses—even takes his socks, and with a smile!—Grady knows for damn sure the shit's about to erupt. She's too helpful, bustling too much for there not to be trouble coming.

When he's under the showerhead Erica says, "I'll set clean clothes out for you, honey." *Honey*, and the hot water, and the dirt he sees collecting near the drain—all this sends Grady's lying heart into a frenzy. The water stings him around his bruised eye and on his banged-up shoulder, a pain bringing into his mind pictures of Kate, how innocent she was, really, and how at that last moment he couldn't control himself, couldn't act like a decent married man with a house and payments. And the funny thing is, Kate is not—no way, na-ah, forget it—a better-looking woman than Erica. If Grady is going to cheat, he should be taking a step up, or a hundred steps up. Never cheat downward or in parallel. It's ridiculous, the whole thing. Stupid. But however bad he's been, no matter what, he can't tell Erica the truth. He soaps himself and rinses, scours his body with a washrag. He cleans and cleans as if the filth will never disappear, and by the time he shuts off the water and towels off, he has concocted a top-quality lie. There was a brawl in the Liquid Forest, and he got smacked good breaking it up. He was a hero tonight, goddammit.

He dresses, puts on the T-shirt and shorts Erica left on the toilet for him, and strides out to the living room, his mind full of bar-brawl nobility, how he can't stand violence in the tavern, how he placed himself on the line for peace.

But Erica is not in the living room. With her head in her hands she sits at her spot at the kitchen table. An open bottle of

Leinenkugel's rests in front of her, half drained, and another open bottle sits across from her, at Grady's spot. When he walks into the kitchen he hears the herky-jerky noise of Erica sobbing.

"Look," Grady says, and he circles around her and sits in his dinner chair. "The fight wasn't what you think."

Under the kitchen ceiling-fan light her shoulders shine. Her head convulses one abrupt time, and her hands grip her head so tightly Grady thinks she's trying to keep it from flying off. She says, "Fight all you want. It's irrelevant to me."

Grady handles his beer bottle with his fingertips, tries to seem relaxed. But his mind swarms with his bullshit: two feed-capped fellows mixing it up, ducks and swerves, steel toe to steel toe, Grady himself soaring across the barroom in his SuperMaintenanceMan cape, getting between the fellows, stopping the brawl.

"I broke it up," he says. "You'd have been proud."

Her right hand drops to her bottle, and she lifts the bottle to swig. When she sets it down, Grady sees a puffiness in her eyes, bloodshot from crying, and a bubble of tears forms on each of her lower eyelids.

"Everything's irrelevant," she says, broken speech, the words coming out in high-pitched chirps and chokes. "We have a major problem, my husband."

My husband: This is bad. She only says *my husband* when it's the worst. Grady regards the cabinetry behind her, the stain and varnish so perfect, each cupboard door hung in precise symmetry with the next. He does good work—that's a No Shit For Sure—but he can't figure out his wife.

His first try: "I don't mean to be going to the bar after work, if that's what's bothering you. I get bored, you know."

Her eyes rise to his, but as soon as they do they turn back to the table. "You know I don't mind you going to the bar." Another convulsive sob: She makes a noise like air trapped in a hydraulic line, a deep blub.

His second try: "Did I forget to do something lately?" When he says this he gnashes his teeth. He's sounding like a moron.

"Nice, nice, everything's been just nice." She sits herself upright, begins peeling the label from her beer bottle. The fingers are long, the nail polish immaculate, and silver flakes of beer label stick to the undersides of each nail.

His third try, an angry try, spoken with much volume and palms pounding on the table: "Spit it the fuck out then."

She jerks back in her chair like he's just slapped her, and the way her eyes widen and dry, the way she swallows and sniffles and folds her hands professionally on the table—hold it the fuck together, Grady; her announcement is about to arrive.

"I know you have a low opinion of Lucky Littlefield," she says.

The word *Lucky* brings a picture of a mushroom cloud into Grady's head: cataclysm, atomization, buildings vaporizing. He balls his hands into fists. "That Beandick ought to go back to the grit-eating country he came from," Grady says.

Erica interweaves her fingers and presses both thumbs, at the knuckles, to her forehead. "And every time I talk about Lucky you get upset," she says. "I mean, look at you."

He knows better than to follow her directions in a moment like this. Never give her the edge; that's the Golden Rule of marriage squabbling. He looks at the kitchen sink: dish-sprayer hose, extra tap for filtered water, everything mounted in place and true and level. Lucky Littlefield could never install sinks like this.

"My husband, I must be honest here." She inhales deeply,

exhales through her nostrils. Her right pinky twitches. "What we did a while ago—well, I practiced before I got home."

Over the sink hangs a tile plaque, which says, GOD BLESS THIS MESS. It strikes Grady odd Erica's hung this plaque, because the kitchen's forever spotless. Even the dish-soap bottle she rinses clean. No crumbs, no germs, immaculate: a retarded cockroach wouldn't inhabit this kitchen.

"Did you hear me?" she says. "I practiced before I got home."

Grady replays his night all over—work, the bar, tantrum in the bar, walk with Kate, French Clamp with Kate, home, crash on the couch—and he can't decide precisely what Erica's driving at. He sighs, rushing the air through his teeth for maximum disgruntled effect, and he says, "*What* did you practice?"

"I did it for you, my husband. I thought if I practiced first, you'd have a better experience."

She *does* talk in circles like this, never getting to the goddam point. Grady outstretches his arms like a priest summoning heaven, and he says, "What the fuck are you talking about?"

In her eyes he catches the first tinge of something awful. She unlocks her hands and says, "I gave Lucky Littlefield a blowjob after work tonight."

Grady leans back in his chair and drains his entire Leinenkugel's, sets the bottle down so tenderly it does not make a sound.

"It was for you," Erica says. "I thought we needed some help." She sobs, regular diaphragm chuffs. She's a sputtering outboard motor.

Grady doesn't look at her, doesn't look anywhere but within. He thinks about who he is. Since he was in high school a man's rule in the world has been this: *You are what you fuck.* He's fucked Erica, all right; she's sucked Lucky Littlefield's dick; therefore, Grady *is* Lucky Littlefield's dick. A great calmness begins in Grady's hands, an opening they do, and it passes through his body. He feels like his soul is leaving his body.

"I think we need to talk about this," Erica says, her voice the butterfly valve over a carburetor, a wheezing opening to an engine gone bad. "I need to have this out in the open."

This is not Grady standing up, not the Grady McCann who whistles while he respokes wheelchairs in the afternoon, who likes Led Zeppelin and Ted Nugent and Molly Hatchet, whose favorite food is kielbasa boiled with onions, whose favorite color is the off-white he sees on certain nurses in the B wing of Shady Glen, who's happy wearing his hair pigtailed because it says *fuck you* to the money-mucks of this world; no, this is a Grady standing who knows of nothing enjoyable. This is a Grady who can't feel his musculature tensing and knocking his wife off her chair. She wiggles on the linoleum, and his foot sidewinds, once, into her buttocks, flopping her body over. This Grady can't hear his wife, in a hollow sob, say, "I am so sorry."

There are Pinto keys this Grady owns and picks up off his living-room floor, and there is a quiet light outside he walks into, the northern lights wavering over the valley, green and luminous, and he can see them vibrating over the home that is no longer a happy Grady home, over the lawn gone bad two months ago, over his dying shrubs and his dented yellow aluminum siding and his roof in need of reshingling, and in the northern lights Grady sees the surge of the earth into space, into the dust the heavens produce, how green the northern lights are, how piercing they are over the moon.

7

LET US PAUSE, PEOPLE, TO THINK: IF YOU ARE WHAT YOU'RE married to, and if what you're married to has sucked Lucky Littlefield's dick and has by process of easy, dipstickproof logic transformed you—a human being with a steady job and a Social Security card and a bank-payment booklet for your own home—*you*, yes—transformed *you* into a six-foot pigtailed likeness of Lucky's Littlefield's dick, what can you do? There's but one option. You park your Ford Pinto wagon one block from Lucky Littlefield's New England home on Westlake Drive, smoke yourself a couple cigarettes, and for a serious while you contemplate killing him.

Two squad cars with their chase lights revolving are parked in front of Lucky's house, nose to nose, and in a semicircle near the squads a crowd, Grady guesses, of fifty folks stands and shuffles their feet and makes skyward-sweeping movements with their hands. In the chase light the crowd looks like it's partying at a dance club on TV, arms reaching upward and bodies moving in hiptwisting shimmers of purple and red and blue. *Lucky, Lucky*, the crowd chants, like a backbeat thumping time to the withering ride of the drought wind.

Grady steps out of his car and glances a moment at the northern lights, a green curtain seething and looking alive, spanning from one edge of the horizon to the other. Beyond the northern lights are stars that have been hidden each night for weeks, and Grady figures those hidden stars probably reveal the Truth there is to all Life: It's a drag. And it's a drag no matter what praying and bellyaching folks do. When that green curtain overhead opens, if it ever does, folks will quit chanting for Lucky, because folks will recognize the Truth when they can see all there is in the nighttime heavens to see. But every night the northern lights curtain off the stars and the Truth they reveal, and folks stay hopeful. Just look at them up the street: chanting and raising their arms. And every night Erica works alongside Lucky Littlefield, believing in God and in miracles, and sure enough longing for Lucky, too, probably the same way she longs for God, admiring Lucky's twangy preaching remarks and how Lucky promises relief will come. And every night Lucky's forecast is one any bonehead these days could make: It ain't raining.

Grady can see this night in laser beams now, what's been going on with his wife and Lucky, with the townsfolk and the drought. He believes he can see each particle in the northern lights and each star in the heavens.

And the sky tells him, *Your wife's been carrying on with a weatherman.*

And *The weatherman makes your wife feel hope when there isn't any hope.*

And *If the weatherman is dead*, the sky says, *your wife won't feel things she shouldn't again.*

And *Everyone's life will be normal again.*

Grady can feel his hands opening and closing, can feel the cords in his arms that operate his hands. He can feel the fluids that lubricate his brain flowing. He has fixed machines all his life, and now he can feel himself becoming a machine, a powerful one that feels sorry for nothing and that he doesn't know how to fix and doesn't, just this instant, want to fix, because the machine he is now is perfectly tuned to do the violent job it's built to do.

He steps behind his Pinto and opens the wagon hatch, glances at the crowd a block distant—praying, chanting—and at the other New England homes lining Westlake Drive—lights off, cars parked in the driveways. Nobody can see him here. He fumbles through his tools—some hammers, some box-end wrenches, some screwdrivers—and selects the proper tool for the job: his oversized thirty-six-inch Craftsman crowbar. About a year ago he bought this crowbar on sale out at Sears. It was too big for any normal job then, and it's too big now. Thirty bucks, this crowbar cost him, and he's never so much as used it once. But just like on the day Grady bought this crowbar, tonight he likes simply the concept of a crowbar thirty-six inches long, weighing over ten pounds, with a claw span wide enough to hook around a cantaloupe and a pry surface longer than a big man's hand. This fucker, yes, is overkill for nearly any job, a quality Grady can't help admiring in a tool. With tools, it's better too much than not enough. He grips the crowbar in its middle, feels its smoothness from lack of use, and he hoists it free into the night air. He holds the crowbar's claw end like it's a shotgun butt, points at the northern lights, and pretends to shoot. Comfortable. Balanced-feeling in his hands. Finally, he's got the proper job for this tool.

He clicks closed his Pinto's wagon hatch and begins a steady walk toward his business, no sneak to his walk, merely one crunch after another through this first crispy lawn. In the second backyard he pauses to stretch, grabs the crowbar at both ends, places it behind his neck like a yoke. He straightens his legs and bends forward a couple of times. All right. The hurt shoulder feels better, looser. The legs have some spring they don't usually have this time of night. When he walks again he hears his breathing, regular, and each crunch he makes on the third backyard's ruined grass is a sound he feels reverberating through his whole body. His muscles are relaxed, his eyes methodically scanning: light on, upstairs, third house; dead maple tree next to the fourth house, Lucky's house, branches bending in the breeze, flickering purple and red and blue. Grady's senses expand and sharpen. His resolve is growing. His power is growing. In his hands the crowbar feels as light as a knitting needle. He can do this. You bet. He can make Lucky Littlefield's skull a goner.

Lucky's backyard has no shed, no fence, no Weber grill, no sign of yardworking equipment, only a small concrete patio without lawn chairs that borders a glass sliding door. Inside the glass door hangs a lamp that shines over a small round kitchen table, and this lamp sends a dim yellow arc of light that stretches into Lucky's backyard to the point where the patio ends. Beyond the patio is darkness. Grady paces to and fro at the edge of the arc of light and looks inside Lucky's house: a grubby kitchen counter with several plates and pots stacked on it, some cheap cabinetry with its sticker cover peeling away from the plywood. Past the kitchen area is a doorway, open door, a carpeted room, with the light on. Lucky must be where that light is.

Grady hefts the crowbar skyward, holding it firm by the claw end, and readies himself to smash it through the sliding door, then bust through the kitchen, freaking the everlasting wits out of Lucky before braining him, but he stops himself and holds as still as he can for a moment. He breathes through his nose to collect himself and wonders, but not long, what's turned him into the machine he is tonight. He never used to be the violent type; never once, not since the fifth grade, has he been in a fist-fight even, never even thought about it. And just tonight he attacked a college girl by the river and knocked his wife off her kitchen chair. And now he's standing outside a man's house with a crowbar, preparing to bash in his brains! Not too long ago, a year or two ago, Grady would give up nearly anything to spend an afternoon with his wife, to hold her hand walking through the park or to sit with her in their living room and watch a movie on videotape. Stupid stuff, sure. But it didn't matter. Grady was happy. But where did that happiness go? Something, whatever it is, has invaded Grady and increment by increment taken away anything that could bring a smile back to his face. Like the rain, the old Grady has evaporated into memory, maybe to return, maybe not.

And Grady isn't standing on Lucky's dead lawn anymore. He's reaching to the sliding glass door, and it's unlocked, and here Grady is: stepping into Lucky's kitchen, smelling it, something salty and greasy, bacon or ham. Music plays quietly from the carpeted room where the light is. It's Molly Hatchet, "Flirtin' with Disaster," a tune Grady recognizes from the juke-box at the Liquid Forest, and he hesitates a second and ponders this notion: Lucky Littlefield listens to the same tunes Grady does.

The room Grady steps into is a decent-sized den-type setup, with pine paneling, a couple of lamps, a drink cart against one wall, a sofa and coffee table against the other, and in a green recliner next to the sofa sits Lucky Littlefield, wearing blue jeans and a flannel shirt with the sleeves cut off, holding a drink in one hand and a cigarette in the other. Lucky reaches his cigarette to a tall freestanding ashtray that's between the recliner and the sofa, taps the cigarette with his thumb, releasing an inchlong clump of ash. Lucky's arms are big and hairy but not muscular, and when he moves them he does so with deliberation, watching his arms and hands, riffling the fingers slowly.

Lucky stares at Grady, at the crowbar in Grady's hand, and Lucky doesn't appear nervous at all. He takes a swig from his drink, squints when he swallows, and says, "I don't rightly recall needing anything fixed. And looky here: Those police out front let me in a man looking to fix something."

Grady says, "That's right. I'm looking to fix your head."

"Cain't be fixed," Lucky says. "You might have saved yourself the trouble of coming on in, and me the trouble of sending you away." He leans forward in his recliner and examines his cigarette with a smile before taking a long, thoughtful drag. His beard looks, in person, about the same as on TV, red and wide, but his hair's messed and downright shabby-looking. "Hell, what am I saying? As long as you're here, Grady, you want you a Jack Daniel's? A little Jack might could improve your evening some."

Grady's grip tightens on the crowbar, and he takes what he believes is a menacing step toward Lucky, who chuckles softly and examines his cigarette again. This afternoon, Kate knew Grady's name before he told it to her, but she'd read it off his work shirt. He's not wearing a work shirt now. He says, "How do you know my name?"

"Ain't a mystery to it, Grady. Lucky Littlefield about knows everything, right? Didn't you know that? See, back where I'm from, folks say The Prophet acquires special powers from immersion in Scripture."

"Prophet, my ass," Grady says, but not in the powerful way he wants it to sound. How relaxed Lucky is—no visible fear, no quivering at the sight of the crowbar—how Lucky somehow knows Grady's name, this ain't adding up how Grady figured it would.

Lucky says, "Likely the term *Prophet* means something different down south Georgia way than what it means here."

"Don't dick with me." But Grady's words are flat and weak. He raises the crowbar a bit to compensate for what his words won't do.

"I offered you a Jack Daniel's. You call that dicking?"

Lucky stands not hurriedly and hikes up his jeans, which, now that Grady can get a better look at them, are not jeans at all but blue painter's pants, exactly the kind of pants Grady likes to wear on his days off. And now that Lucky is on his feet, Grady can see Lucky's got some manly heft to him, not Lennartlike heft, but Lucky is thick, over six feet tall, and he moves in an unlumbering way that suggests possible strength and possible trouble, if Grady doesn't keep control of the situation here.

When Lucky makes a move toward the drink cart, Grady pokes him in the back with the pry end of the crowbar.

"Don't pull any bullshit," Grady says.

"Of course I won't, old buddy. Just fixing to pour you a Jack."

"Pour, then," Grady says, and keeps the crowbar nudged into

Lucky's ribs while Lucky situates himself in front of the drink cart.

Lucky removes the cover from the ice bucket and sets it aside. "Ice, Grady? I'm having me some ice with mine."

Grady says, "Ice will be fine." And he can't figure out why he's all of a sudden behaving so civilized. *Ice will be fine*: ridiculous! Here's the guy Grady's wife's been putting the round mouth to, and here's Grady with the very tool in his hand he should use to bash this guy's brains in, but here, too, pouring two drinks and dropping ice cubes in each glass, is your regular, basic-looking fellow: ripped flannel shirt, wrinkled painter's pants, boots even! Before this, Grady had been certain Lucky was a fraud, that his Hawaiian shirt costume was just that: a costume to wear on the TV. But Grady couldn't have guessed, not for a year's free drinks at the Liquid Forest Bar, that Lucky Littlefield, when he's kicking back of an evening at his house, would be wearing regular-person clothes, would be a normal, guy-with-a-construction-job type guy who drinks bourbon and smokes cigarettes and listens to decent tunes, who doesn't seem like he's ever prayed on TV or predicted yet another rainless week in his life.

Lucky turns around, extends a glass of Jack and ice to Grady. Cautiously Grady lowers the crowbar to take the glass, but he doesn't look Lucky in the eye, looks instead at Lucky's arms, anticipating a sudden movement.

"Pull you up a sofa," Lucky says.

"What?"

"Have a seat, Grady." Lucky gestures with his drink to the sofa. "Let's set ourselves awhile and have us a talk."

With several awkward, jerking steps, Grady maneuvers himself between the coffee table and the sofa, and before sitting he makes certain the pry end of his crowbar stays pointed at Lucky, prepared to thrust out at the slightest miscue.

When Lucky sits he claps his hands together and says, "Cigarette?"

"Why the fuck not?" Grady says, still pointing the crowbar at Lucky like it's a gun.

Lucky places a pack of Marlboros and a lighter on the coffee table and tells Grady to help himself.

When Grady's smoke is going, and when Lucky has himself a smoke going, they don't say anything for a while. Lucky's music comes from a bookshelf stereo that's playing a tape, and the music now is something else Southern rock, an instrumental guitar jam Grady can't ever remember hearing before. Allman Brothers? Marshall Tucker? Pretty decent stuff, but Grady doesn't want to ask what it is. From outside Grady hears the crowd chanting Lucky's name again. They never quit. Never. Grady wonders if those folks know Lucky is having a drink, not wearing a Hawaiian shirt and not showing any concern about getting his life threatened by a maintenance man. Grady wonders if those folks know anything about anything.

He swigs from his Jack, harsher than his usual Beam, and says, "Okay, fucker. Give it up. How do you know my name?"

"Hell, I've been looking at your picture every day for a year. That fine wife of yours—and, boy, is she *ever* fine—she's got you hung there right above her desk. You look just like yourself in the picture, too, except in the picture you don't have that black eye, and you're not brandishing that big hunk of iron you are now."

"No more complimentary crap about my wife, hey."

"I was just saying the truth, Grady. Erica's a fine woman. I wouldn't take me any offense at that."

Grady leans forward and slugs a gag quantity of his Jack, gets the bourbon blur in his eyes and in his mind, and he's got to do this; he's got to get confirmation before going on.

"Well," he says, "she did it, didn't she?"

"Did what, old buddy?"

"I'm not your buddy." Grady thrusts the crowbar toward Lucky, holds it directly in front of Lucky's nose.

Lucky's eyes cross slightly staring at the crowbar, but the rest of him doesn't appear unnerved. His hands don't tremble. He doesn't breathe hard. "Okay then," he says. "I won't call you my old buddy."

Grady says, "Did she do it?"

"Do what?"

"Suck your dick."

Lucky coughs a cough that sounds bored to Grady, and says, without the slightest irritation, "Get that iron out my face, and I'll tell you."

Reasonable enough, Grady thinks. Let him talk, then bash him. He moves the crowbar back a couple of feet but keeps the tool poised for the job.

Lucky says, "She tell you she sucked my dick?"

Grady nods, and the muscles tense in his arms, making the crowbar wobble some.

Lucky laughs without opening his mouth. "There you have it."

"Have what?"

"If she told you she done it, it's as bad as if she did."

"Bullshit. Either she did it, or she didn't. Now, which is it gonna be?"

"Y'all up here in the North are coarse people. You know that? Talking about sucking dicks, cussing every other word and the like — it's ungentlemanly behavior, is what it is."

"Which," Grady says, and now he pushes the crowbar into Lucky's gut, which has some fatty give to it, "is it gonna be?"

Lucky inhales, and Grady feels Lucky's gut moving through the crowbar. "Whichever you want it to be," Lucky says. "Maybe she did. Maybe she didn't. Looks like you decided she done it no matter what I say." Still, Lucky's face is calm, and his voice is as casual as if they were strolling down a country path and talking about the breeze. "Point is, if she gone and said such a thing, how can you be coming over here to my home, threatening me with that hunk of iron, and blaming your troubles on me? It ain't my fault, whatever it is that happened. Put yourself in my boots, Grady. You fixing to turn down a beautiful woman if she's offering? The hell you are. And you can't deny it. Because you by God are a man, and men ain't built to kick anything soft and fine out of their sack for offering to eat their crackers."

Whether he likes it or not, Grady can put himself exactly in Lucky's boots. Just tonight, if Grady wouldn't have lost his composure and gone Clampy with Kate, he'd have given her his whole program: kissed her the correct varied way, groped her long enough and with enough strength and enough tenderness to prepare her underflower for bloom. And he'd have held when they were done, held her for a full hour after, and kissed her like he meant it, because he would have. He would have meant it. The marriage is over; he can see that. And the way Grady's got to look at it is that Lucky's just some stooge gotten himself accidentally in the middle of a marriage ending.

Lucky says, "I'm not suggesting, of course, I had any improper associations with your wife. Take that thought right out of your mind, if you would."

And why should the stooge in the middle admit to anything? Covering his ass, is what Lucky's doing, and Grady's going to let him do it, because Grady, put in the same position, would be covering his ass, too.

Grady reaches over the coffee table and lets the crowbar thud to the carpet. "You know what the problem is?" Grady says, making his voice more friendly. "It's the goddam lack of rain that's the problem."

"Amen," Lucky says, and drains his glass of Jack.

In his arms Grady notices a tingling: adrenaline. He fumbles a Marlboro from Lucky's pack, lights up, and his breath shakes on the exhale. "I was really gonna kill you," he says, and it's a relief to say it.

"I know you were," Lucky says, and for the first time tonight Grady notices a vein pulsing on Lucky's forehead. Fuckhead here *was* scared Grady was about to brain him. "I'm much obliged you're choosing to let me live, Grady."

"Whatever," Grady says flatly, suppressing the shaking in him, because he was scared, too, scared he really *was* going to kill Lucky.

Lucky says, "The drought will do that to people, make them crazy."

"I guess," Grady says.

"But tonight, I'm telling you, tonight we'll have way worse than a drought to worry about." Lucky sits into perfect posture and stares blankly forward, as if Grady isn't even in the room.

"What are you talking about now?" Grady says.

Lucky keeps talking, turning into the Lucky Grady has seen on TV. "I've had a Word of Knowledge. And my mind's eye has foreseen such ravaging of the earth, Mr. Grady McCann, you will not have witnessed hitherto."

Holy shit, Grady thinks. This guy's majorly whacked. And Grady stands slowly, his knees cracking, moves around the coffee table, and he stops to look at Lucky, whose eyes are bloodshot and blue, and who smiles in a suddenly sane way at Grady.

"I just wanted you to know, old buddy, that I'm still Lucky Littlefield, no matter what just transpired here between us."

"I'm not your old buddy, fucker. And I don't give a shit who you are."

"You will. Yessir, you will."

"I'll tell you what, Lucky. Why don't you keep this crowbar, you know, as a little gifty from Grady McCann? A little reminder I was here. Next time, maybe I'll come back with a gun and blast your ass and all your weatherman bullshit with it."

"I'll keep me some good whiskey on hand, just for the occasion."

A flash of weak anger passes through Grady and disappears. He merely wags his head a couple times to demonstrate his disappointment, then he leaves. He retraces his route through Lucky's kitchen, smelling that salty, greasy smell again, bacon or ham. When Grady reaches the sliding glass door he hears Lucky shouting, "Ravaging! Ravaging!" Then Lucky laughs. Insanity: to change personalities like that. Ridiculous.

8

A YEAR AGO, WHEN LUCKY LITTLEFIELD WOULD GIVE HIS forecast on a Friday evening, he would say, "Could be a shower or two Sunday, friends and brethren, but by then we might could need a small break from all the fun we'll be having." And he would smile his bearded smile. And that would be it. Folks would turn off their sets and go about their way, saunter to their backyards again, resume their cribbage game with Aunt Alice, or tell once more that story about dropping two eight-point bucks with one slug. Nobody used to ponder the meaning of Lucky, or think ill of the man, or think he was wonderful. Lucky was the goof from way down South who moved up here to broadcast the weather. Who cared that he did anything but do his job?

But look at what a year does. Look at McCutcheon at tavern close this early Saturday morning. Look at the frenzy Mitchell Street is: three separate brawls in front of the Liquid Forest; a rosary vigil of three hundred souls in the IGA parking lot gone to squabbling over which Glorious Mystery to chant first. Beer bottles fly through the air, along with street dust and windblown pine needles, and rocks and annotated Bibles chucked in anger.

Death threats and vicious prayers mix in the air like an oratorio to the end of the world.

And in the homes husbands beat their wives, wives beat their children, children beat their dogs, and the dogs howl at their screen windows, mournful trombone notes into the windy night.

Everywhere police sirens sound. Everywhere is melee and people crying.

And in the firmament the northern lights waver over the valley, a fabulous display arcing and seething with earthsurge and the dead dust of space. All that remains green of the world glows overhead, but barely a soul looks up to watch.

McCutcheon is one word now, and sporadically along Mitchell Street, and in the neighborhood near the university, and along the streets climbing out of the valley, people begin gathering to chant it. *Lucky*, they chant. *Lucky, Lucky.* Lucky must do something. Lucky's all the hope folks have left.

SATURDAY

1

AT TEN O'CLOCK LAST NIGHT, IN CONDYLE, WISCONSIN—
population eight hundred, a town of one Catholic church, two
cemeteries, and three taverns nineteen miles northwest of
McCutcheon—folks gathered in their living rooms and in their
taverns to let Lucky Littlefield lift their spirits from ruin.

And Lucky said, "Friends, can you still feel what I'm feeling?
Can you feel that rain is finally coming around the corner? And
that all these months we've been devoting ourselves to prayer
are finally going to give us an answer? Yes! I know you can feel
it. Relief at last!"

Folks in Condyle bowed then, moved their minds and hearts
into nearly forgotten territories, where liquid falls from the sky
and where the crops are forever bountiful, and when they
opened their eyes they saw Lucky there, smiling, Hawaiian shirt
pink as a cow's wet tongue, eyes blue as a map of Lake Superior.

And Lucky said, "From the heavens our relief will come.
Soon. Soon. Raise your heads so we may devote our hours now
to rejoicing."

And the Condyle townsfolk left their homes and their bar
stools, and they gathered again just west of town, at the crest of a

giant treeless glacial coulee called Mount Misery. They prayed, all eight hundred, and bore witness to God and His limitless majesty. Folks said their rosaries or spontaneously sang the Lord's Prayer. Some folks wept. Others threw handfuls of dirt to the sky. On other late evenings during the drought, these people had prayed from the crest of Mount Misery, cried out and clutched their crosses and beads, but on this night their prayers demanded a sign. God would speak to them this night, or there was no God at all.

Sometime after midnight the northern lights appeared over Mount Misery and illuminated the bottomland to the west, the vast stretch of dried muskeg and tag-elder thicket known as the Murphy Bottoms. And under the green glow of God the Murphy Bottoms looked like a dark living forest, the tag elder churning in the night wind, the roiling greenness in the sky sending shadowy waves everywhere over the distance. An hour passed, then another, and another. And God did nothing. But His faithful would not abandon their resolve. The beseeching would last till there was nothing beseechable.

And at precisely 3:35 A.M., from the center of the northern lights there appeared a bright star dropping toward the earth, trailing a wide line of sparks behind it. A general cheer rose from the faithful, a yowling heavenward, and folks fell to their knees, crossing themselves, pressing their hands outward into the westerly wind. And the star dropped into a heavy clump of dead thicket a mile from the base of Mount Misery. And the light from the star took on an orangish hue that broadened over the distance, assuming the form of a jagged rectangle expanding taller and wider. Someone in the crowd recognized the light as fire, and what were happy yelps became a great bellow of fright, for the winds were strong, and the flames were growing at a tremendous rate, already in a few minutes four hundred yards across and surging toward Mount Misery. Smoke rose from the Murphy Bottoms, transforming into a mist under the northern lights.

And the faithful panicked.

The eight hundred, young and old and healthy and feeble, clamored down the eastern slope of Mount Misery. Some folks ran. Some hobbled. Some fell. One old woman, Millie Peterson, eighty-six years old and disgusted with God, tucked herself behind a rock atop Mount Misery and was forgotten there. She was the first to be incinerated.

When the last pickup truck sped away from the base of Mount Misery, the fire breached its peak, and the immense fire-light outshone the northern lights and the moon and the stars, and a great wind accumulated within the fire and blasted it downward toward Condyle itself. It came too fast. It came too wide. It came before folks could salvage their precious trinkets from their homes. The fire was in Condyle before the one fire truck in Condyle's station backed from its stall.

And when the fire arrived it obliterated Condyle. The lilac hedges burned like fuses to the clapboard houses and to the three taverns, to Saint Anthony's Catholic Church, which toppled in eight minutes flat, to the Sinclair gas station, which, after a minute of flame, exploded. Fire torched the telephone poles, burned the cars in the driveways, burned the toys scattered in the yards. On the outskirts of town fire killed milking cows and feeder pigs and chickens lickety-split, and in town, just like that, fire killed dogs and cats and parakeets, and fire killed all but a handful of folks in Condyle. Just like that.

And by morning now, when the fire has moved to the east, slowly, the way a thunderstorm rolls, when the westerly wind is fanning the flames from Condyle and through the vast hay fields and pine stands of the western Chequamegon, it's clear that whatever Condyle was is gone. The four streets are covered with black snow. What buildings haven't fallen yet soon will. Smoke hazes the sky over Condyle, and here and there a charred body lies, sometimes two of them, sometimes six in a sooty heap. What living folks remain in the smolder, those who survived by hiding in the Condyle storm sewers, say only this: "We asked God for a sign. We surely did."

And leering over the town is Mount Misery, a black bald head now, proof of what prayer can do. Lucky Littlefield can't speak to folks in Condyle today—there's not a TV set or a power line left—but if Lucky could bring the Word to folks here, no one would listen.

2

NINE A.M. NOW, ERICA McCANN STANDS TWENTY FEET TO the side of the Action 9 set, stands ready to bring Lucky anything he needs—fire-location updates, a cup of coffee, a glass of water, a kind word, anything—because the forest fire is each hour growing larger, more powerful, winds pushing it more furiously toward the valley. Each hour hundreds must be dying out there in the countryside. She sees Lucky in profile, massaging his temples while he waits for the light on Camera One to blink back on. He looks human, capable of failing. Odd, Erica thinks, Lucky has to be perfect today, which means she has to be perfect in order to help him be perfect, that people by the thousands are depending on Lucky to speak to them calmly and to provide them with whatever hope and inner strength they may feel on such a day as this, but Erica is in no physical state to be perfect today. She didn't sleep last night, spent the night instead weeping, hoping that Grady would come back home. She thinks about that: Grady didn't come back. And a weak sob builds in her throat, then fades. This isn't the time or place to come unglued.

Camera One blinks red, and Lucky leans forward in his

chair to speak. "Friends, I want you to consider these words: *more than ever*. No one yet knows how many souls passed into heaven last evening in Condyle, or how many souls are passing to heaven as I speak. In the face of this catastrophe, we must not forget that our prayers are needed more than ever. For ourselves, for our families, for our friends, for those who are dead or dying, we must form our prayers into one unified voice today. The greatest of scourges is on us right now. And we cannot relent at this hour of our greatest need. Let us not run before the fire. Let us face it and pray for our salvation."

As on all the dry days and weeks she's stood in this spot and watched Lucky lead silent prayer, Erica observes with a wince his hands piously gripped together, but she does not bow her head today with the rest of the crew. She stares instead, red-eyed, out into the Action 9 warehouse building: smooth concrete floor shining in all the lights, iron beams jutting from the tin walls and from the tent-angled ceiling lined with silver-coated insulation. Behind the cameras stand Jimbo and Pete, bowing, and behind them several other station employees stand, bowing. The only sound is wind buffeting tin.

She makes her hands into tiny hatchets and hacks at her thighs, considers the fiery end of McCutcheon approaching, and the end of her life possibly approaching. And she has not atoned for her sins. She shouldn't have lied to Grady about having an affair. That was stupid, and she went about it stupidly. But after that girl called, Erica was angry, in no state where her mind could calculate, and all she could think of doing was picking Grady's weakest point and trying to exploit it, to make Grady as angry as *she* was. She'd give anything to relive last night in a smarter way.

And Lucky says, "Amen." He pauses a moment and brings his hands solemnly to his chin. "It is surely not appropriate for me to speak just now. Friends, let us view tape of the destruction in Condyle."

And the tape rolls, appears in the studio on a big TV mounted into the far warehouse wall. The screen shows logs asmolder, taverns and houses gutted and crumbled, humvees unloading National Guardsmen carrying guns, which strikes Erica odd that they should be carrying guns.

"Darling, will you get yourself over here?" This is Erica's cue, and Lucky gives her the summoning eye, a blue flash under the set lights, and he raises his hand and curls his index finger in a slow repetition, like he's tugging her to duty with a strand of fishing line.

"What may I do for you?" she says, and the words have a dagger effect on her heart. Her memory reenters late last night, how Grady rose so calmly from his chair in the kitchen, how she felt nothing when she struck the floor, when he kicked her then, how she could have avoided it by telling Grady the truth: *I got a disturbing call from Kate. What do you have to say about that?*

"Is something wrong with you, Erica? You don't look well."

"I'm fine, sir."

"*Sir*? There *must* be something wrong if you're calling me *sir.*" He breathes heavily through his nose and looks at Erica in a blearing way that makes her believe they're supposed to be sharing a secret. "What we need to do," he says, "hell, you know better than *me* what we need to do."

On the wall screen behind Lucky four National Guardsmen in BDU's kick through a heap of smoking rubble. One of the

Guardsmen pets a sooty golden retriever with its tail between its legs.

Erica says, "We need you to be on the air, keeping people calm. That's what we need to do."

"You're right. Of course you're right," he says, and lowers his voice to a whisper, cuts a glance at Jimbo and Pete, meaning that they shouldn't hear what he's about to say, that he's got some essential information he needs to share with Erica, and Erica alone. "I'm under terrific pressure, Erica. You're the one person around here I feel safe letting my guard down with. I've grown—how shall I say it?—*fond* of having you at my side to confide in."

"Since when have you listened to my advice?" Erica speaks softly, too—she doesn't want other people to hear this.

Lucky leans to whisper in her ear. "I need more from you than advice, Erica. I've got to tell you: I know things about you that you don't think I know. I know what you lie about."

Erica flushes with anger and embarrassment and looks out toward Jimbo and Pete. They stand with their arms folded, both of them absently watching the wall-screen TV, which shows footage of a smoldering pickup truck.

"I don't care what you know about me," Erica says. "This isn't the time for this."

Lucky's whisper becomes a hiss. "I'll determine when the time *is* and when the time *isn't* around here."

On the wall screen: the steaming cross of a burned church.

Erica says, "Good Lord, Lucky. Will you stop for one moment and recognize what's happening out there? Can't you think about all these people dying?"

Lucky bolts up from his chair and stands nearly chest-to-chest with Erica. He says, "Don't preach to me! I'll do the preaching!"

He's a tall man, perhaps two inches taller than Grady, and Erica's nose hovers near Lucky's beard, which gives off a smell that reminds her of the salty whiskey sweat of Grady's crotch last night when she came home from work. She clumps backward, loses her balance when her heel catches on a power cable, and she falls, tumbles off the set and lands hard on the concrete floor.

"Fuck," she says, a word she hates to say, and she stares at the Action 9 warehouse ceiling. In between the iron beams the silver insulation coating is torn at spots, wide seams four feet long, maybe five, exposing pink gashes that look like cuts on a bloodless corpse, and around the hanging flood lamps moths circle and dodge. Dust hangs up there and lines the beams and the conduit and the flood-lamp cords. Now Lucky stands above her: his Hawaiian shirt so loose Erica sees under it a few stretchmark squiggles where his belly lumps over his gym-teacher shorts.

"You're causing an unnecessary fuss here," he says. "You get yourself under control and get to my office. And I mean immediately!"

All that is Erica—the good Catholic girl grown guilty and sad, the married woman who's allowed her marriage to fail—forms into these words: "Fuck you, Lucky." She rolls over, presses her face to the cool shiny concrete, and allows herself to cry, great convulsions heaving through her torso.

Lucky clears his throat and says, "Jimbo. Pete. Please accept my apologies for this unseemly incident. Just keep with the network feed—five minutes or so—and I'll have this problem worked out."

Erica hears Lucky's shoes pivoting on the concrete, a slither over the dust. Then Lucky walks away. Nobody comes to help her. Two days in a row, and here's Erica sprawled on the floor and crying, no one there for comfort, only the sound of a man walking away. She props herself up on an elbow and sees that her forearms have become grimy, and her dress is grimy, and she feels something in her heart has become grimy, but she will not stay on this floor in disgrace. She stands and brushes with fierce strokes at the dust clinging to her, then squares her shoulders and walks toward Lucky's office, thinking briefly of Jesus among the Pharisees and Sadducees, when they come to test Him, asking Him for some otherworldly sign, some spectacular miracle for their awe and delight, and Jesus holds the line for righteousness. Jesus says, "You know how to judge the appearance of the sky, but you cannot judge the signs of the times. An evil and unfaithful generation seeks a sign."

In the periphery of Erica's vision she sees fuzzy outlines of people watching her, the crew, the newsroom people; they are seeing her, thinking she's weak and in disgrace, but she is not weak. She is becoming stronger.

3

GRADY MCCANN—GONE LAST NIGHT LATE WITH HIS PINTO wagon to park by the Shady Glen Convalescent Center utility shed and sleep off his marriage—wakes to hammering sounds on his Pinto's roof, metallic booms that filter into the dream he's having about running along the McCutcheon riverbed in a panic, a mob of angry women chasing him. He hears the thumps on his roof as gunshots in his dream, dozens of women behind him shooting and yelling, *Him! Him! It's him that's made our lives miserable.*

When Grady's eyes open to the oily gray carpet he's sprawled on in the back of his car, he shakes with fright. And his roof booms again. Cops, sure enough, have come for Grady for what he did last night. He puts his forearms over his face, readies himself for the billy-clubbing he figures all wife beaters got coming to them.

The hammering on his roof stops, a sound of feet crunching on the parking-lot asphalt then, and he hears his driver's-side door open, a rusty creak, followed by a whining rush of wind. For an instant he goes so tense he worries he's going to foul his drawers.

But this is what he hears next: "We been calling all over for you, Grady. Three hours we been trying. Stupid me, I didn't think once all this time to look in your car."

Grady's body relaxes quickly, because this isn't the cops he's hearing. This is the alto voice of Jane Schmidt, the weekend charge nurse, sixty years old if she's a day, and a lifer RN at Shady Glen. He sets his arms to his sides, shifts his head to look at Jane leaning over his steering wheel: white smock, gray wiry hair, aviator glasses, a strained smile.

She says, "You're just the man we're needing today, Grady."

His impulse is to tell her, *Ain't nothing in the state of Wisconsin needs done bad enough for Grady McCann to do it today*, but somehow he doesn't have enough energy to start this day surly. He's at work all of a sudden, woke up from a bad night full of bad dreams in the goddam parking lot of his job, and even if his personal life is clogged in the toilet, a certain courtesy is expected at work, no matter if he hasn't shown up here in the regular way, shaved and showered and nicotined up after the twenty-mile drive. He rolls over to his belly, props his head on his palm, and fakes a grin. "You got something needs fixed?" he says.

"We got a major emergency needs fixed, Grady. We need every able body we can get."

Beyond Jane it's light outside. Gray overhead. Beyond the dead cornfields to the east: gray. And the sky between the dying pines south of Shady Glen: gray, not like the parched blue it's been all summer. Near Grady's car a bare maple bends and looks like it might snap in the dry wind, which is a loud wind, more fierce than the wind has been in a long time, the kind of wind that cranks up before a storm.

"Come on, kiddo," Jane says. "Get out of the car." She backs out the door, stands near his dented front fender with her arms folded. A gust comes and blows her hair enough so Grady can see her scalp. She could be his mother standing there in the wind.

Grady performs the cloddish operation of climbing over his driver's seat, grunting and tasting Jim Beam and Leinenkugel's and Marlboros on his breath, and he wiggles out the door. When his palms press the asphalt, a sudden pain comes from his bruised shoulder and makes him lose the strength in his arms. He flops out of the car and rolls a bit on the asphalt, winding up on his back, staring at the sky.

Clouds. You bet. Clouds in the sky all right. It's been so long since he's seen clouds he can barely remember what they look like. And these are sure enough peculiar-looking clouds, more like fog than clouds, none of the soft-angled lines and mounds of clouds he remembers.

"You *are* a graceful young buck," Jane says, and kneels, gets her upside-down face two feet from Grady's, so close he can see her upper nostril hairs and a few crusts of snard clinging to them. "What happened to that eye?"

He tells her the truth, because she'll never believe it.

"I got smacked by a college girl."

"Likely." She lets out a guffaw that quakes through her cheeks and thick neck. "I'm surprised it wasn't your wife smacked you. She says she hasn't seen you since last night."

Jane reaches to Grady's face and inspects his black eye, pulling at the skin on his cheekbone with her thumb, a flowery smell of antibacterial lotion coming from her hands, strong nurse's hands poking and prodding and giving him a good charge of agony.

"Are you goddam trying to kill me?" Grady shouts.

"Don't need to. Your wife'll get you soon enough."

He rears away from Jane's hand, winces at himself for snapping at her, rolls over and stands. Jane stands, too, and though she's almost a foot shorter than him, the way she carries herself—solid arms crossed over her chest, not an inch of her flesh moving—makes Grady feel like she's towering over him.

"It's not like you, Grady, wilding around on your wife like that."

"Held myself together better, I guess. But I done worse—way back."

Jane shakes her head in the disapproving way that only the truly worried can, a combination of brow furrow and nervous laugh. "Your pal Lennart called twice looking for you, and you got several calls now from some girl named Kate." Grady swallows hard and has a sudden urge to light up a cigarette, as if before his execution. "But there's no time to worry about Grady McCann's troubles just now. We got a bigger situation needs dealt with."

He sees a blurry reflection of himself in her glasses, not clear enough for him to make out his black eye, but he can see his hair unponytailed and flapping in the wind. An All-Pro Dipstick is what he's seeing. Dipstick Deluxe.

She says, "Anyhow, I don't think you'll go blind. Your socket's just a little bruised, is all." She hands him a pink hair tie and points to his head. Regulations: Can't leave the hair flopping on the job. "Now get suited up."

"Lennart called, you say?"

"You got too much to do to worry about any Lennarts."

Ah, Lennart. Of course he called Shady Glen to check up on Grady. The guy barkeeps like he's running the Liquid Forest

Day Care Center, making sure each of his drunks is happy and healthy both in the bar and out. This is for sure: Lennart knows everything that's gone down, maybe not the Going Down on Lucky Littlefield part, but everything else, the riverbank clamping with Kate, the leaving Erica. Could be Lennart's got a plan to help Grady's ass out of the sling it's in.

Grady finishes pigtailing his hair and says, "Whatever's up, it can't be that bad. I got time for a couple phone calls."

"You don't have time for anything but hustle. We got the building on Full Alert."

"I don't got the patience to go through one of your frigging drills today."

"Not a drill this time."

"Come on, Jane. Full Alert is *always* a drill."

She cups her chin and tilts her head to the heavens. "Look at all this smoke. That's *not* a drill?"

Grady follows her glance to the clouds, their yellowed look, how streaky they are, how they are a haze, really, without definition.

Jane places her hands to her hips, keeps looking upward. "Big forest fire over Condyle way. Coming right at us, too."

"Fire?" he says, and something in him piffles and feels weak, because Jane's right: These clouds overhead aren't clouds at all.

"This place probably needs evacuated come noontime."

Grady says, "If it needs evacuated, we'll evacuate it." But he says this without thinking what he means. He looks at the smoke, and at Jane, white-smocked, and off to the west, which is all haydeath and wind smelling vaguely, now that Grady thinks about it, like burning.

"What with this wind," he says, "we're toast."

Jane takes Grady's hands in her motherly way, pulling them up near her face. "Grady, whatever you got troubling you inside, you need to leave it go."

"I'm not a mess," he says, but he feels the muscles in his face sagging, feels the weight of everything important in his life vanishing from his body.

"The residents need your help."

The softness of her hands makes him think for a half instant what Jane was like, say, thirty years ago, when she was still in her bed-pounding days. He would have loved her then, her fire-pluggy stature, how kind she is to him. He would have done anything for her, still would.

She squeezes his hands, squints into his eyes. "There's barely an ambulance available. Everything's over to Condyle. National Guard, all that. We're stranded here."

"If the residents need evacuated," he says, "get a couple semis or something, and we'll ship everybody into town."

"They'll die if we can't move them with ambulances."

Grady's professional life: to help the dying. Grady's emotional life: Shady Glen is all that's left. The Shady Glen Convalescent Center building and grounds are his responsibility, as much the solder holding together his life as anything else, and the biggest part of the building happens to be the geezers that fill it, all those grandmas and grandpas, who, in the end, Grady probably couldn't live his life without, even if none of the wizzlers ever remembers his name.

He lets out a long sigh and says, "How many hours we got?"

"Could be four hours, could be six, could be ten minutes." Jane takes his arm and starts leading him to the building. He follows. It's his job.

Another gust blows in from the west, biting and hot, making the dead hay field across the highway look alive. It waggles in the wind. He thinks he sees a herd of deer running out there, multiple flashings of brown and white. From the forest to the south comes a whooshing sound, the wind bending and shaking the pines. Off in the distance Grady hears the mournful drone of an air-raid siren, and closer by the lawnmower sound of what he thinks is either a helicopter or a large turboprop.

"We got problems, Jane. That's for no shit certain."

"That's what we have *you* for, kiddo." She reaches behind him and gently yanks his pigtail, and this fills Grady with confidence. He can still help folks. He still has the ability to fix anything mechanical.

"I'll tell you what," Grady says, and whistles a cuckoo-clock whistle. "We'll get this shit figured out." He pats Jane on the hand but figures there's not much to figure out. They'll live, or they won't.

They go into the building through the delivery entrance, near the break room and the kitchen and the staircase to Grady's basement boiler room. The hallway is narrow, with mops and buckets and cartons of adult diapers leaning against the wall, and it smells of urine and glazed ham. Jane tells Grady he's got five minutes to suit up and report to the activity room. She doesn't even look him in the eye, just barks the order and walks down the hall, a billow of white fading away from Grady's line of vision.

He scoots down the stairs to the boiler room the way he always scoots, both hands sliding down the rail, his feet rumbling the grate steps. At the bottom he tosses his keys in the air, and when they flash just perfectly in the fluorescent light, when he can see each key individually splayed in the air, he stabs out his thumb and index finger and catches the jingle by the boiler-room key itself.

"Business as usual," he says. The chuckle he usually makes starts in the back of his throat, and, just as quickly as it comes on, it stops.

Over the P.A. he hears this: "Housekeeping to the nurse's station." The staff is readying for disaster. Command chains are being reissued. Routine. No frenzy yet.

Grady unlocks the door, flicks on the lights, and here it is, his boiler room, and all the stuff he's accumulated over the last ten years: his red thirteen-shelf top-and-bottom Craftsman roll-around tool chest, lid open and displaying his eight-by-ten autographed photograph of Ted Nugent, *To Grady, Another Wildman of Borneo, From Ted*; his complete set of RIGID pipe wrenches hung on nails next to the chest; his arc welder; his Shop Vac; his collection of antique hacksaws; all of this he's losing in one stroke, plus everything else in his life.

When he opens his locker he looks at the picture of Erica taped to the door, just a snapshot of her in their backyard. She's wearing a pink T-shirt and shorts, sticking out her tongue at the camera while she's placing a bratwurst on their Weber grill. She's beautiful, the thin texture of her hair, that olive skin, her hand so dainty holding that bratwurst. Life with her these last two years hasn't been unpleasant. They've had the holiday barbecues together, the Saturday breakfasts, the Sunday nights watching TV in the living room, the occasional weekend in Duluth. It's been a lovely thing, really, to have a home and someone there to nod and smile when he reels out his troubles.

When he changes into his work uniform—puts on a clean

blue shirt, blue pants, and his steel-toed boots—he thinks of all
the misery he's avoided these last two years by having one
woman, never needing to suffer through the love hunt for
another. He's got it good with Erica. He was a lonesome man
those ten wifeless years before Erica came around. He wanted
somebody other than Lennart to talk to. And when one day
Erica walked into Shady Glen on a research assignment for
Action 9 and interviewed Grady about what it takes to upkeep a
facility like Shady Glen, Grady figured Erica, right when he
first saw her, to be the woman he could say *forever* to and mean
it. She had a bevel to her eyelock, a way of tilting her head into
a side glance and fixing her eyes on him as if everything he had
to say was important, or humorous, or sad. When he joked, she
laughed. When he spoke seriously, she sighed and clasped her
hands. When he misspoke, she wouldn't correct him. And
whatever he said he made sure to use plenty of worldly and wise
jabber of the type he'd picked up over the years, hiding from the
nurses and reading old magazines in his boiler room or listening
to Lennart talk down to the Liquid Forest Bar.

At one point during the interview he said, "Every day we
learn a bit more about life here on Mars. Will you have dinner
with me?"

She said that was a cute way of asking.

And that's how easy his love move was.

When he thinks about it now, he's amazed he lured Erica to
dinner as easily as he did, and how, in the three months that followed, it didn't so much matter to him that her skin was
smoother than any he'd touched before, or that when she held
his hand along the midway at McCutcheon Daze he felt he was
fingerlocking an angel; what he loved about her was the way

she took him for a guy named Grady, not for some guy she wished he was, but for the Grady who laughs about this or that, is crass sometimes and smart-talking others, who goes to the bar when he likes, who putzes with lawnmowers and drainpipes because that's what pleases him, because that's who he is.

One day out sightseeing back then, while they drove along the winding coulee roads of the Driftless Area, she said, "Grady, I'm not a stipulative woman." Grady liked that. *Stipulative.* A woman who used a word like that was prize enough, but she meant it, would take him for who he was, and that day he asked her to marry him. But she couldn't have been telling him the truth. She must stipulate, because look what she's done now.

Grady considers kicking his locker, one wallop for relief, but he doesn't do it. He's a man with more important shit to do.

4

LUCKY'S OFFICE IS A LARGE CUBICLE MADE OF PARTICLE-
board and two-by-fours, flat-roofed and unpainted and window-
less, with ancient TV production equipment heaped on its
roof—old camera stands, a teletypewriter, boxes of frayed
cable—an office so drab and shut off from the flow of Action 9
it reminds Erica of the German pillboxes her father claims he
bullrushed during World War II. She stands outside the office
for a moment, taking deep breaths, trying to pull her thoughts
in order, to suppress the anger building in her. She rubs her
hands together and claps them for confidence, then snatches
the door open abruptly enough to make her believe her
entrance itself will make a statement, will catch the man off
guard.

"We need some things clarified, Lucky." She does not slam
the door, eases it carefully shut instead, so that the only sound
the door makes closing is its metal parts clicking together with
the doorjamb. She faces Lucky with a wide stance, hands to
hips.

He sits in a roller chair behind his desk and smokes a cigarette, examines with relish the funnel he blows in Erica's direc-

tion. He says, "I've got the new fire-location reports here. Got it contained—maybe—five miles west of the valley, at least for now." He drags on his cigarette and on the exhale says, "But looks like Window Falls, most of it up that way, is a goner."

"I see," Erica says, and feels a major percentage of her resolve fading. Her arms drop to her sides, and something swirling inside her guts gives her a quick knife of pain. This office, despite its pizza boxes and crumpled cigarette packs and other artifacts of Lucky—a recent photo of him shaking hands with the governor; a trophy from the McCutcheon Rotary Club; a black-and-white mock-up of a PRAY WITH ME billboard design—despite Lucky himself this is still the office of a certified meteorologist. Various meteorological charts and graphs cover the walls, and next to his desk is his personal radar screen, where the smoke from the fire appears as a green seething mass. The sight of the fire on the screen scares Erica, makes her muscles shudder.

"How long till it happens?" That's all Erica can think to say.

"A couple of hours tops."

"And you think everybody will die up there?"

"In Window Falls? Poof! But look at the bright side. I, Lucky Littlefield, can now, with absolute certainty, put rain in this evening's forecast."

"Rain?" Erica says.

"See, with a fire of this magnitude burning it's for certain that low pressure will move in from Minnesota. The fires will *suck* the low pressure in, if you get my drift, and there we'll have it: rain. My guess is by nightfall the rain will be here."

"But nightfall is too far away to save Window Falls."

He mouths his cigarette and lifts his eyebrows in the affirmative, reaches to a chair next to him, and curls his index finger to her again, drawing her to duty. "Which means we better put together a plan to get those people out of there. That's what you want us to do, right?"

"Of course." This is the involuntary Erica, the Erica that Grady sometimes at home will call *autoChristian*, meaning she has a blind and an instinctual concern for the welfare of others. She moves around the desk and takes her seat the way she always takes it, hands folded in her lap like a schoolgirl.

"Trouble is," Lucky says, "there isn't much we can do." He swivels his chair so he faces her. "Action 9 doesn't exactly have the resources to save all those folks."

"We can tell them to come to McCutcheon."

"The way I figure it, by late this afternoon there likely won't *be* a McCutcheon."

"I thought you said they had the fire contained."

"For the time being," he says, and he taps his pinky on the desk.

"We can't do *nothing*," she says.

"Hey, I'm in the rain business. And tonight that's exactly what we'll have. All in all, I think the forecast is good. Not great. Good."

The fire is a patch of green death on the radar screen, pulsing and growing much in the same way that Erica's stomach is swirling and hurting. She wishes she could make herself vanish.

Lucky extinguishes his cigarette and chuckles in an odd, mincing way that startles Erica. "I know you, Erica."

She unfolds her hands and cups her knees with them, Lucky's eyes following closely the movement of her hands. She says, "Of course you do. We see each other practically every day."

"No, no. I know you more than that. For example: You're not as happy with your marriage as you used to be, are you?" He sticks out his tongue, pulls a tuft of mustache into his mouth with it, and he hums a tune that sounds like "Rudolph, the Red-Nosed Reindeer," oddly enough a tune Grady hums from time to time. Lucky's eyes scan her from lap to neck, never meeting Erica's return gaze. "Everything, darling. You're as transparent as the weather. Another example: The way I figure it, your husband's in the fire path right now, up at that nursing home of his. If you *weren't* having problems with him, you'd have called him to see if he's okay."

"My husband's none of your business," she says, and her gut makes another sour throb, because Grady *must* be at Shady Glen by now. They called for him to come to work early, not long before she got the call to come here. By now they surely have found Grady somewhere, wherever he is, and got him to go to work.

"Come on and admit it. You're having problems with your husband, aren't you?"

"You don't know one thing about him."

"But I know *you*. I can look at *you* and see you're miserable," Lucky says, and reaches his hand to her neck, sliding it under her hair. He begins massaging her, his fingers making her slouch down like a child about to get a belt strapping. "You can't possibly be happy with a man like that. Come on, Erica. The world's coming to an end. You can give me one chance, can't you? I know for a fact you've been thinking about having a chance with me." He gropes along her side, pulling her toward him.

Suddenly she jerks up from her chair to get away, and Lucky

jerks up, too, and grabs her by the shoulders. When he pulls her toward him to force a kiss, she gets a whiff of his beard—the sweat, the cigarette smell, the makeup residue—and all that has been Erica over the last day—the long hours of work and holding in her loathing for Lucky; a peculiar call from a girl named Kate; the long crying sleepless night and the eight bottles of Leinenkugel's she drank waiting for Grady to come home—everything rises into her throat, and she vomits on Lucky's beard and chest. Lucky topples back into his chair, his arms outstretched, and she retches on him again, this time into his lap.

Lucky says the words he's perfected: "Jesus Christ!"

Erica's eyes water from the heavy scent of bile, and she begins swallowing repeatedly. What she sees of the world is a colorful smudge, white charts and big wavy blue isobars on them, the fire on the radar, Lucky rolling off his chair and onto the floor, Lucky bobbing and heaving, and in the blur, she sees, from inside her, a picture of Grady, nothing fancy or unusual about him, just that smart blue-uniformed maintenance Grady she met three years ago, and it strikes her that Grady's about to die. She's about to lose her husband for real, and without getting the chance to make amends with him.

She hears Lucky retching horribly on the floor, a throat-gush and a splatter.

No thinking now: she wipes her eyes with one hand and her mouth with the other. She swallows and swallows and says, "Since you're indisposed, I'll go on the air myself."

And out the office door she walks, the Action 9 set lights moons in her watery eyes. She'll do what's Righteous and Just. With God's help, she surely will.

5

When Lennart was closing the Liquid Forest last night, he asked Kate if she wanted to stop by his apartment, which is directly above the bar, to have a nightcap or two and talk, and Kate—loaded on free drinks and giddy with her night out among the legal adults—agreed to come with him. They had nightcaps all right, gin and tonics, lots of them, and Lennart did most of the talking: about how fond he is of Grady; about how Grady helped him fix up an old AMC Pacer that he keeps parked behind the tavern but can't drive, because he lost his license after his fourth DWI; and after his umpteenth drink, Lennart promised Kate she could take him in the morning for a drive in the Pacer, and maybe, if they were fortunate, they would bump into Grady. But at six o'clock or so, Lennart sprawled on his carpet and passed out. Kate should have left Lennart's then and gone back to her own apartment to sleep, but she didn't leave, and she didn't sleep.

She's too agitated for sleep. For the last three hours she's been giving a close listen to Lennart's TV—Condyle burnt, a big fire burning out of control, general disaster throughout the countryside—but she can't stand to watch the fire pictures the

TV network voices describe. A while ago Lucky Littlefield came on the air and said that the great scourging is here at last. Kate did not watch Lucky, but she did pray with him, not because she believes in God or is inspired to sanctity by Lucky but because praying gave her something to do with her hands, something to keep her from fidgeting for a minute or two, to keep her from thinking about death in a forest fire, or about what the fallout from her phone call to Grady's wife might be. Fire or no fire, she's got to find Grady and figure out what happened to him.

And by now Kate has taken so many laps around Lennart's apartment she's practically memorized everything in it. It's a one-room, fairly small, with a small window overlooking Mitchell Street. Here and there on the walls are framed black-and-white portraits of historical figures, hung at sloppy angles and covered with fingerprints, which makes Kate believe that Lennart regularly takes the portraits off the wall to give them a closer look. Each portrait is marked with a strip of masking tape that provides the name—Commodus, Diocletian, Antoninus Pius, Marcus Aurelius, and so on. The only color picture on the wall is a photograph obviously taken downstairs in the Liquid Forest: Lennart standing arm-in-arm with Grady in front of the pool table, both of them with big cigars in their mouths and wearing tuxedos. They don't look dapper, tuxedos aside, a couple of tavern regulars in costumes—must have been a theme party they were having, or maybe the picture was taken on New Year's Eve—but even in this posed-for photograph Kate can see the blue intelligence in Grady's eyes. Probably the same thing is true of Lennart: not dumb, no way. On one of his walls Lennart's got a tall wobbly bookshelf made out of boards and cinder blocks, and every book on the shelving is a history book: *Alexander's Campaigns Against the Macedonians, Julius Caesar's Greatest Battles, Rome at Sea, Sex and the Centurion,* and on and on, maybe three hundred books, all hardbacks and all looking greasy and constantly read.

Lennart's carpet is a dirty blue, spotted with cigarette ash and sticky to the touch. His only piece of furniture is a ratty green couch, and Lennart is still sprawled on the carpet in front of that couch—snoring, too—while Kate paces and paces. His overall straps are down, buckles by his feet, and his pink boxers expand a half yard each time he takes a breath. His navel is deep enough to hold an olive jar. Twice Kate's kicked him awake and made him call around for Grady. Lennart's made the calls, but Kate still doesn't know where Grady is. She can't take this much longer.

She makes windmills with her arms, walks to Lennart's window, looks up at the smoky sky. This is awful, the biggest forest fire going on maybe ever, anywhere, and here Kate's backflipping for some pigtailed brute with no education, which is proof of what her brother used to tell her is fact: The Scumbag Factor is what women want most in men. Give a woman a nice guy, her brother used to say, and she'll treat him like shit. Give a woman a shithead, and she'll do anything for him.

She stands next to Lennart and gives him three soft soccer kicks to his rear, the blows sending ripples along his belly and into the jiggle of his shoulders and arms.

"Lennart, you've ignored the world long enough," Kate says, and plants her foot into his lower-belly mound. She squishes the foot forward and backward.

Lennart groans.

Kate crams her big toe into his belly button, wiggles his entire massive gut, and says, "I thought you said you'd do anything to help a friend of Grady's."

He giggles, reaches blindly for her foot, and misses.

"You're supposed to help me, Lennart. You promised you would."

"I live to help Grady's friends."

"And you'll do anything?" she says, and jabs and pokes, making Lennart squirm.

"Whatever you wish," he says. "You have my word."

"Then kiss my foot," she says.

He's awake now, eyes wide, nose twitching and sniffing. "I will only kiss a god's foot. No goddess feet for me." He folds his hands over his chest, and on his bookshelf beyond him Kate notices an interesting title. *The Colossus in Antiquity*. Him.

Kate moves away from Lennart to allow him room to sit up. She says, "I didn't *think* you're the kind of man who would kiss my feet."

"Say what you will about Lennart Anderson," Lennart says, and he retwizzles his mustache into a perfect handlebar. "Lennart is always Lennart, and that's a three-hundred percent certainty." He struggles and grunts to sit up. "Besides, if I *had* to involve myself romantically with a woman, I would much prefer the tragic type." He makes a regal gesture toward his bookshelf.

"That's fascinating, Lennart. Now let's go find Grady."

Lennart's smile vanishes, and he stares absently at his hands. "You do have a limited capacity for subject matter, sister." His hair is matted and flecked with ash from the carpet. His eyes are red and crusted with sleep on the lower lids, and each of his eye sockets is dark and puffy. His lips, when he exhales, are gray and bloodless-looking.

Kate steps to the window to calm herself: a miscolory dinge outside, the smoky sky making the valley look like it's a photograph negative. Debris of all sorts—leaves, twigs, paper cups, newspapers—dribbles eastward along the gutters, pushed by the wind that rumbles Lennart's window. And cars and pickups bloodpump the length of Mitchell Street, stopping and starting and sometimes bumping into one another. Horns honk feebly in the wind. In the IGA parking lot a crowd gathers around a squad car. It's odd nothing glints outside; over the past weeks Kate's grown to appreciate to the sun refracting all day off one shiny thing or another. The drought's been beautiful that way. *So long, sun*, she thinks. *So long, McCutcheon.*

From the TV comes a network woman's voice saying something about nowhere to put all the dead bodies from the Condyle fire.

"Look at the TV," Lennart says.

On the far Mitchell Street sidewalk sits a rusty Ford pickup with four slashed tires. Somebody has spray-painted *Lucky* on the hood.

"The whole world's doomed," Kate says.

"Nothing new about that," Lennart says.

Three brown dogs, retrievers maybe, run full bore down the sidewalk, past the pickup, past the IGA and toward the university. The dogs sprint and weave as one dog through groups of folks clutching their rosary beads, through groups of young men holding beer cans, but nobody looks at the running dogs. Everybody on Mitchell Street looks at the sky. But Kate watches the dogs till they veer off toward the river.

"Even the dogs know," she says.

"Know what?"

"The fire's coming into town, Lennart. That's what."

Lennart struggles erect with a great flailing of his arms, creating a cloud of carpet dust when he gets to his feet, but he does not look at Kate, nor does he raise his voice. He grunts and fiddles with the volume on the TV. "Weird that Lucky's not on the air right now," he says, "if the fire is as bad as you say."

"For God's sakes, Lennart. Listen to this wind!"

"I hear it, sister." He steps to his window, gazes sadly at Mitchell Street. "Okay then, let's go downstairs for a while. I better make sure everything's okay down there."

And this is amazing. Three hours waiting for Lennart to get up, and now Kate can hardly keep up with him heading out his door and down the staircase that leads to the alley behind the Liquid Forest, and while Lennart fumbles with his keys to open the tavern's back door, Kate feels the windblown dirt like sharp pins going into her legs and arms.

Lennart opens the door, lets her inside, and when the door closes, when she can hear how quiet the tavern is compared with outside in the wind, Lennart says, "What do you say you give me a quick hand cleaning up the barroom, you know, a little reimbursement for those free drinks I gave you last night. Fair, don't you think?"

"Fair," she says, because she's happy to have something to do, something she can channel her excess energy into.

First, she follows Lennart down the length of the bar, picking bar stools up off the floor and setting them atop the bar rail, and when they have all the stools up Lennart turns on the TV, cranks it loud, then he disappears momentarily into the men's bathroom and returns holding a broom, which he hands to Kate.

So she starts sweeping, and doesn't mind it one bit. She figures Grady would be pleased to see her doing real work, pushing a broom right here in the Liquid Forest Bar, the place working folk call their second home. She's doing a decent job sweeping, too.

After a few minutes, she's got all the peanut shells and cigarette butts swept from the back part of the bar, near the pool tables and the pay phone, and now she's cramming the broom under the foot rail along the bar, getting out even the smallest pieces of crud. It's not bad, sweeping, not difficult, either. Grady should see this clean floor, and how well she's working with Lennart. He would be impressed.

And Lennart is straightening up behind the bar, washing glasses, lugging buckets of ice from the ice machine to the drink-making wells, moving up and down the bar quickly as he works, and he's working up a sweat.

The TV blares, sounds hollow through the empty barroom with all the stools up on the bar, and everything to Kate seems bustling and workaday. She feels the urge, as she imagines working folks typically do, to shoot the breeze about what they'll do after the work is finished.

She says, "Lennart, when we get done here, it sure will be nice to go for a drive."

Lennart sets a rack of freshly cleaned glasses next to the beer taps, begins removing the glasses and lining them up neatly along a rubber mat. He pauses, angles his head toward the glass barfront, toward the blowing outside that sounds like truck engines revving. After a moment or two he bites his lower lip, rolls his eyes in tired red half-circles, and sighs.

"Grady's married," Lennart says. "Why would a reasonable, educated girl like you want to carry on with a married man?"

Kate sees the pay phone under the TV, and the sparkly floor under the pay phone. Oh, that wife sounded so curtsy-curt on the phone last night, a real snootmuffin, that wife, not the type Grady deserves, not in the least way. Kate leans the broom against the bar and assumes the hiphands posture of Wonder Woman, legs wide-planted, chin thrust upward.

"Grady can't be happily married," she says.

"What profound insight leads you to believe *that*?"

"Well, he wouldn't have been so forward with me if his marriage was happy."

Lennart points toward Mitchell Street, and Kate looks with him through the barfront window. A big purple plastic garbage can blows by on the sidewalk. "Kate, like you were saying upstairs, this is some serious wind."

"True."

Lennart resumes arranging clean glasses, swift movements, precise. He's an artist of work. "Let me tell you: I've known Grady approximately the same length of time that any of the more successful late Roman emperors held the throne: ten, twelve years, in any case, an eternity, at least in terms of the ancient world. I have served Grady drinks every weekday afternoon since, well, since he was *your* age."

His eyes scan Mitchell Street for a while, maybe, Kate guesses, to let whatever he's trying to tell her settle into her brain.

Folks wander about across the street, in front of the IGA and in its parking lot, their hair wild in the wind and their faces in ruddy scowls, their Bibles and rosaries clutched in their hands.

Lennart takes the final clean glass off the rack and puts the glass where it belongs. He ambles along the bar, with the rack in his hand, and after carefully setting it down near a sink, he takes up a position in front of the TV. "I'm not leaving till Lucky broadcasts," he says. "I'm awfully fond of Grady, but I wouldn't exactly call him a repository of life-and-death information."

His face is fixed toward the TV, reflecting waves of purples and reds, and his eyes appear moist, his jowls in a depressed slump, his arms lax at his bulging sides. Lennart is obviously dejected, which somehow saddens Kate. She picks up her broom again and sweeps her way beside Lennart, stands across the bar from him near the TV, and when she looks at the screen, from the Buick commercial that has been playing comes the Action 9 logo.

"Ask for Lucky," Lennart says, "and there he is."

"You're a magician," says Kate.

But nothing happens with the Action 9 logo. The jumping buck does not fade to Lucky praying for everybody in the valley. It simply remains unmoving on the screen—thirty seconds, then a full minute—that fence line of nines, that buck jumping, which, the longer the logo remains on the screen, looks like he's smiling human teeth for his television audience.

Another thirty seconds, another minute: no Lucky.

Kate hears the wind chattering the barfront window, and the outside noises of car honks, tire squeals, shouts, the tinkle of glass breaking; she hears an orchestra of sounds, but none of these comes from the TV.

Luckyless minute number three: Quit counting, Kate. He's not coming on.

"This," she says, and grips her broom as tightly as she can, "is not good."

They stand for a time in the silence that is not silence, the sounds of the frantic town dim beyond the tavern walls, and the Action 9 buck suspends in the air like a bird who fears to land.

And Lucky does not appear.

Then from outside the Liquid Forest comes a terrific shattering noise, followed by screams and shouts, and Kate and Lennart scramble to the front of the bar to look out. At long last the crowd's turned ugly in front of the IGA, throwing bottles at the building, hollering and hooting. Just now a shopping cart smashes through a sheet of storefront glass, tossed from inside, and a middle-aged lady, maybe fifty and wearing a red IGA smock, stands where the glass was and raises her pink fists. A cheer comes from the crowd. Hands everywhere in the crowd extend heavenward. Kate guesses three hundred people make up the crowd, and she scans through them, looking for faces she recognizes, but with the yellow sky and the winds so intense she can't place a face. Another cart flying, another window smashing, and a man in a blue flannel shirt and a Green Bay Packers hat emerges from the IGA, helicoptering his arms, and he dances the clog with his big brown boots.

Lennart says, "Okay, then. We needn't debate the issue any further. Let's go."

But he doesn't make his break to leave. He places both arms around Kate, and Kate presses into his side, feels her nerves tingling in the buttery depths of Lennart. Great excitements fill Kate, an enthusiasm for civil disturbance her professors have lectured on at school. This is the common people rising up, all their lives of oppression and misery finally coming to *real* violence, none of this passive prayer stuff. These are *people*, yes, *real people* of all sizes and ages and sexes rushing into the IGA, whooping and yelling *Fuck everything* or *Fuck Lucky*. People yell *Fuck, fuck Lucky* with the same rhythm and pitch that she yelled *Duck, duck, goose* when she was a little girl. She squeezes Lennart with all her strength, because she's pleased to be sharing this moment with someone.

"This is a sad day for McCutcheon," Lennart says, and brings his hands to his face, in the process elbowing Kate away. "I hope they don't come over here and sack the bar."

Kate feels a sudden brutal surge of appreciation for Grady. Grady in the tavern last night shouting, kicking down his bar stool—this was a man predicting what the people of McCutcheon would come to, that Lucky can do nothing for the town, that the people would eventually rise up and uncover Lucky for what he is. It doesn't make sense that Lennart isn't thinking the same way Grady does. And for Lennart's benefit Kate says, "Be a man, Lennart. A man like Grady."

Lennart's jowls sag, arms drop back to his sides, and Kate can tell she's insulted him instead of instructed him. Again. Stupid Kate.

"I *am* a man," Lennart says, and his voice is oddly low, whispery and withdrawn.

"I know," Kate says. "I didn't mean it."

Along the IGA curb six women jump and dance on the roof and hood of a Ford Taurus. They do kicks and knee-raises and spins in unison, and Kate strains her ears for music, but no music propels these women to dancing. This is the noise they hear: glass breaking, folks hollering, horns honking, the howling fire-blown wind, the anger in their hearts against a life marooned here in the wilds of northern Wisconsin, land now of dead lakes and crispy forests, of fire raging through the country-side and about to roar through town. Kate surely understands this Hell of the people, because it's her same Hell, stuck here twenty years and, without money and a degree and a car, for-ever. And she surely understands Lennart's Hell, too, what an awkward life he must lead, the only gay man in a feed-cap and trailer-court tavern. She's not that different from Lennart, prob-ably. She can see the world and understand it, which makes her a rare commodity in this town.

She says, "Any way we look at it, Lennart, you're right. This is a sad day for McCutcheon."

"And the only reasonable thing to do is to avoid taking part in it," Lennart says. "I can almost guarantee you we'll never find Grady, but we must leave. I can't bear watching this any longer."

Right when Kate's heart leaps at the mention of leaving, a squad car smashes into the front fender of the Taurus on which the six women dance. Four of the six fall into the crowd, and in this instant a gasping comes from the crowd, and before the two officers can emerge from the squad car, maybe sixty folks sur-round the squad and begin rocking it. Two young men leap to the squad's roof and kick out the flashing lights and the siren from its bolts. The squad rocks and rocks, its bumpers pounding into the street. Then a gunshot claps through the air, a sound like a whopping firecracker going off. The crowd halts, becomes momentarily a frozen mass of hair and T-shirts ruffling in the wind. On the passenger side of the squad a gray-haired man in bib overalls slaps his hands to his face and falls back-ward. And Kate can't see where he falls.

Somewhere down Mitchell Street a bottle breaks. Crows caw over the rooftops.

Now, without a killshout or general cry for revenge, the crowd closes on the squad, beats its fenders and trunk and roof. Not a face in the crowd has an expression Kate can identify as anger or hate or happiness; these are drained faces doing drained work, people so tired from drought and life they don't care what they do. Arms everywhere in the crowd wave forward. Feet drag absently along the asphalt. In the mass of outstretched arms at the squad's nose, a cinder block appears, and a pair of hands tosses the block through the squad's windshield. Rocks then, and crowbars and hammers appear, and two more gunshots come from the squad, two more crowd bodies dropping, two young men in muscle shirts, hands to their faces and backward down. What Kate watches now is a slow-motion seethe, two blue uniforms emerging through the gone squad windshield like blue babies ripped from the womb. Rocks fly, stuttering in the yellow light. And crowbars thrust down and down again.

Kate's mouth forms an O, and when she tightens her grip on Lennart's arm, his arm drops away, and Lennart stumbles from the window. He says, "I won't fall apart. I won't. I won't."

But he does. He gimps to the bar and plunks his elbows on the bar rail.

"Abominable, abominable," he says.

"Abominable," Kate echoes, but she doesn't believe much is abominable about the crowd in front of the IGA. They're doing what people strapped in sad lives do; they're evening up with the world, because now they have their opportunity. Sure, Kate registers the facts: three people shot down, two cops probably beaten dead, the IGA in the process of ruin. Really sad, the whole business. But what terror and sadness she feels she feels because she's expected to.

And suddenly over the crowd noise rising from Mitchell Street comes a mournful mechanical howling: air-raid sirens. The sirens howl over the valley, not in unison, but in distinct here-and-there rises and falls, and all in the mob pause. Maybe even the wind pauses, for when Kate looks across the street she hardly notices a thing moving. One head, a young man's, looks upward, now another head tilting, and soon all heads peer at the yellow sky, a sky streaky and seeming to descend into a fog. The sirens grind upward to their pitch and drop down and rise again. And behind the mechanical siren howling the valley dogs set to howling, yips of agony along the alleys and in the backyards and from all the McCutcheon Kate cannot see.

And the crowd in front of the IGA disperses like grease racing away from dish soap, scattering at a run or a hobble every which way. In no time all that's left in Kate's view of Mitchell Street are three cars and five bodies and arrays of glintless glass, and leaves and paper trash dribble eastward.

"It's time." This is all she can think of saying, and she grabs Lennart by the overall straps. "Move, move. You got your keys?"

"Abominable, abominable," he says and sobs and sniffles. But he extracts his car keys from his pocket and hands them to Kate.

The cool jingly weight of the keys, the way Lennart's gone hysterical and she hasn't—this fills Kate with an inner muscularity she didn't know she possesses. Her brain is as clear-thinking as she can ever remember it, and she thinks this: *Who says I can't hold it together when the crisis comes?* She notices the evenness of her breathing, how sturdy her legs feel under her, how she might sprint for two hours and not feel a thing.

She maneuvers Lennart down the length of the bar, and in front of the TV he stops still and points to it. There, on the screen, is not the Action 9 deer or Lucky Littlefield but a woman, in a sundress, pale blue. The woman stares out at the world, her eyes wide, but she doesn't say one thing.

Kate says, "Now, who the hell is that?"

Lennart says, "I don't know."

For an uncomfortable time the woman remains on the screen, staring and not saying a word.

"I wonder why she's not saying anything," Kate says.

"Let's not wonder, Kate. Let's get moving." And just as quickly as he left his apartment not long ago Lennart starts hustling about the bar: takes money from the till and puts it into the safe, double-checks the front-door lock, turns the lights out in both bathrooms, turns the TV off, the ceiling fans off, and on and on in an endless irritating holding pattern of Lennart moving with amazing speed and saying, "Wait! I forgot to do this!"

But when they finally step outside into the alley, Lennart has slowed enough so that Kate can maneuver him. He locks the back door, double-checks the locking, and Kate takes him by the overall straps and guides him.

"Where's the car?" Kate shouts, and tugs Lennart to the alley's middle. She scans the up-and-down of the gravel, the line of lilacs extending to the river, the wind bending the dead shrubs into snapping, twigs and brambles tumbling, and overhead the power lines whistle in the gusts. She smells the smoke in the hard wind, a campgroundy smell. The sirens are howling loud enough to make her ears hurt.

He says, "Two blocks." He struggles in the wind, leaning into it.

The walking is difficult, dust dimming the alley like hot dry sleet, needling into her legs and arms and face, and Kate wishes she still had her bandanna, so she could tie it over her face. A slitworld is what she sees, her eyes squinting the alley to near darkness. She tongues at the grit accumulating on her teeth. She wants to guide Lennart but can't, really, because she can't see where to go. She hears a woman screaming off in the distance, a baby crying, a dog howling, a car horn blaring, sirens near and far. She hears rushing.

Up ahead, in a break of hedge, forms appear, rectangles that look like stunted elephants tethered in a row, and after a few more steps she can see these are cars. She takes Lennart's hand, tries tugging him into a run, but he doesn't run with her; he stops walking entirely, becomes a foam-rubber boulder resisting her grip and yank.

He shouts, "We gotta go back."

"No!"

"I forgot to turn off the lights in the storeroom!"

When Kate turns to face him, her head shields the wind from her eyes, and she can open her eyes, see him squinting through the blown dust, his mustache collapsed from its handlebar, jowls rippling.

"Send me the fucking bill for the lights already," she says, and she's not sure if Lennart can hear. Way in the back of her brain, in a spot that stores book learning for special occasions such as this, she recalls the old Zen koan: *What is the sound of one hand clapping?* Kate knows what the sound of one hand clapping is, and she makes it now. She rears back and slaps

Lennart across the jowls with all the force she can muster, but with the sirens and gusts the slap is a sound she's certain only Lennart can hear.

She screams this: "Don't think about the bar. We gotta get out of here."

Lennart places his hands for a second to his face, and begins walking again, yells a desperate *Ah* that rises over the din. Kate places her arm around his midriff, comforting him the last stretch of alley to his car. He brings his mouth to her ear and says, "Thanks. Even Alexander the Great occasionally needed his subordinates to slap him to his senses."

A fact for Kate to remember: There's much to be said for slapping the hysterical.

Lennart's car is covered with a canvas tarpaulin, the back half of which has come loose and is flapping like it's alive. The car is a yellow AMC Pacer, not rusty, with a personalized license plate that says this: DCLINE.

Kate takes one side of the tarp, waves at Lennart for him to take the other side, which he does—they make a good team— and they roll the tarp forward over the hood to the Pacer's nose, all the while Kate getting whacked by whipping canvas, eyes getting gritted and stung by dust, and she stuffs the roll into Lennart's arms. She unlocks the driver's side and climbs in, and after a moment Lennart climbs into the passenger seat.

When both doors are shut and the howl of the valley is, presto, feeble and lost, Kate basks in a feeling she figures is an after-battle glow. They made it this far, which is an accomplishment. Her skin feels like it's been sandpapered for shellacking. She brushes at the grit on her arms and legs.

"I believe this is definitely the occasion," Lennart says, "for some civilization enhancer." He reaches into the glove compartment and produces a full pint of Jim Beam and a cough-drop tin. He snaps open the tin, which contains three cigarette-sized doobies.

"Lovely," she says. A little sedation right now is what they need. "Let's smoke 'n' roll."

She clicks her seat forward so her feet can touch the gas pedal and the brakes, turns over the engine, and pulls into the alley, retracing at a slow pace the route she walked with Grady yesterday evening. The wind buffets the car, chatters the hood, and the dust and flying grit look like brown powdery snow. Fire or no fire, wind or no wind, Kate's unbeatable now. She's got a Pacer under her fingertips, a copilot lighting up a doobie. A little while driving, and Grady will be hers.

6

Sirens. That's what struck Erica dumb. Sirens. The on-air light on Camera One blinked red, the sirens began, and Erica couldn't think of anything to say. A minute, two minutes, for what seemed like forever, Jimbo and Pete, the cameramen, left her in the Land of Dead Air, but she couldn't speak, and what could Jimbo and Pete do but bring back the Action 9 logo in Erica's place?

And the sirens still howl through the Action 9 warehouse walls—a mournful sound, a rising up to a pitch and wailing there, dropping down, rising again, must be dozens of sirens howling out there. And the Action 9 walls shake in the heavy winds. Fiberglass dust floats down from the torn spots on the ceiling's insulation, giving the Action 9 news set, and the spotlights surrounding the news set, the fuzzy look of Christmas. The dust spirals inside Action 9, moves in white sheets and shudders, like snow.

She is no longer seated at the right hand of Lucky Littlefield. She's sitting in his blue Action 9 broadcasting chair, sliding its rollers back and forth on the news-set carpet, making with Lucky's chair slow crucifix signs on a field of all-weather red. These are the facts: Lucky hasn't emerged from his office yet, and *somebody* has to broadcast. She will have to be the one. They'll have to put her on the air in Lucky's place. But Jimbo and Pete won't do it, won't give her another try. They stand behind the control board, both of them with their arms folded, nodding at her, disapproving. She doesn't fault the boys for refusing to put her back on the air, but they simply don't understand that she knows as well as Lucky what should be said to the public under conditions like this: *Remain calm, stay in your homes till you receive official instructions, this is not the time to quit praying.* She hasn't been writing copy here at Action 9 for two years and not figured out what to say. She knows as well as Lucky not only *what* but *why* something should be said to the people, who are out there this moment hearing the sirens and the wind, who are seeing that Action 9 is not broadcasting, and what can the public do right now without a voice coming to them through the TV, telling them anything, no matter if it's fact or lie, no matter if the voice is Lucky Littlefield or Erica McCann—what can the people do without Action 9 but panic?

"Boys," she says, and she squares her shoulders. "You have a responsibility to McCutcheon to turn that camera back on." Her voice, and this disturbs her, has become gravelly. But she *does* have a voice. She *can* do this broadcast, if they'll give her another chance.

Jimbo is the shorter of the two boys, has a gray Green Bay Packers T-shirt on, a camouflage Leinenkugel's hat, and a nose acned so red it looks like it belongs on an eighty-year-old drunk. He says, "I'll wait for Lucky. That's my responsibility."

"Lucky is ill," says Erica. She sucks at the sour taste on her teeth. "I'm taking his place till he gets himself composed. Need I tell you a hundred times?"

Jimbo says, "Lucky will get better."

And Pete, who never says much, who is a long-haired sallow-looking kid wearing a Metallica shirt, nods at Jimbo, then examines the smooth concrete flooring as if for a new place to shuffle his feet.

Erica's ears tune to beyond the warehouse walls, to the rising and sad falling the sirens make.

"The people need *information*," she says.

Jimbo says, "I ain't putting you back on the air without Lucky's okay."

Behind the cameras, nobody stands in the open concrete space usually filled at broadcast time with station employees waiting to watch Lucky. The only movement over the concrete is the dust settling, glittering in the fluorescent light. Everybody has gone home, except her and Lucky and Jimbo and Pete. When the sirens started wailing, folks ran for the exits in a great jingle of car keys. Most everybody at Action 9 has a family worth the going-home to, worth the dying with. Not Erica. She's ruined what she's supposed to call family. It's because of sex that Grady's left her, because Erica believes what the Church says about sex and subsequently has to control when sex with Grady will occur, because how could she possibly handle a split-shift marriage and a baby all at once? And with Grady going to the tavern every night after work? Forget it. He's not ready for a child. He's far from able to handle that kind of settling down. So, sure, she's driven Grady crazy with the Church's Natural Family Planning Regimen: sex only on certain days, at certain hours, and usually, when conditions are safe, she's too tired, and Grady will either spend an entire weekend sighing whenever she walks by, or, if she's not too tired, Grady will spend an entire weekend sprawled on the couch, sleeping off his week's drinking in front of the TV. See how it is with Grady? Everything's *Erica's* responsibility, *Erica's* body, *Erica's* church. Is that *family*? Is that working together? What she should have done is taken the care and shown the patience of character to reach an understanding with Grady, that a good marriage and a family start with something more than sex, but she didn't do that. Instead she simply, over a period of time, had sex with him less and less until there she was, yesterday evening, knowing that Grady was obsessed with sex exactly the way all men she's ever known have been obsessed with sex, and she was using sex to jar him into paying her some attention. She failed with Grady, which is maybe why she can't fail here. She must persuade these boys to put her back on the air. She deserves one more try at *something* in this life.

Jimbo scratches at his nose, some acne oil transferring to his fingers, and his fingers shine under the set lights. She imagines, for some strange reason, the ghastly smell of Jimbo's hands, of Chee-to film and pizza sauce and RC cola and the armpit he's always scratching when he's waiting for something to do. The thought makes Erica feel suddenly clammy all over. She feels a little prickle of sweat beginning at the back of her scalp.

She says, "Jimbo, you might have the opportunity here to do something more than standing there and picking your nose." She can't look at him, looks instead at the wall-screen monitor, at the Action 9 deer frozen in its leap. "You owe the people more than a test pattern. Think of it this way: They're responsible for your paycheck."

"Action 9 signs *my* paycheck," Jimbo says. "I don't know about yours."

7

GRADY MCCANN IS FOND OF DEFINING PRECISELY WHAT bullshit is, because bullshit is what he experiences near to each hour of each day. Work, sometimes, is bullshit. Or drinking is, mostly the hangover part, which is the part he's got going now. Or mounting his wife is, especially when she mentions Jesus Christ at every fourth thrust, a habit of hers, at least back in the days when she was wifely and mountable. Or here's the same thing another way: Mowing the lawn used to be bullshit, when he used to have a mowable lawn. And at the moment Grady's dealing with one of the finest examples of bullshit he's run across in quite some time: Father Mary.

Take a look at this All-Star: six feet tall, maybe forty-five years old, graying close-cropped hair, square jaw with much razor stubble. And wait: Call the Pope. Rome's servant here forgot his priest costume today, no priest collar, no Godly blacks. The priest is ready for tennis—a green plain T-shirt and blue shorts, a healthy tan, forearms veiny from the gymnasium—and his name is Mary. Mary! If there were a God overwatching the Wisconsin flock, He would strike this numbnuts dead on the spot. Having a name like that, it's bullshit. You bet. What else could a guy call it?

They stand near the front entrance of Shady Glen, Grady's pigtail a rope flailing in the wind, Mary's hair too bowl-cut to wiffle one inch, and they both hold garden hoses. They're out to save the building, and this is Grady's plan: Douse the walls and roof with as much water as his pumps will pump, and through as much hose and sprinkler head as he's got, and maybe all that wetness will keep the flames at bay. For sure, Grady *would* work alone, would be happier working alone, but Jane's assigned him this priest for a helper, because Mary's the only other nonwheelchaired man on the property, if a guy could actually call a Mary a man. Sad truth of it is, Grady won't disobey Jane, which is about the only thing, cranky as he's getting, Grady won't do.

"Now screw the fucker into the spigot," Grady says. "You *do* know how to do *that?*" Grady's said this twenty times already, each time they've set up a lawn sprinkler to tinkling on the building. They've got four more setups to do, and then they'll be out of sprinklers.

Mary trots to his position at the wall and he hunkers. The wind blows a cloud of dust up into Mary's face, but still he smiles, doesn't even blink.

Grady says, "A fellow like me, shit yes, has an endless supply of hose. It's the shortage of goddam sprinkler assemblies fucking this operation up."

"You really think," Father Mary says, "you can bother me with that language?"

And Mary, to his credit, twists the coupling threads into the wall spigot with much manliness, muscles rippling on his forearms. Mary's no pussy, but he probably has one.

"I ain't thinking much more than sprinkler nozzles," Grady

says, points to Mary with both thumbs, which is Mary's cue to open the water valve.

"Here we go," Mary says, a guy grinning no matter the grief Grady gives.

The hose bulges, and the sprinkler begins its chick-chicking, the wind misting the water upward and mostly onto the roof. Perfect.

"A beautiful thing, how my mind works. Don't you think, Mary?"

Mary clip-claps his hands, brushing off dirt that's not there, steps next to Grady, and says, "Yes, your plan looks like it will work."

"Fuckin-A Raymond it will."

Twenty sprinklers: same conversation.

Grady begins the stroll to the utility shed for more hose, and Father Mary falls into easy strides with him, whistling some pleasant priestly tune Grady doesn't recognize.

Along this side of the building ten sprinklers chick mist air-ward, mist that mixes with the windblown dust into spirals of light brown fog, and Grady counts the sprinklers, making sure of himself, making sure the plan's going smoothly: ten sprinklers on this north wall, owing to more burnable equipment on this side, the kitchen, the boiler, the 440 box, the propane and oxygen tanks in the storage room; six sprinklers on the south, which could be a fuckup, because the forest's over there; eight sprinklers on the front, the west side, because the fire will blow in from that direction; no sprinklers for the east, because if the fire gets that far, it's too late—might be too late no matter what.

For the first time in weeks the aluminum siding looks pass-ably clean and dustless, something Grady admires after this dreary dusty interval the summer's been. He should have sprinklered his building before, would have kept the place neat-looking, the shrubbery alive, the lawn green as a Grady lawn should be. Hell, add not sprinklering the building to the dollar he should get for all his fuckups this summer, and Grady would be a millionaire.

When they each have coils of hose slung from their shoulders again, a matter of Grady handing the priest the coil and helping it around his shoulder, Mary clears his throat and says, "Grady, I'm certain I know your wife from Saint Joseph's. Her name's Erica, right?"

"Nope," says Grady. "Mouth. My wife's name is Mouth."

"What?"

"Forget it."

Mary snorts and grunts, a faint sound in the wind, and he walks smiling alongside Grady to the front of the building, takes the fifteen steps Grady counts aloud from the last sprinkler they set up. "You imagine your wit to be quite sharp, my son. But the longer you talk the more you should realize how foolish you sound."

"Fuck calling me *your son*, Mary. It's unnatural for a man who is not my father to call me *my son*."

"I was making conversation, is all." Mary takes his place where Grady points, and he eagerly studies the ground at his feet. "Thought you might be thinking of your wife at a time like this. Maybe you want to talk about her."

"What is it with you priests always wanting to talk about women?"

"I wasn't aware that's what we priests do."

"If your head wasn't up your ass, you'd notice all right."

"Please, if you mean to offend, I'm well beyond reacting."

Grady, deep inside, knows he's given the Father enough razz, but Grady can't help himself. What a name: Mary. He can't get over it. Here Grady stands in the wind on which he now can definitely smell the fire, in the wind that each five minutes seems to be blowing twice as hard as it did before, with his building surrounded by sprinklers throwing sheets of fake rain toward a yellow sky, and whatever his last day's been, the whole Kate and Erica and Lennart and Lucky of it, is all reduced to a priest named Mary.

"Now screw the fucker into the spigot," Grady says. That's twenty-one times, three more to go.

Mary says, "Well, this much is for certain: Nobody can say we didn't try." Mary muscles the coupling in place like before, veins popping on his forearms.

Grady fingers his nostrils absently, digging for blood boogers of the sort he's mined for the last hour. "Mary, you *are* a happy bastard." Then the thumb cue: *swoosh*, water spraying. Then a booger: a big purplish one, quarter inch, well worth the fingering for. Grady holds it to the sky for inspection. "A man," he says, "can pluck one of these gems from himself any time he likes. Comes from manly living, rocks like these."

"If you ask me," Mary says, "I would say a *man* might be concerned more for the safety of the building than what he finds in his nose."

This pricks into Grady, because, hey, picking boogers to prove a point is a basically dumbass thing to do.

"Listen to you talk," Grady says, flicks the booger high, tries tracking its arc in the wind, but with all the sprinkler mist he loses sight of it. "You got asshole talk down to a tee."

"I must talk like an asshole to deal with one," Mary says.

"Ho! I been underestimating you. You *can* talk like a man after all."

Mary makes a teethy smile, flexing his jaw muscles. "I appreciate your kind words," he says.

Grady says, "You're a prize, really and truly."

They stride back to the utility shed for more hose, another nozzle.

From the south Grady hears a droning, indistinct and sad, that he thinks sounds like sirens, but maybe he's wrong. He's heard all kinds of noises out here in the wind this morning, none of them provable, except the rush of the sprinklers, the pines cracking in the forest beyond the building, or the hay fields swishing in gust after gust. And his miscuing ears have got him agitated. Well, everything's got him agitated. What's gone autopilot in Grady, what his job is, the man-with-a-plan part of it, keeps him from hopping into his Pinto and driving back to McCutcheon, finding where his life was yesterday. But he just can't go. The building needs saving—his life, too. The marriage, that Kate chippy from the college, Lennart, the other dipsticks at the bar: have to leave them be. Over with. Hard to hold in, all this stuff happening to him at once, and this pisses him off. He's near to explosive, in fact. And all Grady can do to hold his life-anger in is harass this priest. Grady knows he shouldn't, knows it's not the priest's fault that life is fritzed and shambled; knows, even more, that the priest, if Grady asked, would try to make life seem better than it is. But that's exactly Grady's problem with Father Mary: Priests are for the hoping souls, not the souls like Grady, who know Hope is an illusion and a lie. The fire *will* come and toast this building. And Erica *will* keep slobbering Lucky Littlefield's bone. And there is *no* God stretching out on a blue Barcalounger, having Himself a God-sized beer and a smoke while He waits for the best instant to shut off the wind valve and turn on the rain. No way: God would have watered His flock weeks ago. Grady waters Grady's flock. That's all Hope is, and it pays ten bucks an hour.

So here's Grady watering, slinging a hose over his shoulder, and—there *are* miracles—Mary shoulders his own hose exactly the way Grady does, dips his shoulders and levels up like a pro, which brings a smile to Grady. Mary catches on after all. Mimicry is a solid sign of a good worker developing.

Grady says, "If you ever get bored with priesting, I'll get you a gig working maintenance."

Mary says, "Who says I can't do both?" He walks with Grady headlong into the wind, fiercer wind, blasting steadily now a charcoalish and bratwursty smell. Grady thinks he sees deer off to the west again, bobbing and zagging in the dead hay. Near the road a stick breaks free from a maple top, lofts upward and flies an easy fifty yards, lands not far from Grady, and scratches the asphalt the length of the parking lot.

"That stick's come to life, eh?" says Grady, you know, to ease up on the priest a bit, be a little nicer, but while they walk Grady considers why Mary said *both*. An insult, that was, telling Grady anybody can maintenance and only certain folks can priest.

"Mary, you don't think I'm worth much, do you?"

"That's not what I said."

"Hey, it's not like you been telling me I'm a prince."

"What I mean is that if *I* can do *your* job, who is to say *you* couldn't do *mine*?"

"You call priesting a job? Fuck *that*."

"Ah, let's let it drop. You're in too much turmoil, that's quite obvious, for us to carry on a discussion."

"I can goddam discuss anything you please."

"I do feel sorry for you, Grady. I really do." That pleasant face of Mary's, all perfect jawbone and perfect lips, is supremely irritating, the more Grady thinks about it. How could this tweeze-ass hack on Grady with such a pleasant face?

"You know, Mary, I only allow myself a certain amount of fun in life. And if I kicked your face snotless right now, that would be too much fun for me. See, I won't allow myself that much joy in one thirty-second period."

"Looks to me somebody's had the best of you already. That black eye doesn't exactly make you look like a brawler." Mary chuckles and assumes his position at the twenty-first sprinkler, cocks his head at Grady, giving Grady the sign to count off the fifteen steps to where the twenty-second will be. And Grady counts, watching Mary's calves flex at each stride, thinks about melting those calves with an acetylene torch.

He says, "I got this black eye examining my dick yesterday afternoon."

"I'm impressed," Mary says, but he's no longer smiling standing there with his length of hose. Mary points to the ground, spurring Grady to work, to bring the sprinkler over and kick it into the hard dirt.

With a shrug Grady spikes the sprinkler into the ground, screws his end of hose coupling in place. "I *bet* you're impressed," Grady says. "You look like the type that would marvel at a dick."

"You have my one warning, Grady. There's only so far you can push me."

"Hose," Grady says, meets Mary's stare unblinking: green eyes, nothing bloodshot in the whites, lashes brown and full. "Now screw the fucker into the spigot."

That's twenty-two times. But Mary does not move, not a neck muscle quivering, not an arm trembling. His eyebrows jerk—once—and go still again.

Grady says, "You're not gonna make some faggy move on me now, eh?"

Before Grady finishes his thought Mary *does* make a move, a head-dipping and shoulder-bending move so fast Grady can't get his hands up to react, and Grady's vision spins with his body being whipped around to face the road, the hay field blurring in the distance, and he feels a length of hose around his throat tugging him upward so he stands on the toes of his boots. Mary says this into Grady's ear: "Green Berets, 1970. That's the 'Nam, my son. Three tours. And if you'd like me to demonstrate what I did with Gooks over there, I suggest you push me a little more."

Grady's eyesight goes to checkerboardy blotches, his breathing wheezing, and in his inner ears he hears the slunching and hissing of his pulse. Think, Grady, and do it quick. He says, "All right, motherfucker. All right."

Grady feels a kiss on his ear, Mary's dry lips like penny nails sticking in Grady, and Mary says, "What's all right, my son?" Mary's voice so calm—dude just *kissed* Grady—and the hose jams tighter into Grady's throat, pulling him backward and off balance.

Grady says, "I'm sorry already."

"Not good enough," Mary says, but he loosens the hose enough so that Grady can take a strong solid breath, get his feet underneath him, and with the breath his eyesight uncheckers to a view of the road, the rusty-wire fence line beyond it, the wind flattening down the hay field.

Mary says, "Enough squabbling with me, is that clear?"

"Clear," Grady says, but things aren't clear the way he's letting on. When Mary releases the hose, when Grady's certain the hose is no longer around his neck, he rifles his elbow into Mary's ribs, spins to him, grabs the hose from him, and whacks him on the neck, toppling him sideways but not to falling. Mary clutches his hands to his neck, takes a few steps backward, and Grady raises the hose to bullwhip him again. But in that prewhack instant, in that place a guy pauses to consider what he's doing, why he's striking another man, where he's going to strike, Grady notices that Mary's eyes widen not to the hose, not to him, but to some undefined spot behind him.

Mary outstretches his arms in the manner of blessing and says, "There it is." And his eyes glaze somewhere westward and windward.

No way is Grady turning. This look-the-other-way trick is way too obvious. But Grady can't bring himself to belt Mary again. Hell, he's standing there undefended. What good is beating a guy who wants it?

Mary begins shouting the Lord's Prayer, and his head wiggles and waggles. He looks like a terrified child.

Grady takes a few boot-dragging steps away from Mary, far enough to avoid the pouncing he suspects is on the way, and he turns warily to the west, to the wind. Maybe two miles over the hay field, beyond a wooden-spoony indentation in the earth, emerging in waves from the horizon-long stretch of Chequamegon pines is the firelight, a brighter yellow under the yellow sky, the flameyellow nearly white and tonguing upward and from side to side. The fire crowns the pines in what to Grady seems like a half second, and in no time the entire tree line is aflame, walls of fire shooting two hundred feet in the air, by Grady's guess. Now the sky darkens in a smooth fade to a heavy gray, the wind blowing with such power Grady feels himself pushed backward. Up and down the road in front of Shady Glen deer bound from the hay field, slide on their hooves as if on ice over the pavement, and they bound again. Rabbits and fox and squirrels and woodchucks scuttle across the road, and ruffed grouse and pheasant spring from the hay field in bursts and drops. Everywhere birds of all sizes zip over Shady Glen like slingshot stones, and Grady stumbles backward to the priest and shouts, "You're right on one thing, Mary. There it is."

Mary's lips flutter and curl in, and he looks at Grady with squinted eyes. "God help us," he says.

Grady considers smacking the priest again, a little instructional swat, revenge for that kiss, but he figures it's too late, way too late for slobberknocking any sense into the man. Grady says, "Forget God. On the planet Earth, we save our own asses." He grabs Mary by the arm, feels him trembling, a reaction Grady understands, but for reasons he can't put his brain on Grady isn't terrorized much. Numb, probably, that's Grady.

He scans the flaming horizon, the animals racing from the fire, the thin sprinkler mist sheeting over the building top, and he can see the laser-focus truth: Whatever kicking and screaming and baby-acting he might do won't amount to squat. Maybe nothing ever has. He's done ten years of fiddling with this building, thirty years of living, and this is the way his end comes. Knowing he can see the end out there across the hay field fills him not with the guilt he thinks he should feel—not anything about drinking too much, or failing to make anything spectacular of his life, or lying to people, or cheating people, or taking Erica for granted so that she cheated on him—but the fire and the end it brings fill Grady with words he bets Mary says every day: *Go in peace*. Let the struggling end. Have some dignity for once.

Grady says, "Come on, Bud. They'll be needing you inside."

A Green Beret. Ha! Who'd have thought a Green Beret could turn into a Mary? Fuckin-A.

Grady leads Mary around the building to the side entrance, the wind a gale now, the sky blackening like it might before a tornado.

And while Grady guides Mary down the service hallway, his ears tune in on the building for sounds of panic, screams, shouts, women scurrying, but the building sounds and smells routine. Peace, Grady thinks. Ain't nobody falling apart here.

He joggles Mary to facing him and says, "We'll make it through this, eh?"

Mary says, "We did what we could." He shakes his head, sniffs one sharp sniff, and flares his nostrils. On the wall behind Mary a folded-up wheelchair leans; a few of its spokes are bent.

"Fuckin-A, we did what we could," Grady says, pats Mary on the back, and laughs because he's mothering a father.

This hallway leads to the dining room, and from here Grady smells the mashed-bacon and oatmeal odor of second-serving breakfast preparations. Metallic noises come from the kitchen, and the steam blast of the dishwashers.

"I'll tell you what, Mary. When this is over I'll buy you a few drinks down to the Liquid Forest. Fellows at the tavern would like hammering a few with a man like you."

"Thanks all the same," Mary says, and his face is composed now, back to smiling and being hopeful the way it was outside, the jawbone sturdy, the lips thin and taut. "Taverns aren't quite my thing."

"Didn't figure as much," Grady says. But peace is in the asking.

When they walk into the dining room Grady is overwhelmed, as he always is, with the rank gastric stench of the residents eating. Seventeen tables fill the dining room, but there are only enough regular chairs for nine tables. Who needs regular chairs in wheelchairland? This second shift of breakfasting is reserved for geezers who have it the worst: the stroke geezers, or the legless, the speechless, the ones missing fingers or mewling incessantly at the ceiling. Around the tables these residents wear terrycloth bibs over their robes, and they worm and jerk and gargle their prune juice. Some of these rundowns and brokens can hold their own spoon, but most are being fed by a young female nurse's aide.

Grady turns to Mary and says, "Hell, they don't even know."

But Mary's already at work with his flock, on his knees with Mr. Davidson the noseless man, an ex-policeman who had his nose blown off in 1972 in a gun-cleaning accident. Mary blesses Mr. Davidson's forehead, and Mr. Davidson gurgles.

Ah, the great calm in Grady, the way he breathes easy. This is the life he's had, a life with the dying, a life for more than the time clock and the tools he's got downstairs, for more than the bourbon he buys and gags on after work. What's the shame in keeping these wheezers wheezing in comfort? Peace, that's what Grady's given them over the years. You bet.

He whistles walking to the nurse's station, and the calmer

Grady is the calmer he figures everybody around him will be. He focuses on keeping the muscles in his arms and neck and face relaxed.

At the nurse's station clipboards and file folders pass from woman to woman, each nurse concentrating on evacuating the building properly.

Grady says, "Where's Jane at?" And not a head looks up.

Four voices say in unison, "Activity room."

"Good enough," Grady says, which is what he thinks everything is: good enough. Phone lines light up and buzz, and the nurses shout directives at one another, and the world is white and pure and ready, Grady believes, to face its doom.

The activity room is a forty-by-sixty rectangle of drywall Grady painted light blue a month ago. A nice blue, he thinks, a good paint job. But no Jane.

Surrounding the wide-screen TV on the north wall of the activity room are a dozen wheelchaired residents, all slumped or head-bobbing. These residents watch, or they don't watch, the logo of Action 9 news, and the TV doesn't make a noise. On the west wall two picture windows provide a view, through the sheets of sprinkler water, of the darkness outside, and between the picture windows is an oak-cased Wurlitzer organ that the red-sweater lady plays for sing-along on Monday and Wednesday mornings. Two silver candleholders and a yard-high golden crucifix rest atop the organ, because the organ doubles as the altar for mass, which is held every day promptly at 2:00 P.M. Grady's idea: keeps him from having to set up a table each day for Father Mary. Grady wonders if there's time for Mary to give one more mass, but then again, the residents can't tell the difference between mass and sing-along and the TV.

Grady hears, somewhere behind him, Jane calling his name, but he doesn't turn to her. He fixes his eyes on the Action 9 logo, listens to Jane's footsteps shuffling nearer to him on the carpet.

"We're ready to evacuate maybe in a half hour, after the feeding's done," she says, and he can smell her soapy smell next to him. "You and the father get all the sprinklers up?"

"Mostly," Grady says, and from the corner of his eye he watches Jane's small white shoes toe-tapping on the carpet.

"This is a not a time for *mostly*. Why aren't they all up?" Her voice has the drill-sergeant venom she's famous for, blatty and low, and she grabs Grady by the arm.

Grady whispers this: "Go to the window and look."

Inert Grady, Grady at peace, Grady standing without a muscle flexing, Grady watching the Action 9 logo and waiting for Lucky Littlefield to come on the air: Grady wants one last test before death. He wants to look at Lucky Littlefield and remind himself he did the right thing not killing him. He wants to be a forgiving Grady, a better man, a calm one who can accept himself for who he is, which is the kind of man he'd like to be dead.

Jane shrieks at the window now. She's seen the fire sure enough. But Grady doesn't look away from the TV. He listens to Jane running from the activity room, then more shrieks from the nurse's station, feet running behind him in the come-and-go of panic, and more shriekings at the window, and then yelping residents, and from every cranny in his building he hears screechings like a giant alternator belt slipping and fraying. But Grady hasn't a movement in him. Even his eyes won't blink from the TV. He imagines himself transformed into the Action 9 jumping buck, what a powerful leap he's taking over that fence line, how something's frozen his blood and muscles and the air itself, and he will never move again.

Jane's voice comes over the P.A.: "All staff, take your stations now. This is not a drill."

And Grady's body floats over the fence line of his imagination: *Why does the buck jump in the first place? Why does the buck run? Why can't the buck hold his ground and take whatever comes?* From the corner of his eye he thinks he sees a glowing through the window, something flickering like the suncreep from night to day this summer has been, which is what Grady's life has been, asleep for a time and flicker awake, and gripe and moan about waking until it's sleep time all over again, and the griping is over at long last. The louder the clamor behind Grady the harder he concentrates on the buck, the muscles rippled in the leap, how, for that buck's eternity, he's stronger than the dirt below him, yet weaker than whatever it is that scares him over the fence.

8

TIME DOES NOT FLY AT ACTION 9. ONLY THE ACTION 9 DEER does. And Erica sits where she's been sitting ten minutes now, maybe longer, in Lucky's chair. She's watching the deer on the monitor and waiting for Jimbo and Pete to put her back on the air. But Jimbo and Pete won't do it, won't even discuss it. And another terrific gust rumbles the warehouse, makes a buffalo-herd sound that blocks out for a moment the howling sirens, and Jimbo's head jerks toward the walls and toward the fiberglass snow descending from the ceiling. His jaw drops and twitches. Something big clatters across the roof, a tree branch, maybe, or maybe several garbage cans, and clumps of fiberglass cough downward. From the iron beams spanning the ceiling comes a menacing series of squeaks. Jimbo pockets his hands and takes a few sidesteps over to Pete, whose hands are pocketed, too, and they stand there together, their mouths open, their eyes turned-up and glazed.

"Kill the logo," Erica says, exactly what Lucky always says when he's ready to broadcast, "and let's get on with it."

Nothing. They keep staring upward.

She clasps her hands as tightly as she can. Her palms, she notices, are sweating.

A voice, close by the Action 9 set: "You're not planning something foolish now, are you, Erica?"

She snaps her head to a vision she needs to blink and open her eyes again to believe: two Luckys. Lucky One is the standard, neatly coifed, Hawaiian-shirted Lucky, head tilted in an anointed way, and this Lucky is silk-screened in gray on a black T-shirt that says, PRAY WITH ME, FRIENDS AND BRETHREN. Lucky Two, the real man wearing the T-shirt, is not neatly coifed, is haggard and has dark circles under his eyes. He moves with slow, pained steps toward the news set, grimacing with each movement his body makes.

"My darling Erica," he says, and his voice, like hers, has gone to gravel. "Get out of my seat." He coughs violently, bends over and spits on the floor, pats himself on the tummy. Then he pitches himself upright and throws his shoulders back. Erica can clearly see his neck muscles move as he swallows. "I mean it. Out. I've taken enough shit from you today." And he steps onto the news-set riser.

From outside comes a wind blast that rumbles the building enough to make her believe the Holy Spirit has gripped Action 9 and is shaking it. The set lights brown momentarily, then whiten again.

"Now get your self-righteous fanny out of my chair," Lucky says, close to her now, his eyes darkening in a desert of bloodshot. "I've got people depending on me here."

"No way will I move," says Erica, and folds her arms.

Lucky stops near the edge of the desk, and Erica focuses her attention on the T-shirt Lucky. She tries to appear relaxed and unfettered.

"Why do you insist on being belligerent?" Lucky says in a

hushed voice, rolling his eyes toward Jimbo and Pete, probably indicating that he doesn't want them to hear.

"I'm not moving."

"What this is, no question of it, is that you're never appreciative of your opportunities. You think, for instance, that I don't read that copy you write, but you're wrong, darling. I read it all right, every word. Lifeless stuff. I'm doing you a favor by improvising my broadcasts. I'm giving *life* to what you want me to say. Life! You are just the same as your copy, Erica. You're frigid. I'm giving you the opportunity to feel alive. For once! To inspire your life! To let you share your life with Lucky Littlefield, instead of some *common wrench*. And what do you do in return?"

The T-shirt Lucky stares off into the void, a few cigarette ashes forming a filthy halo above the coifed hair. The real Lucky raises his voice from its hush and shouts, "Ingratitude, thou art the inviolate weed that grows."

"That's not from the Bible," Erica says.

"Who gives a shit?" And he sweeps his arms in a regal gesture to Jimbo and Pete, who maintain their ready position in front of their equipment. "What sounds good is what works. Right, boys?"

"We're with you, Lucky," Jimbo says, and fiddles with his Leinenkugel's hat. "All the way."

Pete nods, begins examining again his shuffling shoes.

"Since my crew is with me, and, given the circumstances, which any sane soul would call *an emergency*, I do believe I have the right to throw you from my chair. Jimbo, what do you say?"

Jimbo nods and smiles. Pete shuffles.

Lucky says, "Is this what you want, Erica?"

She knows she can't win. All the stubbornness she can muster will not get her on the air. "No," she says, and stands, steps away from the chair and away from Lucky, moves to the edge of the news-set riser to face Lucky, who watches her, looks somewhere below her neck, probably at her hips or at her breasts. And she drops gently to her knees, holds her posture straight and clasps her hands together. "I'll pray," she says. "Just watch me."

Lucky does watch her for a second or two. He says, "We'll get to that later." Then he sits in his chair, runs his hands through his hair, clears his throat, and says, "Let's get on with this thing, Jimbo. Kill the logo, and we'll rock 'n' roll."

Erica does not cry, only thinks of crying, how relieving it would be to cry. But the sirens cry for McCutcheon now, for Grady, wherever he is, for everybody facing their doom at this moment, out in the waterless wind, huddling before the walls of flame.

"In five," Jimbo says, and he counts backward to Lucky's cue.

Erica clasps her fingers together so tightly it hurts her bones. Her forearms quiver with the force she applies to her hands. She is trying to pray, but no prayers come to her, because with whatever is deepest and hidden inside her she is beginning to question whether prayer is just a useless, uncomfortable gesture the body makes, whether, after all these years of believing, she's wasted her time following the Word of the Lord.

9

AND THE FIRE TAKES THE GOODNESS FROM THE LAND. From Condyle north thirty miles to Gullickson Township, the fire's burnt everything. Same situation southward, from Condyle to Little Oslo, twenty-six thousand acres, it's all burnt. And the thirty-five thousand acres eastward, everything to within a mile of the McCutcheon River Valley, this is burnt, too.

In the open country the fire has erased every acre of bottom-land, every tag-elder thicket and sumac grove, every forested hill. And the Christmas-tree plantations are gone. And the corn-fields, the hay fields, the wood lots, and the orchards, all that was once lush here and bountiful here and worthy of earnest thanks to the Lord—this is not a landscape merely withered from the drought; this is a landscape gone. Even the cranberry bogs of Hutchinson, the largest continuous wetland stretch in the state of Wisconsin, have become a fifteen-thousand-acre series of black depressions in the earth. Smoke wisps about where the cranberry roots once took hold. It is as if this region, passed over as it was by the glaciers of the last Ice Age, is now getting the scourging clean the Lord forgot to give it ten thousand years ago, back in the days of Woolly Mammoths and six-ton bears and hairy men who earned their supper with stone hatchets and atlatls and hickory spears.

And what the Lord leaves behind the fire are salted ashes. And charred deer carcasses litter the countryside. And pickup trucks, tractors, and hay wagons smolder under a yellow sky. Here and there birds circle—crows, turkey vultures, scrub jays, hawks—and they screech and swoop to the ashes, but the ground is too hot for them to touch down. National Guard helicopters hover above the birds, their pilots searching for survivors. But not much moves on the ground, only the occasional flutter of fire from a big stump or from a blackened station wagon or from a barrel of used crankcase oil. When a helicopter pilot speaks, if he says anything at all, he says this: "Jesus Christ." But no pilot believes in Jesus Christ, not today. There is no redemption in a scorching like this.

And in front of the fire the wind reaches sixty miles an hour. It gusts and swirls and snaps tree branches, and in the dry fields huge dust devils form and gain the strength of tornadoes. The devils slam into the wooded draws between the fields, and sticks and entire trees launch toward the unburned wastes to the east. The flying trees crash into roadside power lines, and the power lines fall and start new fires, which tongue down the roadside gullies, and the new fires spread into the pulpwood stands, which become the pitchy expanse of the lower Chequamegon Forest. These new fires crown the Chequamegon pines, and flames shoot two hundred feet into the air.

It is midday, and before the fire is a midnight sky.

And before the fire whatever lives panics.

Animals of all sorts—deer, squirrels, fox, raccoons—stampede toward the McCutcheon River Valley, somehow knowing that this is where the last water is.

And the people of the countryside do their best to stay alive. Some folks take to their pickup trucks or station wagons, packing whatever they can with them, and they drive toward McCutcheon. But with the soot and dust and smoke flying in the heavy winds, no headlights can illuminate the road. No driver can see where he's going. And vehicles careen into the ditches, sometimes catching fire in the crash, and in this way the fire's advance gains speed, as if every vehicle speeding from the fire is tendril of the fire, groping over the withered landscape, torching it. Some folks stay on their farms with their families, trying to wet down their barns, their chicken sheds, their farmhouses, using whatever little water is left in their wells, and these farmers die, and their families die, and their buildings transform into embers flying to the east. When the fire approaches a farm, the flames surround the property, wicking along the fence-line scrub, and the wind blasts the flames from the perimeter to the center. And in the barnyards chickens and geese catch fire, burst upward through the barnyard darkness like flaming cannonballs, and they explode onto the ground, their deaths spreading the fire to the farmhouse. The same pattern with every farm: The fire surrounds, burns somehow inward, and destroys.

10

AT THE WESTERN CREST OF THE MCCUTCHEON VALLEY, since early in the morning, what few Forest Service workers could be mustered—a hundred men—have been chainsawing and bulldozing an open space in the woods, making a fire lane, bordered on the west by a ten-foot berm made of dirt and branches. The berm, according to the workers' calculations, is too high for the fire to jump. But at times during the chainsawing, so many deer have bounded over the berm and into the clear-cut that the workers have had to shoot the deer to keep from getting trampled. If deer can make their way over the berm, the workers think, the fire surely will. Still, the workers keep working. They have been trained to keep working.

At eleven o'clock, when the fire reached a spot three miles away from their clear-cut, it was these men who requested that McCutcheon's civil-defense unit start blaring the take-cover sirens in the valley. From the workers' position on the valley's crest, they heard the sirens begin as a soft moan over the grind of their chainsaws. Some of the workers wept when they first heard the sirens, for the sirens were proof to these men that their labors were useless.

And these men have worked hard, have cut this swath fifty yards wide and bulldozed this ten-foot-high berm a half-mile long through the forest. Their bosses have put in all the distress calls—to the Smoke Jumpers of Montana and Colorado, to the United States Army, to anybody who might come to help—but the fire's too wide and moving too fast. The soonest help could come would be by nightfall. But the skies are black already. Embers sail through the air like shooting stars.

And when the fire draws very close, the winds are so heavy and the sky is so dark that the men can't see well what they're cutting or where the trees will fall. By noon, by the time the fire glow appears near the clear-cut, a dozen men have been killed by falling trees.

And when the flames tower two hundred feet over the ten-foot berm, the men pile into their pickup trucks and drive east, some of them vowing to drive the three hours it takes to get to Lake Michigan, to the big water that even God couldn't set aflame.

11

AND THE SIRENS WHINE IN THE VALLEY. AND THE PEOPLE in the valley huddle in their homes. Lovers make their last love, drinkers drink their last drink, and folks fanatical for His Mother the Blessed Virgin Mary clutch their rosary beads, reciting their Glorious Mysteries in whimpers and gasps. And people stare at their television sets, waiting for Lucky Littlefield to come on the air. And at a few minutes after noon, after all that's been on their televisions for a full hour has been the Action 9 deer, Lucky finally appears in the living rooms of the valley.

The picture is grainy at first, and something about Lucky does not look well, the hair mussed, the beard limp, something vacant in the eyes. He does not wear his trademark Hawaiian shirt. He wears a black T-shirt of himself instead, a T-shirt tight on his chest, and when he speaks his voice is not the horn of hope it has been during these months of drought.

"Friends and brethren," he says, and it's a scratchy voice, and when he coughs and wipes his nose, the people of the valley draw closer to their television screens.

And Lucky coughs and coughs. Every fifth cough or so, he jerks his head away from the camera and mutters these words:

"You stay the fuck there on the floor. I'll deal with you in a minute." And people wonder who Lucky is talking to, and why he is talking in this way. Throughout the valley people begin a confused and unnerving wait, a slow terror that grows with each passing second, each hammering of wind against their walls, each upward whine of the sirens, each moment that Lucky does not look into their homes and tell them that everything will be all right.

"Friends and brethren," he says again, and he coughs again. "We have endured much this summer. We have asked the Lord to bring relief to us. But the Lord has let us down. And you want to know why the Lord's let us down? He doesn't give a shit about us. And don't look at me for help, either. I can't save you. It's too late. We're dead already." He presses his hands to his beard, jerks his head away from the camera again, and he stands, pulling his T-shirt away from his stomach, and he shouts to a person folks in the valley cannot see: "I said stay the fuck there on the floor!"

Lucky begins moving then, hobbling strides that the camera swivels to follow, and for an instant the people of McCutcheon see Lucky Littlefield, weather wizard, man of God, raising his hand to strike a small, dark-haired woman in a sundress. Her arms form a crucifix over her face. She kneels, and her posture is perfectly straight. Around her dust swirls, thick dust, flaky, like pink snow.

But before Lucky's hand strikes this woman, the electricity fails all over the valley. TV screens go blank. Refrigerators stop running. Fish tanks quit bubbling. And in a great descending sigh, the sirens, near and far, whir themselves to silence. The wind howls through the valley, and that is the only sound anyone can hear.

12

WHEN THE LIGHTS FAIL IN ACTION 9, ERICA'S FIRST THOUGHT is that Lucky has killed her, and that she has arrived in the Hell she deserves. She is kneeling, and her knees are beginning to ache. Something hairy presses into her arms, but she can't see what it is. She hears a swishing sound close by and the sound of high winds far off. She hears Jimbo's voice saying, "Goddam emergency lights kicking on finally."

And there are two emergency lights in the Action 9 building, both a long way from the set, both mounted over the exits, on opposite sides of the building. These lights are Devil lights, dim and unearthly. Blurs, odd shadows, are what Erica sees. Right in front of her now an object appears. It makes slight bobs up and down and from side to side. This is Lucky's hard dick in front of her.

Lucky says, "I'll be goddamned if I'm going to die without having my way with you one time." He takes hold of her hair. She struggles to recoil, but she can't get away. Lucky's grip on her is too intense. He slaps his dick right between her eyes.

She tries to scream, but the sound she makes is thin and reedy. She hears feet shuffling some distance from where she kneels. She hears Jimbo clearing his throat. "Holy shit, Mr. Littlefield," Jimbo says. "What the fuck are you doing?"

Lucky says, "I have things under control here. You'd best git while the gitting's good."

The feet shuffle again, a scraping noise Erica hears growing more distant, till a door opens and closes. And Lucky's grip tightens on her head.

She says, "Let me go."

"You've never appreciated me," Lucky says, and he tugs her several feet along the carpet. She had thought she was dead not one minute ago, and now she knows she is living, and only to die again. Lucky is going to kill her, sure enough. Listen to him: "You can appreciate me one time now, Mrs. McCann," he says. "You can be cooperative for once, can't you?"

Maybe at some other time, when she was a more confident Erica, she would not be cooperative and would instead accept death, because death, the way the stronger Erica used to think about it, would give her new life with the Lord. But she saw death moments ago, or what she figured to be death, and she is not ready to accept that kind of everlasting torment. She can still change. She has time. If she can go on living, she can undo what she's done wrong. She relaxes her body, her neck, tries shifting her weight toward where Lucky pulls her, which is to the broadcasting desk, and she knows she must do one more wrong thing before she can realign her life toward the hope of Heaven. She can leave her body for a while, let herself go, and do what Lucky wants.

The desk is black. The carpet was red a few minutes ago; it's black now. Lucky's broadcasting chair used to be pale blue.

"There you go," Lucky says. "I see you're finally coming around."

And here is the movie Erica sees of herself: her hand rising to the penis, her hand making an O-slide over it. She is the woman with the mouth. She is the woman with nostrils, a neck, elbows, with knees numb to the rough carpet's bristle.

Please, no sensations, Erica. Think nothing. Close your eyes. Don't listen to the man grunting and sniffling above you. Don't hear the creakings his chair makes. Move your mouth, your head, Erica, your spine. Make the lesser rhythm of the Angels. This isn't you. This isn't the earth you were born into.

No.

13

OUTSIDE NOW, THE SKY IS A NIGHTTIME AT MIDDAY. THE wind is a vast hissing noise Erica doesn't feel against her skin. When she breathes she tastes something remotely like the way the air tasted when she was a little girl, dancing around the family campsite fire, waiting for the hot dogs to be done. But she never could have been a little girl. She was a woman once. She knows this. She is not a woman now. And it's Lucky Littlefield's hand tugging her through the Action 9 parking lot. She knows this.

And Lucky shouts in her ear while he tugs her. "I knew you felt something for me all along. I knew you'd decide I'm better for you than a maintenance man."

Maintenance. She knows what maintenance means.

Lucky says, "I'll need you to drive now. I can't be driving in all this smoke. My eyesight's bad enough as it is."

She feels her mind thinning into a vapor. She is not human. She is a thing with a mouth. She is a thing that produces saliva.

Lucky says, "We can strap ourselves in, and you can drive."

Lucky's car is white. "This is a 1978 Buick Riviera," he says. "It's indestructible. We'll make it through this, no matter how bad things get. You'll see."

Lucky opens the door, guides her in front of the steering wheel. "Here, my love," he says, and presses his lips to her ear. "I'll adjust the seat for you."

He reaches across her, slides his hand over her leg, snaps her seat belt around her. He touches her breasts. They are not hers.

Lucky is seated inside the car now, strapped in his passenger seat.

Lucky says, "Turn over the engine." And she does.

Lucky says, "Back up slowly." And she does.

14

WHEN FLAMES BLASTED THROUGH THE SHADY GLEN activity-room windows and the ceiling caught fire, Grady made a bee-line for his boiler room, and on the way, for reasons he can't quite now remember, he grabbed Father Mary and took him along. And they're both still alive all right. And they're alive because of the plan Grady's devised to live through the fire.

Check this out: Grady has his industrial Mag Lite handy, best flashlight Sears sells, holds eight size D's, lithium, and this sucker really shines through the boiler-room darkness. He can eyeball anything that needs eyeballed down here. There's Mary squatting underneath the workbench, two red eyes reflecting the flashlight beam. A good boy, that Mary, he's staying put where he was told to. And Grady can shine the beam on his emergency generators, too, or on his two Briggs & Stratton well pumps, which chug, you betcha, and they chug. He's got six hoses nozzled and C-clamped down, four gallons per minute apiece, which accounts for one awful lot of spray, mirrors of water, great cascades of it. He's got water sailing all over the place. Wherever the flashlight shines, water splashes and shimmers, makes silvery blotches the size of flying thumbs. Water sheets down from the ductwork, shoots upward from the hoses. Grady's boiler room looks like it's the boiler room of a sinking submarine. And you're damn straight this is the kind of planning he's thinking about: He waterproofed and double-grounded his emergency generators four months ago. All this water, all this electricity: nightmare-potential factor 28. But with Grady in charge, electrocution is not a possibility.

The water is cold, coming from way down in the aquifer as it has, and it's part of Grady's plan that the water's cold. When the fire burns through the boiler-room ceiling, and it'll burn through for sure, the colder the water is, the better the chances of staying living. And Grady's uniform is soaked through to the skin.

For the rest of the building, well, it's toast. Grady can hear the fire shaking the building all the way to the floor joists. The sound is like what his Pinto sounds like when it goes through the automatic car wash, only it's amplified fifteenfold. The fire's really giving the building a walloping. As to the nurses and geezers, all of them must be crispy critters by now, which is a tragedy, but Grady doesn't want to get maudlin just at this moment, not when his own living is on the line.

And Mary huddles there under the workbench, staying right where Grady told him to stay put, wet and out of the way.

Grady shines the flashlight in Mary's eyes, and with that hair of his bowl-cut so short, he looks like an eight-year-old boy who got caught in the rain. "I don't deserve to live," Mary says.

"Fuck that, Mary. You're alive, which means you don't deserve to die, at least in my book." The building shudders above Grady, a board-scraping and drywall-twisting noise. He shines the flashlight toward the noise and thinks he sees a break developing in the floorboards. Something between the boards doesn't look as dark as it should. Won't be long now, nope, that ceiling will never hold. "You hear that ceiling?" Grady says. "We might go ahead and die just like you want. That'd be great, eh?"

Mary says, "I believe we should make at least *one* attempt to save lives upstairs."

"They're dead as motherfuckers, all of them. Nothing we can do." Grady keeps the flashlight beam on the ceiling, waiting for an orange light to break through, and where the beam shines, even though Grady's holding the flashlight as still as can be, the beam wobbles.

"I'm a failure to my calling," Mary says.

"Tell me who the fuck *isn't* a failure." The flashlight beam begins jiggling violently.

"Jesus didn't fail."

"Jesus did too fail," Grady says.

"How is that possible?"

"When He named you Mary, that was a fuckup extraordinaire." And before Grady gets the chance to laugh aloud and shine the flashlight again into Mary's eyes, the ceiling caves in near the stairwell. It's the meat freezer that's fallen through. Big sucker, that freezer is, and it smashes on top of Grady's new Shop Vac, crushes it into a garbage-can lid. In seconds the boiler room is awash with orange, and flaming floorboards begin cracking down from the gap where the freezer fell through. Heat comes in waves through the boiler room, and the burning noise is as loud as a jet engine.

Grady shouts, "We're done for." But the fire is so loud he can't hear his own voice.

Automatic Grady: He's got to try something. He can see without the flashlight now. The boiler room is lit up like day, and he
unclamps two hoses and yanks them over to the workbench.

"Take this hose," Grady says. "And keep the water spraying
over your head."

But Mary doesn't take the hose. Mary probably can't hear
him.

With each passing second the break in the ceiling grows
wider, and Grady holds both hoses at his hips, like a gunslinger,
and he shoots water into the break. It keeps growing wider.
These hoses aren't going to do shit.

Last ditch now: Grady climbs, tugging the hoses with him,
underneath the workbench. Water gushes everywhere, in his
face, on his chest. Everything is water and heat and jet-engine
loudness, and the underside of this workbench is way too
cramped for two people. If Grady shifts his knees, they bump
into Mary. If Grady tries maneuvering himself so he can shoot
water into the room, he elbows Mary.

"You got to take one of these hoses," Grady shouts. And
Grady can't hear himself.

Flaming boards begin dropping into the boiler room,
tongues of fire following them, and so much flame is everywhere now that when Grady looks up, he sees nothing but
sheets of white and orange. On his face is a heat like the sun.

Water, water, yes, water is the only way, and he takes both
hoses and blasts water on top of his head, cool water, the water
of staying living, so much water running over his face his vision
goes to orange smears, so much water it becomes difficult to
breathe. This is going to work. He reaches an arm out to Father
Mary and draws him close, holds a hose over Mary's head. Arm-

in-arm with Mary now, flames, jet-engine thunder, Mary's body quaking, a much harder body than Grady's, than Kate's was yesterday, than Erica's has ever been, than any body Grady has ever held, two hoses spraying two bodies, two heads pressing together, the air thinning, thinning, difficult to breathe, eyesight fading, sleep coming, Grady can feel the sleep coming. He feels the heat and the cold and the hurt of living fading. He feels the slippery skin of Mary's arm. He feels Mary's muscles twitching. He feels the world withering away into a calm space deep inside his mind, a place where everything is pink and watery and quiet, where what is tra-la and la-la about the world is all there is to living.

15

DURING THIS LAST HALF HOUR KATE MURPHY HAS GRADU-
ally figured out what's going on: She is lost driving on the
streets of her hometown. Incredible. Lost in McCutcheon.
Must be not long after twelve noon now, and the air itself has
turned black with smoke. She can hardly see beyond the roadside, let alone fifty yards up the road. The Pacer's headlights cast
merely two gray baseball-bat beams of light through the black
distance she drives into. Twigs and branches soar like birds
through the headlight beams, and newspapers and cardboard
boxes whisk through the beams, and they disappear into the
whirling murk of the road ahead.

Kate says, "Does this look like Highway Fifty?"

"I guess it does," Lennart says, and Kate can faintly hear him
swigging from his pint.

"You're a real help, Lennart." She watches the road ahead
and thinks this: It's a road. Smoke funnels over it. It has curbs.
But that doesn't mean this road is Highway 50, which is the
road to Window Falls, where Lennart was saying this morning
they likely might find Grady. She is alert to the unfamiliar con-
trols of this Pacer, her eyes pegged on the speedometer and the

blinkers and the mirrors and the road ahead all at once, and she observes the branches flying, the blown garbage, the occasional dogs or deer running in front of the car; and when an obstacle does present itself in the road, she breaks or swerves with, she believes, great skill, hitting nothing, keeping the car at a safe pace. Funny, driving out here is like playing a video game.

All of a sudden Lennart moans loudly and shrieks. "I insist you stop my car this minute!"

She keeps driving, fifteen miles an hour, down a stretch of road with familiar-looking hedges, which, factoring in a few turns and a few previous stop-sign stops, she probably drove along fifteen minutes ago.

"Why?" she says.

"I mean it. I absolutely insist you stop this car."

"I'm not going too fast. Am I?"

"I can't stand this much longer," Lennart shouts, and he pummels the dashboard a few times with his fists.

"Okay, okay, I'll do it." And she does it, eases the Pacer to a halt, changing somehow the sound of the wind battering the car windows, making the sound less violent.

"What's the problem?"

"My book," Lennart says. He stares in an empty way out into the blackness along the road.

"What book?"

"*The Decline and Fall of the Roman Empire, Part One.* I left it in the tavern last night, by the cash register."

Kate sighs a sigh that, with the wind and debris buffeting the car, she figures there's no way Lennart could hear.

"Jesus," she says.

"Edward Gibbon."

Several large objects dart in front of the car, big brownish objects: deer.

"Look at them run," Kate says. "I wonder if they're as lost as we are."

"Why can't you listen to me?"

Kate watches the deer safely bound off into the swirling smoke, and, when she's sure they're gone, that the road is clear, she resumes driving, eases the Pacer back up to five miles an hour. "It was just deer, Lennart. I was just commenting that they were there."

"I can't go on like this," he says. "Stop this car and let me speak."

So she stops again. "Speak already."

"It's about my book. It's a reasonable request."

"We can't go get the book, Lennart."

"We can't. I know that."

"Then why bother making me stop?"

"It's just occurring to me that I've been reading *The Decline and Fall of the Roman Empire* for fifteen years now; maybe today is the day—no, that's not it." He taps his index finger on the windshield. "Go ahead. Drive. You're right."

She goes ahead, touches the accelerator, eases up to ten miles an hour, on the dot.

"No problem," she says. Debris tumbles through the headlights. No problem. Concentrate on driving. The steering wheel is becoming comfortable in Kate's hands, responsive, an extension of her body, and she is trying to tune out what Lennart is saying: *In the beginning there was not Heaven and Earth. There was Mesopotamia. There was the Mediterranean Sea. At the base of Mount Vesuvius, along the seashores of*

Pompeii, was volcanic sand. When the Romans came they mixed this sand with lime and pebbles to make the finest concrete in the ancient world. And with this volcanic concrete the Romans built their empire. The trade in volcanic sand made the city of Pompeii rich. And in 79 A.D. Mount Vesuvius erupted fire and ash and made the city of Pompeii nothing at all. And up the road Kate can only see the blackness where she thinks she needs to get to, which is to Grady, not for love, not to tell him she loves him, but to tell him she came on to him yesterday for a diversion, for a change in her dull life. *And after the empire was built with concrete, Christ came, and the spread of Christianity throughout the empire was its downfall.* And maybe she will sleep with Grady someday. Maybe she won't. What's the difference?

Lennart keeps on talking—*because one God was not many gods, and many gods make the managing of an empire simpler, because one God is a threat to the authority of Rome, because one God portends to be more powerful than the state, because—* and Kate's mind focuses harder and harder on the driving, on what she needs inside her to find her bearings and to negotiate her way out of the valley and away from the fire.

16

Grady dreams he's relaxing on a huge pink towel somewhere on a tropical beach, a scorching afternoon, a sun like an acetylene torch in the heavens, and the sand on this dreamy beach is the kind of black sand Grady has seen on ESPN TV, swimsuit-model sand so black it makes babes look like they're stretched across the nighttime sky. Ah, and how this beach is filled with babes: here a blonde in a pink one-piece, here an Asian chick in a fishnet bikini, here a brunette with boobs the size of Leinenkugel's pitchers. To see them floating in space, that's the way Grady likes his babes, just forming constellations in the void, and nothing of the regular world borders the babes on this black beach: no living rooms they might want repainted or recarpeted, no briefcases full of Action 9 copyediting they might have to fiddle with tomorrow and complain about tomorrow, no thermometers for cervical-mucus testing next week.

This black beach is not Grady's Gone-fishing. It's his Gone-to-Heaven.

He dreams a light dreamy wind, a few coconut trees swaying at the jungle edge of the black sand. The surf pounds the shore with a sound like a thousand Shop Vacs switching on and off. Hawaii, yes, Grady must be relaxing on the best black beach in Hawaii.

And this must be the Number One ESPN TV Hawaiian Swimsuit Babe in his grip. Ho! She's baby-oiled and muscular, wears a one-piece, a blue one. Her hair is as short as a Cub Scout's. Her legs are like shafts of six-inch PVC mainline, sturdy at the thigh, flanged at the knee. And Grady's got the French Clamp real good on Miss Hawaii: got his thumb planted solid between her cheeks, plenty of torque from his bird-flip finger to the thumb pinion on that hard bone over her snatch. He's applying ten pounds of torque easy. Hawaii will not be wriggling free, not on this dreamy Grady day.

The light wind, the hard sun, the roiling the waves make at his knees, the babe's roiling, the flex and shimmy of her arms and legs—Grady's giving her all cylinders the way only a maintenance man can.

He is the suave babe-maintenancer, saying, in a French Clamp accent, "I am fellow most debonair, no?" And he is suave with the tiny tender pecks he gives her ear. Her kisses her ear with the rhythm of the waves. One kiss, then a long pause, then he applies another kiss, and another, till the pauses don't come that far between.

And he is the babe-maintenancer with a two-year certificate from McCutcheon Valley Trade & Mechanical. You betcha, Grady knows his mechanisms well. Watch him twist her and maneuver her and make her waggle her knees. Watch him, without a slide rule, calculate Miss Hawaii's thrust-capacity numbers and make the appropriate adjustments with respect to her PSI and her surge transduction limits and how many cycles her system can perform in a minute. Go to work, Grady McCann. Do it for Wisconsin. The Badger State adores a maintenance man in his prime.

And in that second before the heave and before the ho begins, when Grady gazes down at his manhood to admire its great dive out of the sun, he notices with pride that his manhood bears, along its shaft, the capital-letter stamp of the finest drop-forged pipe wrenches God ever made: RIGID.

A professional never chintzes on tools.

Ah, the dreamy Grady.

But wait. What are these shadows filing in front of the sun? Why is this hot day growing suddenly cool? He glances heavenward—clamping Hawaii still, never slack on that grip—and he sees a row of puffy clouds. One cloud takes the shape of Lucky Littlefield, beard in a partial profile and shaking in the breeze. The dude Grady's wife sucked off is a bearded cloud, a weatherman cloud, and look at that cloud smile. Will Action 9 come to Grady even when he's at the black beach? And Action 9 is Erica, too, a wifely cloud with its arms folded, with its head cocked in a curious way, the mouth open and looking like the stuffing cavity of last Sunday's chicken. That Kate girl from the college, she's in the sky, too; she's a cloud smoking a cigarette and blowing smoke rings that become new clouds, new clouds that become new faces. And more new clouds emerge from the ocean, clouds forming more faces and shoulders and arms, hundreds of clouds, then hundreds of thousands of clouds watching him. The sky is the world watching Grady, and the sky is a crowd going wild for Grady. Can't you hear the applause, Grady, the hollering, the whistling, the victory horns blaring? Nobody's pissed off at you, Grady. The clouds love you! You're doing it, Grady. You're

mounting ESPN's Number One Swimsuit Babe, and not just on
Action 9, on worldwide TV. And everybody is proud of you! Why
wouldn't they be? You're happy.

He revels a moment too long in the cheering, a moment that
stretches into a sequence of odd pictures flashing before his
eyes: the applauding clouds, the black beach, the surf, Miss
Hawaii, then a silvery light shines at his feet, and something like
rain in a spotlight flashes into Grady's eyes. He sees Miss Hawaii
again, then cold water splashing like millions of minnows over
his body, and Miss Hawaii is close by and wriggling. And Miss
Hawaii is not Miss Hawaii; she is something clammy and hairy
and twitching in his arms, and Grady's eyes open into a world of
spraying water, of concrete and two-by-fours, and the silvery
light at his feet is his industrial Mag Lite shining strong, and
Miss Hawaii, holy shit, Miss Hawaii is Father Mary. Grady's
been Clamping Father Mary!

Grady jolts to his feet so quickly that he slams his head into
the workbench he's been hiding under. Blotches of purple fill his
eyes, and he rolls out from under the workbench, rolls over
Father Mary's legs, and Mary lets out a lingering and multi-
pitched squeaking sound, a sound like a bird singing in spring-
time, when the meadows are quiet, when the lilacs are in bloom.

And after a purple moment of indeterminate length, Grady
finds himself awake and sprawled on his boiler-room floor, his
hands submerged under a few inches of water. He is looking
through a bright hole in the ceiling. Nothing is orange in the
bright hole. The light is gray and wispy. The light is the light of
the sky. The fire has evaporated the building, and Grady is alive.

And Grady begins shaking with life.

17

A SHORT DISTANCE UP THE ROAD, THROUGH THE BLOWING smoke that rushes everywhere in the headlight beams, Kate recognizes the Highway 50 sign. The sign bends and flaps, is a battered silverish color, and beyond it she sees the stop-and-go lights wobbling over the intersection of Highway 50 and Midland Mall Drive. She knows these stop-and-go lights, knows even the manhole cover in the middle of the intersection, because that's the manhole her older brother climbed down two summers ago, when he was drunk and yet another of his girlfriends had dumped him. Kate remembers her brother, after the police found him, saying, "I deserve to live in the sewer. Nobody gets a broken heart in the sewer." But her brother got over that girlfriend, whoever she was, and Kate is getting over being lost in her own hometown.

She hoots again, and says, "I told you we would find our way eventually."

And Lennart hoots, too, but for getting over a different type of lost. "Fifteen years," he says, "these ideas have been running around in my brain. It took a day like today for me to put it all together."

Kate surveys the intersection in front of her, watches for other cars passing along Midland Mall Drive, but everything is too black and too windy for her to tell if there's traffic. Sticks and newspapers and plastic milk jugs sail by, but no cars drive by. It would make sense that Kate's not the only person in town trying to escape the fire. But she can't recall seeing another car on the road since she's been driving. Visibility is steadily worsening, every second a bit darker, a bit windier. Streams of smoke funnel around the Pacer, and smoke tumbles through the intersection in front of them. In the stands of trees surrounding the intersection, Kate can see only a few trees—some pines, a birch, a willow— but she knows from memory that thousands of trees occupy this part of town.

"It's good not to be lost anymore," she says.

"Does it matter?" Lennart thoughtfully rubs his hands together. "I mean, anywhere we'll go the fire will catch us."

Kate adjusts her ears to the wind, hears it twing-twangling the stop-and-go lights, and she notices, in the warped music of the gale, that the sirens have stopped.

"Lennart, listen outside once."

He keeps rubbing his hands together.

Kate says, "No sirens. Don't you think that's strange?"

"Sirens. No sirens. What's the difference?"

Kate pictures Grady's ponytail, the jut of his jaw, his thin-lipped half smile, the respectful way he treated Lennart in the tavern yesterday afternoon. "Grady would be crushed if you died, you know."

"He'd only be sad that I couldn't pour him any more two-for-one bourbons."

"I think you sell him short."

"I sell him drinks, is what I do."

Kate experiences a dim rush of sad affectionate pity for Lennart, and she reaches across his shoulders, strains her arms around his neck, slides herself past the steering wheel, and gives him a squeeze. His neck smells oddly sweet, like a field of fresh-cut hay, but he does not hug her back. He merely tenses, seems to quit breathing. She moves her hand down his shoulder, down the arm, which is much more solid than it looks, and his arm trembles. She eases her hand to his leg. She can feel her juices working, can feel her underside doing that opening-up of arousal. Funny. She giggles in an awkward way. She whispers into Lennart's ear. "I don't know why, but my body really wants you right now." When she reaches her hand to his crotch to give him a soft tug, Lennart takes her hand and squeezes it.

"Please don't," he says.

She recalls the riverbed, the log, the stars, Grady. She felt a dim rush of sad affectionate pity for Grady then, and Grady couldn't understand the nature of her affections, either.

"I don't know what's come over me," she says, and eases away from Lennart, past the steering wheel, slouching down a little, but she keeps a hold of Lennart's hand.

His head cocks slightly in her direction, and his hands quiver. Beyond him, the wind snaps branches off a bare weeping willow. Kate watches the branches sail: snakes soaring off into the void.

Lennart says, "Too quick. You're too quick."

"I'm ridiculous, is what I am," Kate says.

Lennart pulls her hand to his mouth and dryly kisses it.

In the intersection a large white picnic cooler scuds eastward along the asphalt.

"Lennart, what can I say?"

"Nothing. Living is crazy enough as it is." He lets her hand go, claps his hands, says, "So drive already."

Kate is confused and little embarrassed. Maybe Lennart is right. Nothing. There's nothing to say. She touches the accelerator and maneuvers the Pacer into the intersection, veering north, which is not the direction to love or any foolishness like that. The way north is simply the way to drive so that she might go on living.

A white flash then, this is all Kate sees in the darkness, a white flash swooping toward her from the south, and the white flash slams the Pacer. A huge crunching follows, and a jolting from underneath throws Kate's head up to Pacer's ceiling. Everything in Kate becomes electrical and groaning and shattering, and suddenly still.

And then comes the silence that is not silence: the wind riffling the Pacer. The hood has popped open and is flapping, making rusty-spring sounds in its back-and-forth. Steam cascades from the vents near the steering wheel, and the motor is not running. The steam reeks of antifreeze. She reaches for the keys and turns the ignition, but the motor makes merely a few miserable clicks.

The windshield is cracked on the passenger side, and the view of the intersection comes intermittently: sooty and whirling when the Pacer's hood is blown all the way down, yellow when it's sprung back up. But Kate does see a large white car next to the Pacer, crunched, in fact, together with the Pacer. Vapor flows sideways from the white car in the wind. A woman sits behind its steering wheel. She is delicate-looking, wearing a sleeveless top. The woman does not move. Kate thinks she sees a beard in the passenger seat. The beard does not move, either.

Kate says, "This is really the shits." But Lennart does not say a word, nor does he seem to be moving. His body slumps toward the door, his head turned so only his hair is visible, and something is odd about his arms; the hands splay out in a bizarre angle from the forearm.

Hissings fill Kate's ears, and along with the antifreeze smell comes a butcher-shop smell close by, an odor of fresh meat, not quite the same cut-hay smell she's come to associate with Lennart. And Kate's thoughts are blurring. She's been in a wreck, okay, okay. Something's wrong with Lennart, okay, okay. She runs her hand through her hair, feels a large bump at the crest of her scalp, but when she examines her hand, she doesn't see blood, which must mean nothing's too terribly wrong with her.

She reaches to touch Lennart, places her hand to his stomach, and feels its heave and gurgle. He's alive.

"All right, Lennart," she says. "Let's have a look at you." She cautiously grasps the back of his head, feels the slickness of his hair, and when she swivels his face into view, Lennart lets out a bubbly exhale, his lips spattering out so much blood the sight makes Kate dizzy. She feels blood rushing into the bump on her head, sees blood bubbling from Lennart's mouth. Her eyes go watery with wooziness. The distance beyond Lennart is black, windy—a willow out there loses branches—and one side of Lennart's face is a red cherry pie. His face is crushed from the forehead to the right cheek. The right eye socket contains no eye, merely two crimson flaps of eyelid, and between the flaps a chunk of gray matter wobbles like a goose gizzard on a string. The mouth coughs three groaning coughs, and several teeth spurt through the lips. One tooth sails to the dashboard and splats there.

Too much, way too much. Kate has to have fresh air. She releases Lennart's head, and it slaps into the passenger window the way a soaked sponge might strike a mirror. Several lines of blood dribble down the glass. The windshield in front of Lennart is spiderwebbed, which must mean Lennart crushed his head at that very spot. Too much, she can't stand looking at him, way too awful, the gore, the antifreeze fumes wafting through the air vents, the butcher-shop blood taste in the Pacer air. No! She's ready to faint, and, with a blind reflex, she scrambles out of the Pacer and into the wind.

She bends over to catch her breath, to organize her brain back into a thing that functions, but nothing is sweet and refreshing about the air. Dust wallops her like driven hail. Her hair flails about her face and over her ears, muffling what she can hear, making her feel smaller and smaller.

She tries gazing to the west, into the wind, and down into the valley, but her eyes can't maintain the gaze. The wind's too fierce, too needly to look into. She thinks she sees something bright down in the valley, a redness overriding the black skies. Kate's McCutcheon, all Kate's memories, her mom, her dad, her brother, everything that has formed Kate into the woman she is—this is burning, Kate. Your McCutcheon is already gone, Kate.

White car, white car, forget about McCutcheon—what's gone is gone—and do something about these hurt people. She strides awkwardly around the Pacer, keeping her back to the wind so she can attempt seeing, and the white car is very big, a luxury boat of the trailer-court variety. Its hood is folded in half like a newspaper. She worries the vapor streaming from its engine might be gasoline fumes near to exploding. And behind the wheel the woman sits, hands still gripping the wheel, eyes still locked forward as though to memorize the road. Kate opens the door to get to this woman, says to her, "My God, I hope you're all right." She is shouting but can only hear herself faintly.

The woman has black hair, thin-stranded, pigtailed tight to her head and scarcely moving despite the gale. Her sundress is pale blue. She does not look at Kate, keeps staring forward. "I want you to understand me," the woman shouts.

From the valley comes a furnacey sound, a sound of melting and pouring, of bubbling and crackling and embers snapping everywhere in the reddened gloom, and when the woman moves her lips to speak, her head doesn't move, doesn't show the slightest strain to make her words boom, but they boom to Kate nonetheless: "Do you understand me?"

"Don't talk! You're not making any sense!" Kate yells. "You need to get out of this car before it blows up."

The woman reaches her hand to Kate and says, "I knew you would understand."

Kate takes the woman's hand, and the woman squeezes in a limp way that suggests desperation.

Before Kate has the woman upright and unwobbled enough to stand on her own, a man's voice shouts nearby: "Be careful with her. She's the most important thing in the world."

The man's voice it's a voice she's heard a thousand times before: "Hell, I don't know how she missed seeing your car in front of us. Really, really unfortunate, all of this." He puts his arms around the woman's waist, pulls her away from Kate, and

Kate feels the woman's body shirking somewhat, a quick tensing through the woman's arms.

"Darling, are you all right?" the man says, and he kisses the top of her head. "I only bumped my arms a little."

And the sky transforms into a dazzling orange cloud. Brightness is everywhere, and what Kate sees is not the light of day, but the light of fire, which is a light that turns the intersection into a crumbling old-time movie: a willow losing branches, the power lines doing circles like jump ropes, deer bounding along the sidewalks and over the road, the two cars mashed together, Lennart slumped inside the Pacer, an artwork of his blood smeared on the passenger window, the woman feebly standing with the bearded man whose voice is so familiar, who wears gym-teacher shorts and a black T-shirt of Lucky Littlefield, the man who has a beard flapping in the wind; this man *is* Lucky Littlefield, no question about it.

Kate hollers, "You're Lucky Littlefield, aren't you?"

Lucky says, "I will not allow this woman to die. She means too much to me."

He holds the woman tightly to his chest—a limpness about the woman makes Kate wonder, for a split second, if Lucky has drugged her, or worse—and he scans the intersection with mechanical flips of his head.

A short distance down the road, emerging from a flat stand of jack pine, the wall of flame towers into the sky. The wall is bigger than Kate ever imagined a fire could be, giant like a tidal wave, and full of moving colors—reds, yellows, purples—that make the valley horizon more beautiful than any she has ever seen. The flames breathe and shoot in bursts of veinwork that form the shapes of human hands and human heads that tumble

into themselves and burst upward again in new forms—here a
blast of fire that is Jesus in profile, here a blast that is a Mongol
on a galloping horse—always something new coming from the
fire, which is what fire is, a shifting and shimmering that draws
the eye and holds it, lets the eye see what is forever about the
world: how trees can burn into moving pictures of what we have
always known the world contains but have never seen before.
Fire is not rage. Fire shows us the mystery of living. And Kate
has no muscles to propel her body from the flames, for these
flames are what she has lived her whole life to see.

A hand tugging her arm then, jerking her away from the
panorama of burning, and it is Lucky Littlefield's hand, and he
is screaming: "Come on. You gotta help me. I got a way we can
get out of this."

The fire makes a trashing noise, a tumult Kate tries fixing
herself to accept, to hear the earth's symphony, but Lucky will
not let Kate stay still. "Please, don't stand here. You gotta come
with me. We gotta get down into the sewer or we're goners."

Lucky pulls. Kate follows, but she can't figure why she does.
A blur on the brain is what's wrong with Kate's resolve. Lucky's
woman stands near the trunk of the white car. The trunk is
open, as are the woman's arms. She faces the fire like a priestess
making blessing, and her expression, a smile that flutters and
radiates in the fireflicker, is something Kate can plainly tell is
ecstasy. The woman is seeing the same mystery Kate sees in the
fire.

In the Pacer, behind the reflection of the flames on the passenger window, Lennart moves. His hands touch his head, drop
out of sight, and his body slumps down farther into the seat.

Lucky shouts, "My wife is too fragile just now to be of any

use. I mean, look at her. She's falling apart. Now, I've got a very large crowbar in the trunk. I'll need you to help me lever up the manhole cover. Probably too heavy for me to do all by myself."

"What about my friend Lennart? He's still alive."

"Listen to me. This is *me*. Lucky Littlefield." He jerks Kate so she can get a good look at him, the beard, the serious blue eyes. "There's no way we can lug that big man down the sewer. We'll have to let him take his chances out here."

Lennart makes another movement, a shuddering, maybe a seizure setting in, maybe a few last thoughts of Rome crossing his mind. If he stays in that car, he'll be torched for certain, which might be the kind of death he would like, to burn the way the ancients did, but on the other hand, if Kate leaves him out here, maybe she's contributing to his death, maybe becoming a murderess. But she hasn't the time to reason this out. She can feel the heat of the flames now; they can't be a hundred yards away.

She follows Lucky to the manhole without feeling herself following, watching her movements as if her eyes are a camera recording events for a TV disaster show: crowbar in the crack, hoist, manhole moving aside, Lucky running to the woman, a brief struggle with the woman, her arms flapping like a bird trying to take flight, Lucky hoisting the woman by the waist, her legs doing a swimmer's kick in the air, the fire fifty yards away now, purples and reds and greens appearing and disappearing in the flames, Lennart squirming in the Pacer, Lennart living, and down, down into the sewer, the woman first, then Kate, her palms sweating and slippery on the iron ladder rungs, everything brown now and smelling of must.

Lucky comes through the manhole, fixes the cover back in place.

At the bottom of the ladder is blackness and a hushing sound, a rushing wind.

Lucky says, "Darling, I told you I would keep you safe."

Overhead the fire sounds like a giant stamping his heels on the earth.

And Kate has a heart that's still pumping.

The sewer-pipe wind carries dirt with it, sometimes in clumps that sting Kate's face, and the wind smells the way a dirty sock does, salty and dank.

"The fire is sucking oxygen from the sewer system," Lucky says. "Breathe carefully, and we'll live."

And Lucky's woman is not careful. She lets out a throaty laugh, says, "I remember it now," and begins whistling "Turkey in the Straw" like a professional whistler might, tonguing to one precise note or the other, making long warbling phrases that echo down the pathways of the sewer. When she takes in air to whistle another long phrase, she sucks it in through her teeth, making a squealy, sandpapery noise.

But Kate takes her air in tentative sniffs and chicken breaths, her lips stiff and snapping open in brief jerks. She counts to ten before each new small breath. If she dies here, she doesn't want her dying to be caused by carelessness.

The sewer-pipe concrete feels cool to the touch, and she can feel through the concrete the firestorm vibrating the ground. From down the tunnel come low moaning noises that sound to Kate like farm animals bellowing in death. She thinks the animal sounds are odd, mournful in their way, maybe too mournful to be real animals dying somewhere down the tunnel, but she does not think about her family dying or the thousands of folks who are dying in McCutcheon just now. Her thinking just now is as simple as listening: The sound of the fire is the sound of terror; the woman whistling is the sound of joy.

And Kate hears two distinct explosions overhead, each sending struck-gong noises through the sewer pipes.

"That would be the cars blowing up," Lucky says. He's whispering, saving his air.

"Yes, that's it," the woman says. "When we were camping, it was always Dad whistling 'Turkey in the Straw.' *That's* what Dad whistled when he cooked us hot dogs over the fire." And she whistles again. Her whistling sounds like an electronic bird.

Kate can taste the concrete grit on her lips whenever she takes a breath, and counts once more to ten. She can feel the tunnel rumbling. She knows Lennart is dead, but she doesn't give it much thought. She's certain she's about to die, too, which sets her body to shaking, legs moving involuntarily, arms flapping around. She can no longer count to ten. She can't quite tell if she's breathing at all. She feels her brain thinning into brightly colored fumes, sees tapestries inside her head like she saw forming in the fire when she stood above ground and watched the wall of flame approaching from the valley—men on horses, giant birds—and the only thought her brain gives her is to relax into death, which is a death already buried many feet beneath the ground, with the ground shuddering as if to keep her under, with a woman whistling an oddly happy tune over and over, a woman gulping huge mouthfuls of air and saying, "I died when I was no longer a little girl," and Lucky Littlefield saying, "Breathe carefully," and Kate lets herself die. She lets go of life without a struggle, when not long before she wanted so much to go on living. We turn ourselves off that easily.

18

And from death comes a gray light in the sewer—
maybe this is an hour later; Kate doesn't know; she passed out—
and the voice of Lucky Littlefield clangs everywhere on the
concrete around Kate. "We made it," he says. "Folks, the fire has
passed over."

Then, simple as that, they climb from the sewer, and they
are alive.

The woman says, "The air is so white."

And it is.

It looks like Heaven does in the movies, fluorescent and
pure. The wind has calmed to a breeze, and the smoke around
the intersection has the quality of fog being evaporated by the
sun. Over the intersection, where the power lines and stop-and-
go lights used to be, vapors gently swirl and wisp about. The
vapors smell like an old fish-smoker, sooty and tainted with salt.

Lucky says, "I'll tell you what: You can trust Lucky Littlefield
to pull folks through something like this. I wish all
McCutcheon was with me. I could have saved them all."

The woman says, "You have never saved a soul."

And Kate says nothing.

In the middle of the intersection are two huge steaming black lumps, one bigger than the other, the cars, of course, mashed together as before, and extending from the two cars are several thick smoking logs, a couple of which seem to have fallen, during the worst of the fire, on top of the cars. The logs were trees once. The cars were cars once. And Lucky Littlefield was a respectable man on TV once. Who knows what Lucky's woman once was? She no longer whistles. She stands near the manhole they climbed from, a couple of feet from Kate, and places her hand on Kate's shoulder.

"What's your name?" the woman says.

"I'm Kate."

The woman's head cocks in a peculiar way, and her eyes widen, just for a few seconds, then she speaks in monotone, like she's reciting a prayer: "I am glad you are a Kate. Kate is a nice-sounding name. Me, I don't have a nice-sounding name."

"What is it?" says Kate.

"I don't have a name at all," the woman says. She presses her palms together, interlocks her fingers, and closes her eyes. "When I was a little girl, my dad used to call me Skeeter. I don't know why. Do you understand what I'm telling you, Kate?"

Kate does not understand, but she mumbles that she does. The woman smiles and sighs and tells Kate that the Lord has given her a message to deliver to people who survived this fire, but she does not say what the message is.

Lucky paces near his burnt car, shaking his beard, stopping from time to time and thrusting his fists outward in the posture of crucifixion. He keeps saying, "My car, my car. Of all things to lose, it would have to be my car. A car would be so useful just now."

Kate can't get over it that *this* is Lucky Littlefield: beard much shaggier in person, kind of a blubberish midriff, shoulders kind of slumpy. His eyes look the way a little boy's do when he's had a rotten Christmas, fixed and angry and near to tears one moment, circling and disoriented the next. Whenever Kate has watched Lucky broadcast on Action 9, the on-the-air Lucky has appeared to be a man of strength and confidence, the kind of person who wouldn't fall apart no matter the miseries life produced for him. Kate has taken him to be a man of feeling—maybe even, despite the fake personality she knows it must take to face folks on TV, a man with genuine compassion. But here he is: He paces behind his car, points at his car, swears at his car, says, "And you crashed my Riviera" to his woman, spits at the ground and into the air, but he does not look once at Lennart's Pacer.

But Kate looks, walks to the Pacer and stands there, not shaking, not feeling much except for a wee thrumming inside her veins. Her heart moves her blood, but just now she's not sure she wants it to. Lennart is dead. A lump of dried black tar is what Lennart is. He has melted into his passenger's seat.

Off in the distance a few trees remain standing, blackened and looking like human hairs do through a microscope, scaly and teetery, and the smoke has begun receding back into the valley, revealing, as it withers away, acres of blackened valley slope and endless rows of singed trees, some standing, some toppled over. Not far from the intersection, three large piles of debris smolder on the only treeless stretch of ground Kate can see. These piles were houses once. Three ranch homes is what Kate remembers they were. Each has two gutted cars in its driveway, and a chimney still standing, and near the chimneys stand rigid rectangles that were once fridges and stoves. She didn't even know Lennart twenty-four hours, but she knows he would say a smoke-clearing always comes after the worst destruction imaginable, and people will be alive to witness the damage done and to tell others what they saw. That's History: to see what happens now and to compare it with what happened before. But Lennart didn't make it to compare this sight with some other nobler disaster of the bygone type. Kate sees this destruction before her, the houses gone, the trees gone, the everything gone, and she doesn't feel sad, not really. She'll miss Lennart though, even if she barely knew him. He was an interesting man.

But to Lucky Littlefield, Lennart might never have existed. Lucky's ruined Riviera is all that matters to Lucky.

They don't stay long at the intersection.

Lucky finally finishes ranting, and his woman says, "I must go down into the valley. I have a message to deliver to the survivors." And she begins walking so slowly and effortlessly she appears to float away from the intersection. In front of the woman is the pale and luminous smoke cloud over the valley, which, the farther away she walks, seems to swallow her up.

Lucky says, "Just where in hell you going?"

She keeps moving away like a ghost into the void, and Lucky shakes his head and follows. Kate follows, too, doesn't hesitate to follow; she merely starts walking.

For a long time they walk downhill, down the middle of Highway 50, and no cars pass. Not a bird flies over. The breeze moves, but that is all that moves. While they walk, the sky grows dimmer and dimmer, and the smoke becomes thicker the farther they descend into the valley. But they can still see. Along the highway are more ruined houses. The yards of these houses are black and crisscrossed with downed and burnt trees. Sometimes Kate sees a body among the fallen trees, or on the sidewalk in front of one of the houses, or next to a charred Winnebago. Bodies, one after the other, some partially burnt, perhaps a chunk of flannel shirt unburnt on the corpse's back, some are wispy human-looking piles of ashes—she wonders why these bodies are outside, why these dead folks didn't pick more intelligent ways to run from the fire than to stand out in their front yards and let it come. Whenever Kate sees a body she swallows hard, tightens up her face, and keeps walking. She does not feel sad for the dead, not exactly, or feel sick to her stomach; the dead she sees are like artwork in a gallery. The dead are the dead, and Kate Murphy is not among them.

19

BY LATE AFTERNOON THE GREAT WINDS OF THE FIRE HAVE subsided. A light westerly breeze puffs over McCutcheon, the kind of breeze, Lucky Littlefield used to tell folks in the valley, that makes for a comfortable evening, a breeze so faint it barely prevents the air from being still. Lucky Littlefield used to tell folks that this evening's weather will be proof of perfection in Nature. Lucky used to say, The temperature, folks, is sixty-eight degrees, looking for a low in the midfifties. Clear skies later tonight. Lovely stars. But if Lucky could broadcast his five o'clock update just now, if there were a power-line pole left standing or a TV set left unburned to bring Lucky to the people, this is all he would say: Friends and brethren, this evening's weather has been canceled. McCutcheon has been canceled.

Throughout the valley, trees topple and create burstworks of embers that arc through the air and drop into the ash, and small fires flare up briefly and die off. The great fire has become a campground of many little feeble fires, safe fires, foot-high flames that won't spread and become great fires again, for nearly everything in McCutcheon has given up its burnable gas to God. The broad stands of pine and birch that once stood along the valleysides have either vanished entirely or have had their branches burnt away. Every building is gutted, every car. Everything smolders or flickers or is nothing at all.

And along Mitchell Street the burnt-out taverns let off lazy columns of smoke. This smoke drifts east, past the telephone poles and siren poles knocked over in the burning, past the pickup-truck carcasses sputtering grease flames beside the Mitchell Street curb, past the IGA, where the goods from the cleaning-supply aisle burn with yard-high flames, sending up another column of smoke, this one as big around as a barrel, and this joins the smoke flowing down the valleysides just as the great fire did hours ago, down the ravines and the side streets and over the neighborhoods, and it flows toward the river, moving in gentle spirals through the ruins, as though each new spreading puff is an old woman come to place sheets on a battlefield's dead.

Over the river the smoke settles in and hangs there, becoming whiter and thicker. Animals by the hundreds, deer, cows, dogs, squirrels, overcome by the smoke and the heat of the fire, lie where they dropped in the river shallows. The river is too weak to wash the dead away. Here and there among the dead animals a fish jumps, twisting and straining itself to stay in the air, and splashes back into the murk.

All summer Lucky Littlefield told folks that prayer would bring on the rain. But it is fire, in the Kingdom of God, that brings on the rain. For the grand design of firestorms is that they will rage for a time, and, by the strength of their raging, they will extinguish themselves. A firestorm as large as this one creates wind, and wind creates instability in the air behind the fire. And at the peak of the firestorm today, at noon, when Lucky broadcasted his last appeal to prayer to the valley, the winds drew their air from many miles west of McCutcheon, from over the plains of Minnesota, where the pressure has been low and the system has been occluded for months, and the winds set this low-pressure system to moving toward Wisconsin, pushing the high pressure that caused the long drought slowly eastward. Folks, Lucky Littlefield used to say, instability is terrific for the atmosphere. Instability means weather systems are moving. Instability is what causes the rain.

Six o'clock, folks: We currently have thunder over McCutcheon.

Seven o'clock: We have rain.

And the rain is not violent rain, a dribbling at first, merely water washing the smoke from the air. Then the rain gradually falls harder, becomes a strong steady shower that douses the last patches of fire. By nightfall the gutters contain water the way they used to, months ago, in spring, and this water finds the drains it's supposed to find, and flows into the sewers, which are where the survivors of the great fire hide. Manhole covers around town start popping open, and survivors begin poking their heads up from the concrete tubes that have kept them living. Two hundred survivors, and they stand in the rain and stretch their arms to the watery sky.

Rain. After all these months of cloudless skies, this really is rain. How cool rain feels against the skin. How rain washes the air clean and makes the ground soft again. This is the rain Lucky Littlefield promised all these dry months. This is the rain

Lucky promised would bring joy. But for the folks who live the rain is not joy. Full dark now, not a streetlight to illuminate the gloom—rain is a thing that makes the night as dark as the sewers were. Rain is a thing that proves Lucky Littlefield, for all these months, was lying.

SUNDAY

1

No moon, no nothing to light up the countryside, Grady McCann is blind out here walking on Highway 50. Blind. The night is totally black, and it's totally Grady's fault he can't goddam see. Since the moment Grady and Father Mary climbed out of the boiler room at Shady Glen, Grady's Mag Lite's been on battery-fry, which is a grade-B boneheader directly blamable on Grady, because he left that Mag Lite shining when he passed out under the workbench, didn't plan ahead for passing out by keeping spare batteries handy, and here he is: Look at this shit, complete frigging darkness, and he has no tool to help him see.

Worse yet, it's raining sheetrain. The sky is a gigantic invisible cold-water showerhead soaking Grady. And he's soaked bad. He's way past the drowned-dog stage. Water runs down the insides of his shirt and into his pants and collects in his work boots, putting the big-time squish into each step he takes. And boots like these, they're meant for working, not walking. Blisters already, and Grady's figuring him and Mary got ten miles walking to go before they get to McCutcheon.

With each soggy clop Grady makes on the highway, he lets

out a groan. But get this: Ain't the blisters—or the sore legs or that he's hungry and cold and needing a cigarette—that do the groan-bringing in Grady. Grady can 75 percent tolerate suffering bodywise; the body is in misery, but it's functioning. But in his mind Grady has gone beyond the point of letting go who he was yesterday, because to let something go a guy's got to *have* something to let go, and the marriage is history, along with the house, the job, and the fine tavern to attend when the day's maintenancing is done. No, Grady is operating from a far darker sector of his brain than the part that does letting go. He's figuring he flat-out *isn't* anything anymore, at least anything he wishes he was, and walking through the rain with Father Mary next to him, this about breaks the last bolt holding together Grady's mind.

Here's Mary in the midst of his hiking homily: "I can understand a logic to the Lord's work here. Drought, fire, rain—of course, this is the natural order." Mary's strides are a *swish-swish* through the puddles. "Surely this is a tragedy, but there must be a reason for it."

Grady hasn't said a word to Mary since waking up giving Mary the French Clamp, which is the there-it-is that keeps Grady quiet. *Going French with Mary.* There it is. Was thinking Mary was Miss Hawaii, too. Grady has managed to be inside a nursing home getting completely rubblefied by fire, and he's managed to live through it, only to discover he's got a bone-on for a priest. It's one thing to put the shuck and shimmy on that Kate girl by the river. But with Father Mary under a workbench? There it is. It hurts, but there it is.

"In one sense," Mary says, "you have been the Lord's instrument, too, taking it upon yourself to save my life as you did."

Rain, groan, clop, the same, the same. Mary talks. Grady can't.

"I'm finding a strength in walking I didn't know I have. I feel like He's leading us toward doing something really important."

They started walking to McCutcheon a while before dark, after they had stood in the Shady Glen parking lot maybe a half hour, dropjawing at the sight of what was left of the building, scorched wheelchairs and melted mattresses, and what was left of the cars in the lot, charcoaled upholstery and melted rubber and glass. They didn't come out and decide to walk to McCutcheon. Grady simply couldn't look at the rubble any longer, started walking so he could look away, and there was Mary, walking right next to him. Maybe they have been walking three hours, could be four.

"The Israelites, it's worth mentioning, suffered through all sorts of winnowing and all sorts of carnage, and this is because the Lord wanted only a *select few* to occupy the Promised Land. I can't help wondering why He has selected us."

The first hour, when it was still light, was a walk through something that looked like the type of ancient ruin Lennart always babbles about at the tavern. Along the good fence lines, the unburnable metal ones, were dead cows, one here, two there, sometimes six in a pile, and in the pastures the ground was black and smoldering and speckled with objects the size of small pine logs, probably dead deer, maybe pigs. In the air was a whispery death sound, a breeze seething over the razor stubble the fire had made of the countryside. The breeze smelled like an ashtray.

"This is not to say all those who died in Shady Glen are being denied Heaven. I can't presume to say *that*. But for *us* to be the ones living? Neither of *us* is extraordinary. I find it terribly troubling that the Lord would pick two ordinary men to survive a catastrophe like this."

By the second hour walking, lightning came, but only a few strikes far to the south, likely over McCutcheon. Grady didn't hear the thunder, only saw the flashes. His heart made a sound it seemed like he had never heard before, something battering and metallic. His heart was rain beating down. Rain. Grady had forgotten the sound of rain. It sounded like the machinery of God. Ten miles, it must be ten miles walking so far. The rain doesn't sound so miraculous anymore. It sounds like rain.

And Mary sounds like Mary. "I imagine one of the Lord's plans for today was to make you take life a little more seriously."

The rain beats into Grady's eyes, producing miniature silverish lights with each drop.

"And I can speculate the lesson you have learned today is not a happy one. Just look at the way you refer to your wife, or the disrespect you show to a man like me. Perhaps you won't make the spiritual changes you need to make right this instant, but your silence certainly suggests to me that you're aware of what you've done. A man shown his Sin, who comes to understand his Sin, this is a man making a move toward salvation."

A voice is what Mary is, little more than that, but Grady can understand what Mary is saying. *Grady is a piece of shit. Grady has lost everything because he is a piece of shit.* And if that's not bad enough, his body is so out of shape he couldn't get thirty-five bucks for it at the junkyard. His legs are not used to striding for hours on end. Near his kneecaps, his bones give off acetylene pains, and the cords in his inner thighs twang and pop, giving him an aching sensation he feels all the way to the tip of his

dink. His fingers are ballooned with blood, and he flexes his
hands to squeegee the puffiness out, but the puffiness will not
go away. He tells himself to stop walking, but his legs will not
stop.

He feels his mind floating away from the highway, sees the
little lights the rain makes in his eyes, sees, in the nothing of the
road, other little lights, small and low to the ground and jagged
in the rain. Torches up there, that's what they are. Grady is hallucinating torches. They are bluish red and beating time at the
identical rate Grady's legs move. And from his chest, presto, and
through his neck, his voice begins functioning again.

"Do you see the lights up there?" Grady says. His voice is
geezerish after all this time not talking. Silence and walking
have made his word maker frail.

"I see one light," Mary says, and Grady hears an irregular
swish-swish next to him.

"A light like torches?"

"One torch."

The lights are alternately blue, then red.

Grady's voice makes words again: "Be straight with me,
Father. You seeing one torch or two?"

"Could be two. I don't know."

The rain all of a sudden seems heavier, lead sinkers bashing
into Grady's eyes. He has to squint to see the imaginary torches
blinking blue, red, blue, red, forming a torch line on the
asphalt. These torches are the lights of a squad car.

"So you seeing that squad car I'm seeing?" Grady says.

Mary sniffs and chuckles and tip-taps his feet. "I'm seeing it."

The torch is a squad all right, and it's parked maybe two hundred yards up the highway. Its headlights are on, shining two

raindroppy beams on a fence line. Grady tries hurrying his strides but can't, because his body is locked on Gradypilot. He wonders if he's going to walk right past the squad and not be able to stop. Up ahead, the chase lights whir their reds and blues, making the highway an asphalt stretch as bright as the midway at McCutcheon Daze.

"Perfect," Mary says. "Just the help we've been looking for."

This is the first time Grady has been able to see the priest in hours, and the sight of him in these revolving lights is unsettling. Father Mary is shirtless, broad-chested, his pectoral muscles flexing in the squadlight. His chin is square, lips fixed in a watery smile, the nose small, and his hair is so short he seems bald. Father Mary is not fazed by what it is that makes up living, how things go wrong and wrong again, how droughts come and make fires, how marriages go bad and jobs are vaporized in the stretch of an afternoon. He is a man forever looking forward, a man who sees life as something endlessly fixable, because he never dwells on what is broke. Grady is exactly the opposite: What Grady has done his whole life has been to dwell on what *just went to shit*, rather than to see what *will be just fine*.

The squad is not on the road but nosed instead toward the ditch. Its motor isn't running, and inside the dome light doesn't shine. With a couple of springy steps Mary reaches the squad first, and he leans to peer in the driver's side window. Mary doesn't move for a while, merely bends there.

When Grady's legs stop walking, he feels a dizziness—not like the regular around-and-around dizziness—a forward-to-backward dizziness.

Then he hears Mary's voice through the rain: "I'm going to need your assistance, Grady."

Mary stands up straight and crosses himself, mumbles something religious-sounding that Grady can't make out, and Grady shuffles to Mary, who opens the squad door, and the dome light snaps on. In the driver's seat sits a cop, a thin fellow, legs barely filling out his dark-blue uniform pants. His uniform shirt is loose around his middle. The fingers of both hands are bony and hairless and are white-knuckling a shotgun, the barrel of which is directed at the officer's head. And this officer has no jaw, only a line of meat and gray matter below the cheeks and below the closed eyes and the shiny plastic brim of his hat.

Grady feels Mary's hand grasping his forearm and shaking it, but Grady does nothing to take the hand away. He stares at the dead officer and thinks how, despite the blown-off jaw, the officer looks the way he might if he were sitting here on the highway waiting for speeders. The shut eyes give what's left of the face a hopeful aspect, like the guy's dreaming about a long weekend fishing the good walleye lakes near Duluth. Maybe the dome light is too dim to show blood, because Grady isn't seeing any. The officer's shirt is dark, probably blooded through, but everything is soaked out here in the rain, and for some reason Grady doesn't feel as shocked by this suicide cop as he thinks he should be. Grady has seen geezers die, or geezers who just died, every day for ten years at Shady Glen. Hell, they *all* died today.

SCHWARTZ is engraved on the officer's name tag.

Grady says, "You know this guy? I never seen him in town."

Mary lets go of Grady's arm and says, "I don't *know* if I know him." His voice is matter-of-fact, doesn't have the slightest edge of alarm to it.

"The guy's name is Schwartz, see?" Grady fingers the tag so

Mary can get a good look. When Mary leans to the officer's chest, Grady notices the grimace lines tightening around Mary's eyes, not a look of horror exactly, more a workmanlike way of examining something grim. Mary obviously is a professional with this type of shit, too. He stands away, tugs Grady by the arm a few feet from the squad, where the chase lights are hard on the eyes. The chase lights send a billion raindrop diamonds refracting into the night.

Mary says, "I guess I do know the name. There are several Schwartz families at Saint Joseph's. But to look at this man, well, who could *recognize* somebody in that mess?"

"You got a point there, Father." Their eyes meet, and, with all the shifting shapes the rain and the blinking lights make out here, it's hard for Grady to get a fix on what Mary's thinking. Mary squints in what could be a smile, but yet again there's so much water running over Mary's head that, were the man crying, Grady couldn't tell.

But when Mary talks, his voice is steady. "I have to be honest. I don't think the Lord put this squad car here for nothing."

"You're right. The Lord *didn't* put it here. Officer Schwartz did." Grady tries not to smile and in the trying feels a little of his old self coming back.

"Perhaps the Lord wants us to *have* this squad car."

"No fucking way did the Lord make this guy blow his jaw off."

"True. The Lord wouldn't do *that*. But it looks like the squad's ours anyway."

Grady sticks his head inside the squad, glances momentarily at the officer, whose jawless head looks like an upside-down plunger, and then checks for the squad keys, which are in the ignition, and the ignition is turned on. The gas gauge is a quarter inch past E.

Grady says, "Schwartz, why didn't you goddam turn the car off before blasting yourself?"

Mary's voice comes from behind Grady. "What did you say?"

"You can forget the Lord giving us the squad, Father. Fucker's out of gas."

Mary mumbles something Grady can't understand.

On the passenger seat is a semiautomatic pistol, a Beretta .45, a quality gun, in Grady's estimation (in last month's *Guns & Ammo* Grady read that the Beretta .45 is the Utility Sidearm of the Decade; why didn't this cop use the proper tool for the job?), and under the pistol is a small notepad and an ink pen. Grady leans over the dead officer, bumping the shotgun, which the dead fingers grasp so tightly it hardly moves, and he picks up the notepad. It's covered with green scrawling, and Grady about has to climb into the squad with the corpse to hold the pad near the dome light.

This is what the scrawling says:

Anybody:
McCutcheon is all gone. Thank you God for my 27 years of good living that end today.
Sergeant Lawrence Schwartz

Grady reads the note over a few times, making sure what it says, trying to decide if it's true that McCutcheon is gone. On the squad roof the rain sounds like lazy applause, and on the police radio, when Grady turns up the volume knob, the squelch sounds like applause, too. But Grady's heart, when he presses his hands to his ears to listen for it, sounds like nothing at all. His heart is doing too much thinking for it to make noise. All evening walking, what he was considering *gone* was a hypothetical *gone*. If he were to find Erica, well, figuring that it was Grady's fault she cheated on him, he would have taken her back. You bet he would have. But she's dead for sure. Grady thinks about that: Erica is dead. And from the bottom of his belly comes one violent hiccuppy sob, a sob he feels like a sudden cramp seizing him.

He returns the notepad to the passenger seat and maneuvers himself from the squad interior back out into the rain. Mary is holding both hands on top of his head, and he's flexing his biceps back and forth in an even rhythm. His face, as it was this morning, when they were rigging the sprinklers that failed, is content-looking. He stares at something on the ground, his feet.

"Read the guy's note," Grady says, and the words barely come out before he sobs again, this time a sob so powerful through his chest he has a tough time breathing.

"Are you all right?" says Mary.

"The note." Grady chokes on his words. "Just read the fucking note."

And Mary does, leans into the squad, picks up the notepad and holds it under the dome light so he can read it.

After a time, Mary stands away from the squad and says, "Looks like we're walking the rest of the way, all right."

Blackness is the road ahead, must be ten miles.

Mary leans into the squad again, tries tugging the shotgun from the officer's hands, but the corpse is too rigored-up to let it go.

"We don't need a gun, Father. There's only the two of us."

"True."

And they begin walking south again.

"Can I tell you something?" Grady says.

"Anything you like," Mary says.

"I mean, it's you and me now, right? I mean, we're *it*."

"Go ahead. Tell me something."

"I never treated my wife very good. I mean, it was terrible how I was around her."

Grady's feet sting, but he keeps them moving, so much slower than before, walk-in-the-park strides, casual. There's no use walking fast when there's nowhere to get to. He starts telling the priest about his life, about Erica and Lennart and the ten years at Shady Glen and what he did to Kate the other evening by the river, and soon the squadlight fades behind him, and the road is totally black again. But Grady doesn't wish for his Mag Lite. Grady is finding a light inside him, a glow of the heart-changing kind. While he talks to the priest, Grady begins thinking maybe the Lord can help him after all. And without actually mouthing the words, Grady begins to pray: *If You pick up my feet, O Lord, I'll set them down.*

2

NOT FAR FROM THE BANKS OF THE MCCUTCHEON RIVER, Kate, Lucky, and the weird woman mill around a City of McCutcheon oil-drum garbage can. They are shielded here from the rain by the Highway 50 bridge. They are warm here, and dry and resting. Rain batters the river and the rocks along its shore, making a hiss that resonates off the concrete over their heads. And in the oil drum is fire, a small fire that Lucky Littlefield made, not God, and this firelit rocky space under the Highway 50 bridge is the only place left on the planet that Kate can call home. This is it: an oil drum, a concrete bridge pillar to lean on, and a bunch of rocks. In a finger-snap stretch of time, anybody, even Kate, can turn into a hobo.

She stands far enough away from the oil drum that she can't feel its heat—she's had enough heat for one day—and she shifts her weight from sandal to sandal, trying to keep blood from settling in her legs and to keep her feet from falling asleep balancing on the lumpy riverbed rocks. She wishes she wasn't too tired to start walking again.

And near the oil drum the weird woman stands, holding her hands in prayer over the little fire, nodding her head and fluttering her lips in a rhythm with the flames. Her face is serene, neither a smile nor a frown working its way over her cheeks. Her shoulders: steady. Her sundress: not filthy, not like Kate's T-shirt, which has been sooted through since they climbed from the sewer hours ago.

"Kate," the woman says, "wouldn't it be wonderful if Lucky Littlefield's television audience could see him now?"

Kate doesn't have the energy to agree or disagree. "I guess so," she says.

"It would make for a terrific human-interest piece," the woman says. "Tonight at ten: Lucky Littlefield gathers wood in the land where all his promises came true."

"Darling, why don't you shut up and do something useful?" Lucky says. His face looms in and out of the firelight in the same spiritous way it used to appear in Kate's mind, when she used to believe in Lucky, when she would sit near her TV, close her eyes, and pray with him. But when Lucky speaks, the TV is gone from his voice, a rougher voice now, sadder somehow. "See, there's plenty wood here. Say what you want about me, I can find firewood in a place where no man normally could."

He pitches a stick into the oil drum, producing a sudden rise in the flames, a stronger light shining on him: hair plastered down with sweat, crow's feet around his eyes making him seem squinty and ornery and old. His nose is smudged with soot. His eyes zip and dart: from Kate, then to the woman, to the oil drum, to the dark hollow spaces somewhere over the river. He looks like he's waiting for something to pounce on him from the shadows or to drop down on him from the underside of the bridge.

"Considering the circumstances," he says, "I've done fairly well looking after you ladies today."

He bumbles among the rocks again, in and out of the firelight searching for more wood. Beyond the bridge's edge, beyond the narrow orange area where the firelight meets the rain, the night is completely black out there, darker than any dark Kate has ever seen. It's amazing how black night is without the electrical lights shining in the valley. It's amazing how loud the rain is on the river, how it hisses.

Lucky drops another stick into the can, sending a few sparks into the air. He says, "That's right. I've provided for you ladies right well."

"Please join us tomorrow evening at six," the woman says, "when Lucky Littlefield reveals his personal secrets for bringing women to their knees."

He makes a rough horse-sounding snort in response, and stalks away from the oil drum to hunt for another stick. He kicks rocks while he searches, and the tumbling rocks send metallic echoes down the underside of the bridge. He ranges in and out of the light.

When the fire dies back again, the woman moves her hands over the oil drum and folds them again into prayer. She says, "Lucky is not concerned with your friendship."

Kate says, "Doesn't matter to me if he is or if he isn't."

"I have serviced Lucky Littlefield," the woman says. "With my mouth."

"*Shut up!* That's none of my business."

"It should be. It certainly matters to Lucky."

Lucky stumbles back through the rocks, chuckling and carrying a log the size of his leg. He says, "You'll have to excuse my wife, Kate. I've never known her to be disagreeable such as this."

The woman steps aside long enough for Lucky to hoist the log over the oil drum and drop it in, causing a large brief wave of sparks to whiz upward. She wrings her hands over the fire again, screws her wedding ring off. "This," she says—and she holds the ring high so Kate and Lucky can get a good look at it glinting—"is what I think of marriage. The Lord hereby absolves me of any claims to matrimony." Then she releases the ring into the fire.

"Darling, you're taking this too far," Lucky says, but something is oddly calm about the way he says this. In fact, when Lucky smoothes the sweat back into his hair, Kate notices that he's not even wearing a wedding ring. And since the three of them climbed out of the sewer Lucky has been ogling Kate the way a single man might ogle her, shameless glances up and down her body, particularly at her legs, and he's been doing this in plain view of this woman he calls his wife. Something's wrong with the facts Kate's getting.

"Darling, you blow everything out of proportion. Who else are you going to rely on but me?"

"Soon it will be daylight," the woman says. "Help will come then."

"There won't be *anybody* coming to help us! Haven't you seen what's happened here?"

"I have seen." The woman opens her hands and examines the finger where her wedding ring just was.

"Forget it then," Lucky says. "I'll just let the oil drum burn all damn out then. See if you don't get cold." He moves away from the fire, kicks halfheartedly at a few rocks, and with a plaintive wheeze he sits down, splays his legs out on the rocks.

"I don't need fire to keep warm," the woman says, and she steps back from the oil drum and sits a flagpole-length from Lucky, easing herself fluidly down as if she's taking her place on a meditation pillow. Then Kate sits down, too, on some uncomfortable rocks the size of softballs, which, the longer she sits on them, don't feel so uncomfortable after all.

And nobody says anything for a while, which is a relief to Kate; she's sick of listening to these folks bicker.

In the garbage can the fire crackles. Rain hisses on the river. When there's a splash in the river, she can't decide if the splash is a fish jumping or a deer fording around in the shallows, and from somewhere in the distance beyond the bridge she hears occasional loud popping noises, probably burnt trees falling down or burnt houses collapsing under the weight of the rain. She scans the distance for movements, for people maybe alive, but as soon as she starts scanning she gives up. Nobody lives out there. She catches Lucky staring at her, not exactly with his eyes, because the light from the small fire is too poor for Kate to see his eyes well. His head points at her. When she stares back at him, he tilts his head toward the weird woman, whose eyes are closed, whose lips move in what appears to be prayer. Kate can't hear the prayer, but she closes her eyes, too, puts her hands over them to block out all light. For a while she thinks about Lennart, and already she's having a hard time remembering exactly what he looked like and what he said. Her brain is getting too exhausted to remember anything except in vague flashes of people, of things she has heard or seen or said or done before today.

She can hear Lucky stumbling about on the rocks now, hunting for another piece of wood. She thinks she hears him saying,

"Where's that woman gone off to this time?" But she isn't sure that's exactly what he says. He moves in arcs behind her, sometimes comes very close to her. She keeps her eyes shut tight, tries to pretend she's sleeping.

Then right on the rocks in front of her Lucky's feet shuffle to a stop. He says, "Looks like it's you and me, Kate."

She doesn't want to open her eyes, but she does. Lucky is dim at first, two hairy legs in the glow of the oil-drum fire, and he is standing over her. She stares into his abdomen, which his black T-shirt makes hard to see.

"I didn't *think* you were sleeping," he says. His beard is quite dark now, not red. Above him the reflections of the oil-drum fire dance and dart on the underside of the bridge, and at the bridge's edge the rain is an orange curtain concealing the night beyond. A tangy smell comes with the breeze, Lucky's sweat.

"Are you intimidated by me?" he says.

She shakes her head, scans the lit ground around the oil drum: no sign of Lucky's woman. Rocks are all there is to see.

"A lot of folks are nervous when they first meet me, you know, because I'm a public figure around here." He squats, groaning through his teeth as he does. He gazes at her, but she thinks he might be looking at something moving behind her, the way his eyes circle about in their sockets.

Kate says, "I'm not nervous about who you are."

"I've been lying to you, Kate. I believe if we clear up some issues between us, we might could get along much better." His elbows rest on his thighs, and one hand twitches slightly, maybe preparing to reach to her and touch her. "That woman I've been calling my wife is not my wife." He takes a long breath through his nose, and waits.

"That's none of my business" is the only reaction Kate can give. She is tired—speaking saps her—and she has seen too much today to care about anything.

"Don't you think that changes things, that she's not my wife? I mean, doesn't that make you look at me in a different way?"

"No."

"Don't you hear me?" Lucky says. "Doesn't that make you look at me in a different way? I mean, that woman is not my wife. That's got to change *something* in you."

"Where did she go," Kate says, "this woman who isn't your wife?"

"I couldn't tell you," he says. "Hell, you've seen her. For all we know she might this instant be walking *on* the river, casting her net for fishes and loaves." He lets out a muted laugh, sighs, and his beard rises into his TV smile. "Go ahead and talk to me. Once you start talking you'll feel much better."

His hand makes a spasmodic move toward her thigh, suspends momentarily a few inches over her skin.

"Don't," Kate says, and the word is an effort, "touch me."

"You're sitting there, thinking to yourself, 'Here I am with Lucky Littlefield. What could I possibly say to a man like that?'" His fingers riffle the air.

"Don't," Kate says.

"You think I'm *too strong* to need any comfort."

Kate is shrinking. She tries listening for the woman in the black distance. "Do not," she says, "get any closer."

"See what I mean? No comforting for Lucky Littlefield."

Then his hand does touch her, a chunk of rubber on her skin, and he leans toward her as if he might tip over on top of her any second. "That feels good, doesn't it? Human touch is a beautiful thing." He kneads her thigh, and she winces at the sting and scratch of his fingernails. "But this just isn't going to work between us, if you won't touch *me*."

"The rocks are uncomfortable," she says.

"Forget the rocks. Touch *me*."

She wants to stand and run, tries straightening her leg to roll over and squirm free, but he pushes her thigh down.

"I would like to stretch my legs," she says, smiling her words. If she can con him into letting her up, she can run, if she has the strength left to run.

"You can stretch them right here. You've walked enough today." Lucky grabs her shoulder, pushes her backward toward the rocks, and says, "It's not a difficult thing to comfort me here at the end of the world. Just ease back."

When his legs prop back so he can place his torso on top of hers, she sees a shaft of firelight between his legs. And in the firelight are her own legs, golden and shining in the small space underneath his crotch. She summons all the strength she has and shins him in the balls. He makes a squeaky noise and collapses on top of her. He's heavy and soft and smells like rotting trash, and his arms strike at her and miss. Strength, strength, Kate possesses enough strength to flip over, elbowing Lucky as she does, and he rolls off her, holding his crotch and his chest.

"Won't be anybody coming to help you," he gasps.

Kate is quick now, is surprised at the lightning of her reactions, but when she springs to her knees, she whacks her kneecaps into the rocks. Sharp sudden pains pass through her thighs and into her abdomen, pains so pure her eyes begin seeing Lucky in speckly flashes: Lucky feebly howling as he tries to rise, Lucky collapsing, then standing again. He takes a few steps toward her, wheezes and doubles up, bending his head forward. And with everything that is still strong in Kate and still living, she rears back her leg and sandals him full-force in the teeth.

Lucky drops to the rocks, flails his arms blindly groping for her legs, and becomes calm.

All is buzzing in Kate: veins, nerves, her double-pounding heart. She scans Lucky for any sign of him coming at her again. His head is cocked slightly, angled into a rock the size of an oblong bowling ball. In the soft flutter of firelight Kate sees the glint of blood on the rock.

She is seized with the urge to throw out her arms and roar. And she roars. And she hears her voice echoing under the bridge, fading off into a thin noise in the rain, which makes a bubbling-soup noise on the river. For a moment she listens to the night so hard her ears begin to ring. A stick snaps behind her, and she spins to the sound.

And there the weird woman stands near the oil drum, next to which is a small bundle of wood. "I had to leave you alone with him, Kate," she says, and drops a stick into the fire. Sparks spiral up like bees around the woman and fly out of sight. "You would never understand what I'm talking about unless I left you alone with him. Now you know."

Lucky's back rises and falls. Once in a while his feet twitch.

"All I know is I didn't kill him," Kate says.

"I'm glad." The woman dips a large stick into the fire, brings it back into the air flaming weakly: a glow that fades promptly out. She examines the stick's end, shakes her head sadly, drops the stick to the ground, says, "You can't die till you've learned all your lessons, Herod."

"What?" Kate says.

With a glide the woman walks to Lucky, hunkers near, grips the back of his gym shorts and underwear and yanks them down to his ankles.

"What are you doing?" Kate says.

Lucky's ass, in this poor light, looks gray and sickly.

"Please feel free to join me," the woman says, moves to Lucky's feet, tugs off his big white shoes and his socks. When the socks come off Lucky lets out a little coo, then he becomes quiet again. "Lucky's always wanted me to undress him." She drops the shoes and socks in the oil drum. Sparks rise, followed by a steady funnel of discolored smoke. Now she pulls his shorts and underwear off in one tug. The shorts she drops in the fire, sparks, more thick smoke, and with a dust-rag–waving flourish she twists the underwear into a blunt gray rope, which she winds carefully around the end of her large stick.

"You can't die till you've learned all your lessons." She dips her stick into the oil drum again, and the underwear flames into a nice torch. She waves the torch, testing its flame, then gestures with it for Kate to follow her. "I think we should have a private word, Kate. He might be listening."

Lucky is still breathing. With each breath he takes his T-shirt rides a bit higher on a ridge of fat above his buttocks. He might not be dead, but Kate doesn't for a second think that he can hear anything they might say. He is *out cold*. But Kate nods and follows.

They walk to the curtain of water falling from the bridge's edge.

"Take this," the woman says, and thrusts the torch at Kate. The stick is remarkably heavy, coarse-feeling, big enough around that Kate can't touch her fingers to her thumb when she grips it. The word *Jockey* is melting in the center of the flame.

"Now hold the torch so I can see my hands," the woman says.

Kate extends the torch, with both hands to support its weight, and the woman smiles, thin lips, friendly eyes. In the light of the torch her teeth are pure white. She shows her hands to Kate—they look like butterflies—and steps to the curtain of rain.

"Filthy," the woman says, and thrusts her hands out into the rain. The reflection of the torch off the falling rain makes it seem as if she is a ghost putting her hands through an orange wall; she brings her hands back in from the rain and wipes them over her face and around the back of her neck. "Okay, Kate. You can give me the torch back now."

And in the split second they both hold the torch Kate can feel, through the wood, the woman trembling.

"I know who you are," the woman says.

Kate steps backward and says, "Just talk to me regular, will you?"

"Please don't get upset with me." The woman's face is serene as ever, her voice a soft flute in the night. "We've been through enough today."

"True," Kate says, and she takes a quick glance at Lucky. He hasn't moved.

"But I really do know who you are. You called me about Grady. It *was* your voice on the phone. I'm sure of it."

The woman's hair is unmussed, her eyes steady, her arms supporting the torch as if it has no weight at all. She is stronger than Kate, is better-looking, finer-featured than Kate, and *this* is Grady's wife? "You *are* the Kate that called me, aren't you?"

"I didn't call anybody," says Kate. In her brain she sees Grady again, just a muddled flash of him, a side glance of him and his pigtail and the sturdy line of his jaw, his callused hand reaching to his forehead, the wedding ring on his finger.

"If you and Grady have something between you, I can understand," his wife says, nods and cuts a glance in Lucky's direction. "Grady isn't a bad man, really—but you know what I mean, don't you?"

And Kate does. She remembers the way he would look at her and see right into her brain.

"Of course you know. Grady carries himself in a way that hides the size of his mind. That mind of his *is* exceptional, I guess. But once you get to know him—well, it doesn't matter. Men have their needs, whatever the size of their minds might be."

Out beyond the bridge Kate thinks she sees the river finally, speckly with rain. Dawn has arrived. She has a sudden urge to strike out at the woman, to slap her and tell her where she can stuff Grady's *needs*, but she's had enough brawling for today, for a lifetime. "Why don't you just leave me be for a while?" she says.

"I understand," his wife says, and gives Kate's shoulder a gentle squeeze, which, despite all the anger building in Kate, is a comfort. The woman's touch feels like friendship, plain and simple, a thing Kate somehow, after all she's been through, wants.

"I'm unhappy," Kate says, and feels her eyes sting with the beginning of tears.

"Come with me. Let's deal with Lucky."

Lucky still sprawls on the rocks. The woman jimmies her torch in between two of the bigger rocks and kneels carefully down beside him. The torch doesn't seem as bright as it did before, but it is bright all the same, like a miniature sun shining on Lucky. His legs and buttocks are covered with fine hair, and blood has clotted along the gash on his head.

"We can work together," the woman says, and when she makes a sweeping gesture for Kate to kneel with her, Kate does, assuming a position beside Lucky. The rocks do not give Kate's knees any pain; her body feels brand-new.

"Of course we can," Kate says.

"Now take off his shirt and bind his hands with it."

Kate starts to say, *Why, he's already immobile*, but doesn't. No more bickering. She pokes his ribs with her thumb, feels the thumb mushing a bit into him, and the T-shirt is moist with sweat, or maybe it's rain; she can't decide. She says, "He's way unconscious."

"He won't *stay* unconscious. He'll wake up eventually, and the moment he does, he'll be looking for"—she picks up a small stone and thumps Lucky's buttocks with it —"another victim."

Kate says, "Did Lucky do something to *you?*"

The woman thumps Lucky's buttocks once more, rotates her head in a dreamy way. "Lucky Littlefield raped me today."

No questioning now, no niggling over the whys and wherefores of what Lucky did to this woman—Kate grips his T-shirt, tugs it to his armpits, lets the woman hoist him to each side, extending his arms so Kate can pull the shirt all the way off. The moisture on his shirt is rapist's sweat, and Kate twirls the shirt into a rope just the way the woman twirled his underwear into a rope to make the torch. The woman holds his hands, and Kate binds him. When Kate cinches the knot tight, she feels the sweat seeping from the cloth. In her chest Kate feels the machine-gun pace of her pumping heart, feels what's wrong with her life beating away.

"Stand aside," she says, takes a long step over Lucky, brushes past the woman and her smooth arms, and extracts the torch from the rocks. The torch does not feel heavy like it did before. It is merely a stick, and its flame is smaller than it was, a sputterish flame now, and daylight is coming in full now, the rain more like a mist than the steady rain it was all night. And she straddles Lucky's feet and touches the torch to his groin.

He squirms at first, thrusting his crotch upward into the torch, making it difficult for Kate to hold the torch in place, but she keeps her grip tight, stabs at his groin with the torch, tries to skewer him with it. His pubic hairs melt and curl away from the flames, and his mouth forms a scream, starting low and working upward to a high note, a scream that is the same scream Kate heard in the sirens yesterday—the scream is a bugle echoing along the undersides of the bridge—and at the moment when Kate feels the scream invigorating her and releasing all that's gone wrong inside her, Grady's wife grabs the torch and yanks it from Kate.

"Enough already. What's done is done."

Lucky's scream becomes, after a moment, a whimpering that dwindles off into the distant mist.

Grady's wife walks with the torch to the riverbank and javelins it into the water. It sizzles and begins its gentle bob downstream. "We need to bring him to the people now," she says.

Kate takes nice even draws of the morning air through her nose. Somewhere overhead is the sound of a plane engine droning. Down the river some distance is a thumping sound like a helicopter. And below Kate comes the sound of a grown man wheezing and crying. Lucky's eyes are open, and his head strains forward. In this new light of day Kate can see that most of his skin has turned bright red. Where his penis was a sooty open sore is.

Kate says, "Look what I've done."

Grady's wife squats near Lucky and grabs one of his arms, gestures for Kate to grab the other. Lucky gurgles, spits up some fluid that dribbles over his beard and onto his chest.

Kate stoops to Lucky, takes an arm, and helps Grady's wife drag him over the rocks to the river.

"Heave," Grady's wife says. And Kate heaves and heaves again.

In the water dead deer float, and Lucky floats as easily as a log.

3

ALL NIGHT GRADY AND FATHER MARY HAVE BEEN WALKING, and during the dark hours Grady has told Mary maybe each one of the twenty thousand fuckups that wrecked his marriage. Getting the fuckups off his chest has kept Grady walking, has made him feel lighter, better. And Grady doesn't exactly know what the Holy Spirit is, but when daylight finally comes to brighten the ruins along Highway 50, when he can see that the intersection not far up the road is the intersection of Highway 50 and Midland Mall Drive, he feels what might be the Holy Spirit flowing like clean fuel through his feet and his legs and his arms. He holds himself broader, taller, puts more power into his strides.

He says, "It's a damn fine thing to see again."

"I'd rather not see this," Mary says.

Scorched pebbles line the road, and the gutters are gunked up with ashy water. The distance on all sides is black stubble: trees, in the far distance, made branchless by the fire; grass, close up, made into dirt by the fire. In the intersection, two gutted cars—a big one and a small one—are smashed together, burnt paintless: no windows on either car, no steering wheels.

"Jesus," Grady says. "That accident looks bad."

"Jesus," Mary says.

A couple of large trees have fallen and burnt on the cars, and when Grady gets close enough, he can see the seats in each car have become gridworks of wire. Near the cars a manhole cover sits a few feet away from its hole. Grady figures a methane explosion knocked the cover off, probably during the worst of the fire. And when Grady gets behind the small car, he jerks to a halt, because the small car is an AMC Pacer, and the license plate has not been burnt of its paint like the rest of the car: DCLINE.

Lennart. Think it again, Grady: Lennart. And DCLINE reads in red letters as clearly as it did the day, four months ago, Grady helped Lennart screwdriver the plate to the car.

Grady lets out a howl, moves to the Pacer's driver's side and looks in. A heap of greasy soot occupies the passenger seat. Strings of grease hang from the seat's wire.

Lennart.

Grady puts his hands to his knees, stares at the constellations the stones make in the asphalt.

"I knew him," Grady says. He thrusts a hand to point at Lennart.

"You did?" Something sounds weak in Mary's voice, something scratchy and stuttery.

"Lennart Anderson."

"Never heard of him."

"Don't matter." A big black ant runs between Grady's feet: a survivor. "Lennart poured my beers every day at the tavern, hey. I hung out with him sometimes weekend mornings, helped him fix the shit he broke. You bet: I worked on this Pacer for Lennart dozens of times. Would have gone fishing with him, too, if he wasn't holed up reading history books all the time. I guess you could call him my best friend."

"I'm very sorry," says Mary with a wobbly voice.

"He was a fag." Grady feels strong enough now to stand upright again, to take another quick glance at the clump of ash that is Lennart now. Until this instant, Grady never would have admitted about Lennart what is the truth: Lennart was his best friend. Beyond Father Mary the landscape is empty and lumpy, like a dark section of the moon. Mist swirls over the wastes, the long stretches of yesterday's dry forest that are stretches of wet nothing now. From somewhere in the valley comes a thumping sound, a helicopter.

"If Lennart's in Heaven," Grady says, "ain't no use in us standing here looking at what's left of him. The *real* Lennart ain't here anyway."

"I believe you're right." Mary's eyes stay fixed on the valley beyond, and something creased in his jaw makes Grady think Mary is listening to the helicopter's thumping.

"You're hearing it, aren't you?" Grady says.

"I'm hearing it."

"Well, let's get ourselves moving."

"Let's."

"And if there's a helicopter, there's probably survivors, right?"

"Probably."

And Mary starts limping toward the valley. And Grady, after three painful steps, walks in alongside him. Grady does not once look back at Lennart's Pacer. No, this is not the time for looking back. The asphalt is as hard as it was all night. His feet hurt no less, but pain is no reason to stop walking, not yet. A ways from the highway, across a space of blackened ground and lightly falling mist, Grady sees the three ranch homes he's checked out every day driving down this road for ten years. Grady has always wondered who lived in these homes, always admired what a nice view they must have of the woods and of the valley below. Today the view from here is oddly beautiful — the mist hanging thick over the intense black ground like foam over a dead lake — more beautiful than somehow Grady can remember it. With each stride Grady takes toward the valley floor, he concentrates on being a better man, a man who can find the good in the bad, a man who can endure living without complaining, and he wonders when his time to go to Heaven will come.

4

AND WHILE FLOATING LUCKY LITTLEFIELD DOWNRIVER, Kate and Erica watch two large green army helicopters descending into the city park, landing on opposite ends of an open space where the picnic area used to be. The helicopters settle to the ground, and when their blades spin gently to a stop and the air along the river becomes very quiet and still, Lucky tenses up with sudden violence, a full-body spasm, and Kate loses her grip on his neck and shoulders. His mouth submerges and fills with water. Kate hoists his head back into the air and turns his head to the side to let his mouth drain, Lucky spitting and coughing and shivering. Kate grips the back of his head tighter, waits for the next tremor to shoot through him. He's been seizing up like this, one quick spasm and calm again, every few minutes or so since they started floating him. Must be he's close to dying. And Kate will be the one who killed him.

"Do you think we'll get arrested?" Kate says.

Erica's arms strain under Lucky's torso to keep him floating level with the waterline. "Nobody," Erica says, "not today, will think a man with a severe burn is unusual."

Lucky moans in a sad, reedy way, eyes rolling in their dark

sockets. His skin is bruise blue. What remains of his dick and balls sways lazily in the water, like a thick dead leech attached to him.

Not far from the picnic area—near the band shell, which the fire did not destroy—are a few green army vehicles, a few humvees, a couple of trucks with Red Cross banners on their sides, and soldiers in fatigues and helmets walk about the park, stopping from time to time to speak with small groups of survivors—could be twenty-five survivors gathered in the park, could be forty, which is about twice the number of soldiers up ahead.

"Those people," Kate says, "will know we did this to Lucky."

"Trust me. They'll be more concerned with what Lucky did to *them*."

Kate scans through the survivors—this man in a torn shirt and holding an empty booze bottle in his hand; this middle-aged woman in a sweat suit and holding her hands together, clutching her rosary; these two little girls holding their filthy dolls; these three little boys in their pajamas—but she doesn't recognize anybody. She considers the possibility of her mom or dad or brother being among the survivors, but she knows they must be dead. It's improbable enough that she lives. But she knows this now: Living is punishment enough. No one needs to arrest Kate. Her punishment will last a lifetime.

When they reach the boat landing at the park, they pull Lucky halfway up onto the shore, leaving his legs in the water, and they stand above him a moment, watching him shiver and roll his eyes.

"Okay," Erica says, and gives Kate a friendly touch on the forearm. "We have delivered him."

"Yes, we've done what we could."

"And we've worked well together, Kate, haven't we?"

"That we have," says Kate. "That we have."

Now Erica takes a step or two away from Lucky, extends her arms, and shouts, "People of McCutcheon! People! Listen to me!"

At first the people merely turn and face Erica—not much expression on their faces, just bland, drained faces staring the way cows would at a car stopped next to a pasture.

And Erica shouts, "This man here, naked at my feet, is Lucky Littlefield." She lowers her hands, holds them like cleavers at her sides. "All of you were swayed by Lucky Littlefield. He manipulated you into believing your lives would improve if only you turned on your TV each evening and prayed with him. But I ask you people now: Is there any good that's come from your praying? Is there anything that leads you to believe Lucky was not, in fact, bringing evil and doom to us?"

A small woman with thick glasses says, "I recognize that woman. That's the woman Lucky beat up on TV." And others in the crowd nod, their faces gaining expression, their eyes looking in much sharper focus than they did a moment ago.

"I am that woman," Erica says. "And Lucky Littlefield has done more to me than beat me up."

Other people in the crowd now begin muttering to one another or to themselves: "It's true. That *is* the woman."

"Come and look at Lucky Littlefield," Erica says. "Come and see what becomes of a man who presumes falsely to be a man of God."

And the people come and see.

They stand over him, making small humming sounds of

recognition, small noises of revulsion when they bend over him and see what's left of his dick and balls.

Erica says, "Lucky told you people to stay in your homes, and he *knew* you would die if you stayed in your homes. He just didn't care. Why should we care if *he* dies?"

A large man in a Green Bay Packers T-shirt elbows Kate, knocking her off balance, and he moves to Lucky, straddles over him. "Goddam right," the man says. "Where the hell was Lucky when we needed him most?"

Blue shirts and green shirts and yellow dresses smeared with soot, and thick arms and thin arms, and Lucky is naked, and all of a sudden this is a mob picking Lucky up, holding him in the air, and carrying him ashore, across the riverbed rocks and sand, over the dirt to the band shell, where a line of soldiers, for some strange reason, blocks the way to the stage, the very spot where Lucky led his prayer rallies during the drought months. Lucky's got the rain he prayed for now, but the mob doesn't care.

Some folks in the mob shout, *"It's Lucky's fault!"* Others shout, *"Lucky Littlefield is no prophet!"* Others stoop to the ground and pick up rocks and burnt sticks.

One of the soldiers, an older-looking man with a mustache, produces a pistol from his uniform and fires it into the air. The shot claps down the river, and the soldier stares at his pistol, as if he's surprised he fired it.

"Enough," the soldier says. "Let's be reasonable here."

The mob halts, and Erica steps to the front and says, "Sir, this is not a matter for you to settle with your gun. This man is our problem, not yours. We'll do with him what we wish."

"Miss," the soldier says, "*I* will tell you what you can do and what you can't."

"You have no rights over us," Erica says.

The mob grumbles agreement, shifts and coils, looks ready to spring.

"I'm just warning you," the soldier says. "My orders say I can use whatever force is necessary to deal with civil unrest. Now, I'm ordering you people to set that man down and step calmly away from him. If you do not comply, and get yourselves under control—well then, you know what we'll do."

The man in the Green Bay Packers T-shirt says, "Fuck that shit! You can't do shit to us worse than what's already happened. We've already lost everything!"

And a general yell rises from the crowd.

"Goddam right," someone says.

"Go ahead and kill us," someone else says, a tall woman in her thirties. "We're already dead."

And Erica says, "You'll never stop us with guns."

The soldier grips his pistol like it's an extension of his fist. "I have issued my warning, people." He shouts several commands, and the other soldiers in the line produce pistols, too, and from behind the line of soldiers come other soldiers carrying rifles, and at the sight of rifles the crowd roils, shaking Lucky high in the air and shouting, "This is our problem!" Or "We'll do with Lucky what we want!"

Howls and cries keep bursting from the crowd, and Kate won't watch, not today, not for a long, long time. She's done enough participating.

She turns away, walks upstream from the mob a short distance toward the McCutcheon Bridge, and along the riverbank she sees two men limping toward her. One of them wears tennis shorts and is shirtless, thin and muscular, has a narrow sad face and very short hair. The other man wears blue pants and a blue work shirt, has a jutting jaw and a ponytail. This man is smiling a half smile, and this man is Grady McCann.

5

A MINUTE AGO GRADY HEARD A GUNSHOT IN THE CITY park. He could see that people were clustered near the band shell—some National Guard troops, some regular citizens— and the part of Grady that's becoming a better man surged at the gunshot. He wanted to get up there and help people. He tried to run but flat-out couldn't. He's really in pain. His body is crumbling, not much gas left in the tank. But he's moving forward, which makes him somehow happy. He will help people when he gets to the park. He will. He's lived his life to discover this: A maintenance man's gift is to help people.

"Mary," he says, "when this is over I'm going to start going to church again."

"Go. Don't go. It's not my decision."

"But I think after all this I'm starting to believe. Really. I mean that there's a God after all."

"Maybe you believe," Mary says. "Maybe you don't. I wouldn't know about believing anymore."

Not very far up the riverbank stands a young woman, all alone, who wears a wet gray sleeveless T-shirt and wet blue shorts and sandals. Her hair is blond and raggedy. Her face is smeared with ash, and Grady thinks she's waving at him, or maybe at Father Mary. And Grady gimps a few strides till he's standing right in front of the woman.

"It's me," she says. Her eyes are gray and wide-set and tiny. "Kate."

Grady feels life cycling through him feebly, has a feeling of lightening in his legs and in his torso, can hear the crowd of people in front of the band shell hollering, and sure, sure, this is Kate, kind of a filthy likeness of Kate, but it's Kate just the same.

"Before all this," she says, "I really wanted to see you again."

Grady is good now. Grady is honest. Grady seeks forgiveness without delay. "I didn't mean to grab you like the other day. It was a mistake."

Kate smiles a blackened-face smile, revealing her teeth, which are black, too, like she's been eating charcoal. "It doesn't make a bit of difference to me anymore what *anybody* does," she says.

"You're not understanding me," Grady says. "I'm a better man. Father Mary here will testify to this being the case." He reaches for Mary's slack arm and tugs him close. Mary's arm feels about as muscular as a blob of axle grease.

"Mary, you okay?" Mary's mouth is open, and a thick line of drool drops from his lower lip and strikes his chest. "Mary, this is the Kate I was telling you about all night."

Mary forms garbly words: "I am going to sit down and go to sleep." Which is exactly what Mary does, he squats into Gandhi position and nods off for a split second, dips his chin to his chest, bobs his head back up, and says, "I am sleeping, but I am seeing everything."

Grady pats Mary on the head and fixes his eyes on Kate's,

which are grayer than Grady remembered them. He pictures Lennart serving Kate drinks two days ago, and remembers how Kate could quaff doubles like a lumberman.

"A priest," Kate says. "Yesterday I wouldn't have figured you for hanging out with a priest. Now that I've met your wife, I'm not surprised."

She scuffs the riverbed with her sandals, has muscular flexing legs and long-fingered grimy hands. Her breasts don't seem exciting like they did two days ago; they look like sad potatoes inside her grubby shirt now. Father Mary dips forward, snaps himself upright again, rolls his eyes, and dips forward again. From the band shell yells rise into the misty skies, and the crowd seethes and is a patchwork of dirty street clothes and clean camouflage. Grady thinks he sees folks in the crowd holding a naked man in the air.

"What do you mean—you met my wife?"

"She's over there," Kate says. And her smile is not a smile, more of a squint. "You can't miss her. People are saying they saw her on TV."

A small crowd at the band shell, could be a hundred folks— they yell and clap and bitch the way a small crowd would at an umpire making a bad call at a softball game.

Grady's eyes are tired, but over there, in front of the crowd, that's Erica all right. She stands before the National Guard line, and she lives. Grady thinks he hears her voice blaring above the crowd.

And Grady shouts, "Erica, I've come back to you." He tries to spring forward, to run to his wife, but he stumbles and falls. The riverbed is sandy and wet and black, and he feels a hand on his arm.

"I'll help you to her," Kate says. "But I don't think she wants much to do with you anymore."

"She'll forgive me," Grady says. "I know it."

When Kate pulls him to his feet, his mind races through Friday evening, when his nose bled, when Kate helped him walk down the slagstone levee on the other bank of the river. Nighttime was setting in then, and he was in a Clamping mood; but nothing is dark now, bright gray everywhere, and the smudgy colors of the crowd ahead fill him with hope. And Grady is a mechanism moving toward his wife, his legs moving but feeling nothing, his body held up by a young woman half his size, his ears taking in the shouting: *"We aren't afraid of your guns."* And *"We'll deal with Lucky Littlefield however we want."* And *"If you want to shoot us all, what's the difference? What else do we have to lose?"* And God has sent Kate to help Grady. And God has assembled these survivors in the park. And Lucky Littlefield must be among the survivors: forgiven. And Erica: forgiven. And Grady: forgiven. And the world is scourged clean now, and is purified by drought and by fire. And the Holy Spirit is inside a maintenance man come to force his way through a small shouting crowd. Elbows jab Grady in the ribs. Feet stamp on his feet. He smells sweat and smoke, and he pushes through, feels the aches in his body turning into strength. He passes a naked bearded man who a dozen big men in filthy clothes hold in the air like a bluish-white battering ram. A long blur of camouflage appears ahead, a parting of the crowd, a sundress is there ahead, pale blue, and the face above the sundress is Erica's face, narrow nose and smooth cheeks, brown eyes, serene. She is looking at Grady.

"I have met your Kate," she says. "She seems like she'll suit you well."

Grady looks for Kate, sees the men holding the naked man in the air, secs other men and other women, some young, some old, some holding rocks or brandishing large sticks or clutching their rosaries, but he can't see Kate. He didn't notice her letting his arm go, but she certainly let go, because she is gone. Something seems hushed about the crowd, something frozen; these folks are staring at him. He tries putting his lips around the word *God* and around the word *forgiveness*, but his lips make a blubbering sound instead. Overhead is pure gray. Underfoot is pure black. Around Erica is a radiance Grady can't identify, something luminous, like the northern lights glimmering, not as they did all summer, not over the nighttime drought sky, but like the northern lights glimmering right here, over this cloudy misting day, and this is the radiance of the Holy Spirit blotting out the bad zones of Grady's heart. He shakes his head at Erica and points to his mouth, meaning that God has filled his heart with goodness but has filled his mouth with mud.

"Yes," she says. "I did not lie about Lucky Littlefield."

Then her voice is a megaphone: "Look around you, people. Who are we to blame for all this?"

"*Lucky!*" says the crowd. And arms and elbows prod Grady, nearly knocking him over.

Grady tries to say, "I don't care what you did with Lucky. I would have done the same thing, if I were you." But the words won't come out. Erica looks beyond him, points at the naked bearded man, who Grady can now see is Lucky himself. The beard is red and ratty. The hair is wet and scraggled. His face is carbon-monoxide blue. Grady wonders if Lucky is already dead.

Erica says, "People, we put our faith in Lucky Littlefield. And Lucky manipulated us into believing he could save us from this. Just look, people, just look at what's happened."

The crowd: *"Lucky!"* And louder formless cheers burst from the crowd, a general howl, followed by much jostling and waving of rocks and sticks. Grady drops to his knees in order to show Erica that his God is her God, that it is God's business what happens to Lucky Littlefield, that God doesn't give Erica the right to stir this mob into wildness. But Erica won't look at him.

She says, "These men have guns, and we have Justice."

And the crowd begins stamping the riverbed together and chanting, *"Lucky! Lucky!"*

Another gunshot now, and Grady sees a National Guardsman pointing a pistol at the crowd. "That's my last warning," the Guardsman shouts.

All is loudness and the mob chanting, and the two helicopters off in the distance start their engines, an electrical grind at first, then an earthquaky rumbling Grady can feel in his chest.

The first rock thrown from the crowd is the size of a football. Grady watches it arc over him and strike a small Guardsman in the chest, knocking him backward, and his gun goes off, makes a puffy sound like a popgun, for the helicopters are so loud. Then more rocks fly, and more gunshots ring out. The man standing next to Grady, a guy in a Green Bay Packers T-shirt, puts his hands to his stomach and drops to the ground. And another man drops, and another. Someone falls into Grady's back, and Grady slams to the riverbed. He feels sudden heavy weights on his back, feet stamping over him, rocks striking him, and what he can see are feet scuffling, work boots, tennis shoes, sandals, army boots, and bodies dropping, more gunshots. And

God sets Grady to crawling toward a pair of bluish-white legs, Lucky Littlefield's legs, which aren't far away, not a far crawl, and a white light comes, two tennis shoes near Grady's face, and one of the shoes rears back and kicks Grady in the jaw. But he keeps crawling, wants somehow to get to Lucky, to get in the way of his blows, to help him. Now Lucky's legs, hairy and cold, Grady tugging the legs, pulling himself along Lucky's body, something striking Grady's shoulder now, must be a stick hitting him over and over—Grady sees boots kicking Lucky and sticks beating Lucky, and Grady pulls himself to Lucky's face, tries shielding Lucky from the blows. More gunshots, and around Grady bodies drop, one, two, three, and another boot into his ribs, another stick beating the back of his head, and another body dropping.

Lucky is smiling and bleeding from the nose, and Grady holds Lucky tight, presses his face into Lucky's beard.

Lucky says, "I knew, friends and brethren. I knew all along I was Damned."

And "Help" is all Grady can say. "I want to help you."

But Grady isn't certain the words come out.

Redness comes to Grady now, a dimming in his eyes, and the thump-thump on his back and on his legs is fading, and all is calming. He is finding that quiet space he found yesterday, with Mary, under the workbench, in the boiler room at Shady Glen, that pink space where the breeze is forever friendly, where the surf laps on a black-sand beach, where eternity is that place the Lord takes us, where Grady will never worry again, where everything bad about Grady is gone, and where living is only goodness and silence.

HEREAFTER

BEFORE VOWING TO THE PRIESTHOOD TWENTY YEARS AGO, Father Mary's name was Joseph Clark, a name he never liked, for Joseph, the way he thought back then, was a second-rate figure in the Bible. Joseph was merely along to tether the mules. Mary had strength, bore the Son without complaint, raised the Son to be the finest man who ever lived. And Mary was assumed into Heaven in a spectacular way, not like Joseph, who went to Heaven in the regular fading way, if he went to Heaven at all. But when Father Mary watches the riot in front of the band shell, he is Joseph again. He is the Joseph Clark who used to enjoy tennis, who used to hunt deer with a bow and arrow, whose favorite food used to be the marshmallow-and-fruit salads little old ladies brought to potlucks at the church. And he is Joseph Clark sitting on a boulder on the banks of the McCutcheon River, Joseph Clark, forty-four years old and shirtless, with ruined feet, and with weak eyes watching National Guardsmen shoot the survivors of the great fire by the score. White puffs come from their guns, and bodies drop. Men and women beat each other with rocks and sticks, or run to the line of military men as if begging to be shot. And then they are shot.

On the far bank of the river he sees a young blond woman emerging from the water, climbing the levee rocks and walking off into the mist, gliding.

He sits on his boulder for quite some time, watches the riot end with no drama; merely a moment comes when everybody by the band shell stops fighting. Many lie dead, or nearly dead, seventy-five people, a hundred — it doesn't matter. Surely they have not died to go to Heaven. For Father Mary is now Joseph Clark forever, and Heaven, for Joseph Clark, is the stuff of fairy tales.

In the middle of the dead Joseph Clark can see Grady McCann sprawling arm-in-arm with a naked man. And Grady McCann might have thought he found God, but he was mistaken. The God Grady found was the God that made Joseph Clark take the name Mary twenty years ago. That God has always made people susceptible to foolishness, always will.

The military men search through the bodies, and pick up a few of the living, and the living are brought, limping or on stretchers, to the helicopters. One of the living is the woman in the blue sundress, Erica McCann, Grady's wife. Joseph Clark recognizes her from church. She was always among the happiest in believing the fairy tales he retold each Sunday. She walks with easy strides to the helicopter. She appears to be unhurt. And when the helicopter rises from the ground, Joseph Clark rises to his feet. He can see her dress in the helicopter's window, watches the dress moving out over the river, and then the helicopter flies west and out of the valley, and he watches the helicopter till it's a green dot disappearing into the hazy distance.

He walks, slowly at first, north on the riverbank to the McCutcheon Bridge, and from the bridge he follows Highway

50 into the center of town. He walks ignoring the blisters on his feet. He walks watching the black heap of ash that McCutcheon has become. He does not weep. This is the natural order: drought, fire, rain. It is not God who showed him the natural order. The natural order is merely what it is, nothing more, which is enough for him to know.

At night he stops to sleep on a sidewalk, and he does not dream. When he wakes it is day, and a woman in army fatigues tells him there are shelters available. There are clothes for him. The fire is over now. Everything is over. He accepts shelter. A doctor bandages his feet, tells him to eat and to rest. He eats soup and thick black bread, and he sleeps but does not dream.

And weeks pass in this way. People offer him food, keep him clothed, let him rest in a trailer. Every day at noon a counselor from the Red Cross comes to the trailer and asks him what he did before the fire. Every day he says his name is Joseph Clark and that he did nothing at all. When he can walk again, he walks, circles McCutcheon and watches people he doesn't recognize cleaning up the town. Bulldozers move the rubble into heaps, and dump trucks haul the rubble away. Men in hard hats stand in barren spaces, pointing scrolls of white paper to the treeless valleysides. He can hear their voices, gruff and confident, saying that McCutcheon will be great once again. He walks and he listens, and his feet become hard as stone.

All fall the rains come and go as they once did. All winter the thick snow falls, and the river freezes over. In spring McCutcheon is green again. Grass grows on the valleysides, and big men from Vancouver arrive and replant the valley with oaks and maples.

And Joseph Clark will walk here every day. He will walk

among the new buildings, among the people from Illinois or Iowa who will come to start life anew in the pretty green valley town of McCutcheon. He will see children playing in the rebuilt park. He will watch families going to the rebuilt church on Sundays. He will grow old walking and watching the oaks grow tall. And when, one day, somebody asks him what life was like here in the time of the great fire, he will say, "As it was in the beginning, as it is now, and ever shall be."

And this is the world without end.